IF WISHES WERE HORSES

SILVIA VIOLET

If Wishes Were Horses by Silvia Violet

Copyright © 2014, 2019 by Silvia Violet

Cover Art by Cate Ashwood

All Rights Reserved. No part of this eBook may be used or reproduced in any manner whatsoever without written permission except in brief quotations embodied in critical articles or reviews.

Published in the United States of America.

If Wishes Were Horses is a work of fiction. Names, places, characters, and incidents are either the product of the author's imagination or are fictionalized. Any resemblance to any actual persons, living or dead, is entirely coincidental.

CHAPTER ONE

Ken wrapped his hand around the ornate door handle and tugged. He was not going to ring the bell at his childhood home, though that was what his parents expected. Even as a kid, he'd been treated more like a visitor than a member of the family.

He stepped into the foyer and glanced around. His mother had redecorated since he'd been here last, but the style still screamed ostentatious wealth like it always had. He strode down the hall and into the dining room where his parents were already at dinner. He was an hour late, and his mother wouldn't have risked upsetting Renata, the cook. Thinking of Renata made Ken smile despite the tension pulsing through him. She was perhaps the only person on earth his mother was afraid of.

"I'm sorry I'm late," he said as he took a seat.

His mother sniffed. "It was to be expected."

His mom was justified in starting without him. He'd never been enthusiastic about family gatherings, but he'd shown up late or failed to show at all since he'd stopped hiding who he really was—a gay man who disagreed with the way his father ran Carver Corp.

Of course, if his family had ever given him a warm reception, he might have tried harder to be punctual. Tonight, though, his tardiness had been unpreventable. He'd been stuck in a meeting for hours, finalizing the sale of the company he'd built, an offshoot of his family's conglomerate. He grinned as he laid a starched linen napkin in his lap. His parents were going to be pissed even though he had sole ownership, and the capital he'd invested had all been his. The idea of anything bearing the Carver name being sold outside the family would give his father a heart attack, if he had a heart.

Ken had arranged to have dinner with his parents so he could let them know before the news became public, more courtesy than they deserved considering they'd have taken the company from him in half a second if they'd had legal grounds to.

His mother looked up from her plate wearing the cool smile she used for public appearances. "How have you been, Kenneth?"

"Just peachy, which you'd know if you ever called," he responded, giving her the false look of graciousness he'd been schooled in from infancy.

"I'm not the one who broke off contact." Her icy calm infuriated Ken.

"If you hadn't insisted—"

His mother interrupted. "The only time you called even before the tacky airing of your private business was when you needed something, so don't try the guilt trip with me."

His father cleared his throat. "You said you had something important to tell us."

Ken nodded. "Yes, sir. I do."

"Then let's get down to business before we all lose our goddamned appetites."

That's how it had always been. Business first. As far as his father was concerned, his family was just another arm of Carver Corp, a public relationship requirement.

Conversation stopped as the main course was brought in. Ken acknowledged the kitchen staff member servant who'd just set his dinner in front of him with a warmer smile than he'd given his parents, even though he didn't recognize the woman. He looked down at the steak, grilled asparagus, and creamy mashed potatoes with gravy on top and nearly sighed. This might be the last meal of Renata's he'd ever have, and he doubted he'd get to eat it.

"I sold Carver Pharmaceuticals."

"What? That's impossible," his father stammered.

"I assure you it's not. I put out the word that I was looking for a buyer. I found one, and we just signed the paperwork. That's why I was late."

His mother pinched the bridge of her nose as if trying to fight off a headache.

"I'll top the offer," his father said as Ken had predicted he would. That was the main reason he'd kept things silent until the deal was done.

"The deal has been finalized, and my buyer will not be accepting offers." He'd given the man, an old friend from boarding school, a good price, a steal really, and he'd put a clause in the contract that his friend could not sell the business to anyone in Ken's family.

"He'll take mine," Mr. Carver insisted.

"He can't. The sales agreement won't allow it."

His father narrowed his eyes, then almost smiled. "I hadn't given you credit for being that big of a bastard. You've got bigger balls than I thought to try this shit with me."

"I learned from the best."

"Why?" his mother asked, giving her patented hurt look. "Why do you need to hurt us?"

"I don't," Ken said, though that wasn't exactly true. "I sold the company because I decided to retire. I've bought a horse ranch."

"What?"

"I used the money I earned—my money, not yours—to buy a ranch. I'm moving there, and I'm going to run it."

"You're going to run it?" His mother looked truly appalled at the idea that he might get his thousand-dollar cowboy boots dirty.

"Well, I'll need some help. It isn't exactly a one-man operation."

His father shook his head. "He always did love your mother's damn ranch. Would've stayed there all year if we'd have let him."

His mother glared at his father. Ken loved how his father tried to blame her for the fact that Ken's grandmother had taught him to love the outdoors and horses and dirt and other things that didn't fit into their society life. They might dress like urban cowboys, but they were as far removed from anything to do with ranch work as someone in New York. Being Texans didn't make them cowboys, but Ken had always loved westerns, the old black and white ones, and now he was going to live that life. To hell with what his parents wanted.

"You're serious, aren't you?" his mother asked.

"I am."

"You have absolutely no concern for our family, for what we've worked for," his mother insisted.

The woman hadn't worked a day in her life unless you counted the muscles she built up smiling and cooing at charity events. "I'm running a horse-breeding operation, not a meth lab. I hardly think ranch ownership is going to ruin the family reputation. I'd have thought you'd prefer I make myself scarce."

"I'd prefer—"

"Lydia," his father interrupted. "There's no point getting into it with him. He wants to be on his own, wants to block us from our own company."

"Carver Pharm was never yours."

His father snorted. "As if you would have gotten so far with it without the Carver reputation behind you."

He had Ken there. He probably wouldn't have been as successful without his family name, but damn it, he'd conceived of the company, developed the business plan, and given the last five years of his life to proving he could be as good a businessman as his father, on his own terms, without screwing over everyone he came into contact with, or hiding the fact that he liked to fuck men. When he went to a charity event representing Carver Pharm, he had a pretty young man on his arm, not some debutante hand-picked by his mother.

"I owned the company. I sold it, and now I'm moving on."

"Then you can move on without any more help from us."

"Even you can't erase your mark from me. I'm a Carver, and that's not going to change."

His father narrowed his eyes. "That may be, but you can do it without the Carver money."

"Fine."

His mother's eyes widened. Had she really thought that would make him stay? He had more than enough money to live comfortably between money his grandmother had left him and the money from the sale of his company. He wouldn't be as rich as his parents, but he'd didn't need a goddamned cent from them.

"So you're really going to walk away?" his mother asked.

"I am."

"Then do it now," his father said. "You're no longer welcome here."

Ken pushed his chair back from the table. No matter how dictatorial his mother acted, his father always had the last word.

"Consider yourself disinherited. You can expect paperwork removing you from all dealings with Carver Corp tomorrow."

Ken gave his father a curt nod. As he stood to leave, the only thing he regretted was not getting to taste the gorgeous steak Renata had prepared.

CHAPTER TWO

Three Months Later

Detective Andrew Wofford took a stool next to a beautiful curly-haired woman and dropped a file on the bar in front of her. "I want in on this."

Maria-Jose Gomez had been his partner before she'd left Houston PD for the FBI, and she was still his friend. When she'd been assigned to a drug task force involving Houston PD and the Harris County Sheriff's Department, she'd used Andrew as an undercover agent. That assignment had fucked him up so bad he'd still not recovered. He done some time on suspension, but she'd intervened to get him reinstated.

She glanced over at him, not bothering to ask how he'd tracked her down. "Absolutely not. Do you remember what happened to you when you went after this man?"

"Every fucking day." He'd not taken an undercover job since, but no way in hell was Gomez going to leave him out if this bastard was back.

"The risk of him recognizing you is too high. And I'm not at all certain you're ready for another case like this."

"He never saw me before. I know him better than anyone. You've got to bring me in on this."

"No."

"Think what a major break it would be for you if I bring this bastard down."

She scowled at him. "Don't make this about me. You're still fucked-up from your last go at this guy. I'm not putting you back in the field."

"If this is him, then he's killing his customers too this time, not just those foolish enough to work for him." The bastard had been diverting Vicodin and other prescription painkillers before, but now things had escalated. The drugs were in powder form, placed in capsules that kids were opening so they could get a faster rush. The dosages of the capsules were higher and uncertain, and at least some of them were mixed with toxic chemicals. Five kids had died in the Houston area so far, but no one had gotten any serious leads on the sellers until now.

"I want this guy as much as you do, but your head's not in the right place for UC work."

She was probably right, but the nightmares and the doubts and the fucking flashbacks hadn't gone away in almost a year. How long was he supposed to wait?

"I've worked on a ranch."

Gomez rolled her eyes. "Fifteen years ago or more."

He glared at her. "How old do you think I am?"

"The answer is still no."

Andrew wasn't letting go of this. He'd sworn the night everything went to hell that he would get justice for Charlie. Memories started to crowd his mind.

Not now. Can't think of him now.

The last thing he needed was Gomez realizing just how crazy he was.

Gomez frowned and took a sip of her bourbon. "I'm sure there are other qualified detectives who can handle ranch work."

"Possibly, but Kenneth Carver is gay." Andrew gave her a knowing look. Gomez was the only person who'd worked with him who knew Andrew was too.

The drug trail had been traced from Houston to a ranch several miles out on Highway 290, a ranch owned by Kenneth Carver, a wealthy Houston businessman and playboy who until recently had owned a pharmaceutical company.

She raised her brow. "As if that's going to convince me. Part of the problem last time was that you got in too deep."

"Is that meant to be a pun?" Andrew had to laugh it off because otherwise he'd have a breakdown right there at the bar. An image of a young man came to his mind, a young man he'd taken to bed so he could get information out of him, a young man he'd last seen lying in a pool of his own blood because Andrew had failed to save him.

He shook his head, trying to send the darkness away. "I'm not saying I'll—"

"Then what are you saying?"

"That he's not going to hire some homophobic asshole you dredge up, but he'll hire me."

She downed the rest of her drink, then picked up the file and flipped through several pages. At least he had her considering what he'd said.

"How did you get this file?" she asked.

"I have my ways." He'd never been one to follow the rules.

She shook her head. "After all the shit you've pulled, you still manage to charm people. It's just... wrong."

He laughed. "I use what I've got." Which wasn't much anymore. The assignment from hell had taken his sanity and —though he didn't often show it—most of his confidence. "I'm suffocating here."

"You're not ready for a UC assignment."

"When am I going to be?"

She sighed.

"Never?"

"Honestly, probably not."

"Bullshit. Quit fucking babying me." A few months ago, he'd have sworn he never wanted another assignment like this, but after months of wasting what talent he had left and realizing that no amount of therapy, either with a shrink or out of a bottle, was helping him, he'd decided going back to what had broken him was the answer. Either he'd get better or he'd implode.

"Are you trying to get yourself killed?"

"No, I'm trying to get the fuck over what happened to me. I'm the best man you're going to find for this. And while part of it is about finishing what I started, I meant what I said. If I break this case, you're going to get the credit you deserve. I owe you that."

If it hadn't been for Gomez, he might have descended into hell and never come back, even to the sorry-ass existence he had now.

Gomez frowned. "If you go in there and pull your usual stunts, it could take us both down."

He gave her his most charming smile. "I can be a good boy."

"No, you can't. And most of the time, that makes you a damn fine cop." She sighed. "Are you really fit for this?"

Maybe. "Yes."

"You're lying."

"And you're going to put me in anyway."

She looked back down at the file and nodded. "Yeah, I am, if the Special Agent in Charge agrees to it. But you're going to have to get close to Carver. He's connected somehow. He's got to be."

"Maybe, but something about this feels off. He doesn't seem like the type."

"Where's the cynical cop I know and love? I thought your MO was to assume everyone was guilty."

"Oh, I'm sure he's guilty of plenty, but I'm not convinced it's drug running. Buying, sure, I could believe that, but running an operation like this… He's already rich as hell. Why bother?"

"For the thrill. And he's been disinherited."

"But he's got plenty of money of his own according to that." He pointed to the file she still held in her hands.

"No matter what you suspect, you're going to have to get in tight with him. If he's not running the show, he may know who is."

"I hope he's not as big of an asshole as he's made out to be in the papers."

She grinned. "Right. I can see how you'd have a terrible time working with someone who's arrogant, flaunts their abilities, and doesn't give a fuck what others think."

"Touché, Special Agent." Even if Carver was an asshole, he was hot as hell. Every time Andrew had seen him on TV or in a news article, he'd imagined what it would be like to fuck that cocky look off his face. Carver was a man who expected to get exactly what he wanted, and Andrew would love to turn the tables on him.

Gomez rolled her eyes. "Whatever you think of him, I expect you to get under his skin and figure out his secrets. Someone on that ranch or one of the ranches nearby is the focus of this distribution ring. The faster we find them, the more lives we can save."

"Yes, sir." He grabbed the file, slid off his stool, and walked out.

ANDREW GLANCED down at his copy of the job application he'd submitted under the name Andy Watson. His new identity kept with the rule of using a name enough like his own that he wasn't likely to forget it—maybe it was too close, but while he'd occasionally been called Drew, he'd never been Andy—and his background was mostly truth with a few embellishments like recent ranch experience. He'd learned that Kenneth Carver, rebellious rich boy, had taken a hands-on approach to running his ranch. A shiver ran down his spine as he imagined Carver's hands exactly where he'd like them. Hopefully, Carver was just playing cowboy, and he didn't have any solid ranching knowledge. Andy didn't need the man noticing how little he remembered from a few summers spent on his uncle's ranch.

He slammed the door of the truck the department had given him for the assignment, and a rusted-out patch caved in. Fuck, the truck had been seized from some asshole they'd locked up, and it was so old and beaten up Andy had doubted it would get him to the ranch. He hoped to hell there were ranch-owned vehicles he could drive, or he'd likely find himself walking wherever he needed to go.

The front door of the traditionally styled ranch house was solid dark wood. Andy knocked and waited. A few seconds later, Mr. Carver opened it. Andy had been expecting a maid, not Kenneth Carver himself, live and in person, wearing an expensive white button-down, worn jeans—that were probably designer—over his fine ass, and cowboy boots with actual dust on them. He was more rugged than he looked on TV, his face angled and craggy. His hands looked like he was due for a manicure appointment, but that would only make them sexier wrapped around Andy's dick. His smirk and his knowing eyes, though, were just as Andy had expected. The man was a walking fantasy.

"Andy Watson?"

Andrew almost forgot and said his real name instead, but just in time, he caught himself. "Yeah, that's me. I'm here about a job."

"Do come in." Carver bowed slightly and swept his hand out to indicate that Andy should enter.

Fuck. Was the man flirting with him? Andy's dick said it liked that a whole lot, but his other head knew that could lead to serious trouble. Despite what Gomez thought he might do and no matter what answers he would get from fucking Ken, getting that close would compromise him. The last thing he needed was a flashback in bed.

But oh my holy God, Carver was even sexier in person than he'd been when the media had spent day and night detailing the events of his coming out. The man moved like he knew he could have whatever he wanted, and wow, that ass. His jeans fit it perfectly, and Andy wanted to reach out and test its firmness. Carver was dangerous, like a jungle cat, ready to leap down from the trees and devour him. All Andy's senses told him this man was shrewder than anyone gave him credit for and far more in his element on a ranch than Andy had thought he'd be. There was little or none of the ridiculous city playboy in him. That must have been an act for the cameras. This man played for keeps which meant Andy was in a fuckload of trouble.

He followed Carver into his office. The heavy oak desk

spoke of power and the wall of glass with French doors said he enjoyed looking at the land he'd made his own. Carver sat in his leather swivel chair, and Andy stood, facing him down, pissed as hell that he was so fucking nervous. He was no rookie. Sure, the last time he'd been undercover he'd lost big. A good man had ended up dead, and he'd been left so screwed up he might not actually be fit for police work anymore, but he'd gone back in and busted his ass to put more assholes in jail. So why was he acting like such a fucking baby now?

Ken studied Andy for several seconds before speaking, and Andy's face heated under the inspection. "I've looked over your application. I'm glad you've had some experience, but frankly, a man can learn how to work a ranch fairly quickly. You've got to be willing to follow my rules if you want to be here."

Andy nodded. Arrogant son of a bitch. At least he wasn't questioning Andy's history. Gomez assured him his background was solid, but Ken was a billionaire whose fact-checking resources no doubt exceeded the FBI's.

"What are your rules?" Andy asked, not quite succeeding in keeping his annoyance out of his voice.

Carver grinned at him. The asshole knew he was pissing Andy off, and he liked it. "Forget everything you've heard about me. This ranch is my life now, and I take it very seriously. I have every intention of being involved in running it."

"Yes, sir. I can't see how that would be a problem for me."

Carver ignored him and continued. "If you have a problem with who I am—a gay man with an asshole for a father and too much money—then walk out that door right now. I do not tolerate prejudice on this ranch. Everyone pulls their weight and respects all the other employees."

Andy fought not to show his surprise, but the way Ken's sexy mouth quirked up and his hazel eyes mocked him told Andy he'd failed.

"I can handle that, sir."

"Good. And call me Ken."

"Okay." But it wasn't. Andy didn't need to get any more familiar with this man.

Isn't that your assignment?

Yes, but while it was still based on nothing but instinct, his belief that Kenneth Carver wasn't guilty had only increased since meeting him.

All the man has to do is smile at you, and you'll believe anything he says. I thought you were better than that.

Andrew hated that sanctimonious voice in his head.

Ken smiled seductively. He had to be flirting, but how had he guessed Andy would be receptive? Did he assume anyone, gay or straight, would be taken in by him?

"Mr. Carver is my dad or King Carver as he'd have it. I'm Ken. That's all I've ever wanted to be."

Andy nodded. "Good enough, sir. I mean…"

Ken laughed. "You'll break the habit eventually."

Andy was pissed at himself. Why was he acting so submissive? Sure, he'd expected Ken to act like a dictator and treat his ranch hands like lowly servants, but he was reacting to Ken like he was a superior officer. Usually his military and police training didn't spill over like that. He respected the badge or the uniform, but outside of the chain of command, people had to work to make Andy respect them.

"If you're okay with my expectations, you've got the job on a trial basis. You have two weeks to show me what you can do, and then we'll consider a longer-term employment contract."

Andy nodded. "I couldn't care less who you fuck or who

your family is. As long as you don't mistreat the horses, I'll be happy to work for you."

Ken studied him for long enough that Andy began to worry he'd gone too far. Then he smiled again. "Done."

He pushed some paperwork across the desk. "Have a seat and look over this. After you sign it, I'll show you where you'll be staying and give you a tour of the barn."

Andy picked up the papers and scanned them. Basically they said he'd work there for two weeks with the option to stay on and laid out the standard pay—more generous than he expected—and other compensation. The most interesting clause had to do with Ken's family. He wasn't allowed to speak to any member of the Carver family or their representatives about his work on the ranch nor was he allowed to speak to the press. So Ken really was cutting himself off from his family. The man had pushed Andy's buttons as a local celebrity rich boy, but as a decent human being, he was far more devastating. Andy loved that he wanted to help run the ranch rather than sitting on his deck sipping cocktails and watching the hands work up a sweat, but working side by side with Ken might be too much for his self-control. Andy needed to crack this case fast and get out.

"Pen?" he asked.

Ken handed him one, and their fingers brushed as he took it. Had that been deliberate? He forced himself to keep his eyes focused on the paper.

His hand tingled as he signed and handed the contract and pen back to Ken. He fucking hated that the man made him react so easily. It would pass though. Surely, Ken would do something asinine soon. Rich boys always did, no matter how real they seemed.

CHAPTER THREE

Ken motioned for Andy to head out of the office and down the hall toward the back of the house. He'd intended to grill him about his resume. His references had checked out, but there were details he'd tried to confirm and couldn't. Something wasn't quite right, like the fact that Ken could find only the barest bit of information about two of the ranches he'd worked for. But he'd failed to find many men willing to work for an openly gay rancher, and he'd had to run off a few of the hands he'd hired because they'd either thought they could get him to pay them ten times what they were worth, or they found the idea of him actually working the ranch hilarious or, worse, cute. He was sick of interviews and sick of second-guessing everyone.

Two weeks. Andy wouldn't ruin the ranch in two weeks, not with Ken right there to keep an eye on him, or better yet both eyes and his hands. Damn, the man was gorgeous, cagey and rough, just what Ken liked.

When he'd played the role of Kenneth Carver, business mogul, he'd gone out exclusively with overly eager twinks who were ready to do anything he said, anything but fuck him through the mattress the way he wanted. Mr. Carver, CEO, didn't cede control no matter how much he wanted to. That was something he only allowed himself on the rare occasions when he'd slipped so deeply into the dark side of town no one recognized him. But all his senses told him Andy was a man he could let go with.

Fucking one of the hands would play right into what all the homophobic assholes who'd refused to work for him expected: that he couldn't be around a good-looking, or even not-so-good-looking, man without trying to stick his dick up their ass. He did not want to prove them right, even if Andy was pure fantasy material. Ken watched the man's ass and the way his thighs strained his jeans as he walked down the hall. Oh, the power in those legs. He could fuck a man hard and fast with no mercy. Dammit, Ken had to stop thinking like that, or he'd have a hard-on while trying to give his new employee a tour.

"I'm having some renovations done on the bunkhouse. Only half the rooms are usable, and all of them are occupied right now, so I'm going to put you in the guesthouse." He gestured toward the cottage-like building across the yard from his office.

"You sure that's okay?" Andy asked.

"Yeah, there's a ton of room in the house, and I don't really have many visitors." He'd learned that most of his "friends" didn't like him so much when he was no longer their ticket to Houston's high life.

Ken unlocked the door and pushed it open. He grinned when he heard Andy's small intake of breath.

"Not what you were expecting?"

"Not at all. It sure as hell beats a loft in the barn like I had at the last place I worked."

Ken smiled. "Good. There's a kitchenette, as you can see. One of the household staff will keep it stocked with basics, and you're close to the house if you need anything."

Andy gave him a look Ken couldn't quite read. Had the implication that Ken could fulfill all manner of needs been clear? He wasn't sure if he wanted it to be or not, but he couldn't stop himself from flirting with Andy.

"If you're set, let's go look at the barn."

"I'm not about to turn down a room like this."

Ken laughed. "I didn't think you would."

"I suspect you're used to people agreeing to whatever you say."

Ken couldn't deny it, no matter how much he wanted to. And there were several things he'd like Andy to agree to. But would he? Just because Ken told him to? "Guilty as charged."

Andy raised a brow. "I'm not going to roll over to just any demand."

What exactly were they talking about? "You did sign on to work for me."

"Do the employees really have to jump for you like trained dogs?"

Ken held up a hand while chastising himself for enjoying how easy it was to rile Andy up. "I give my employees plenty of autonomy."

"You just know how to be a bastard when you need to."

Ken laughed. "I sure do, so don't give me a reason."

Andy gave him a once-over. "You'd do well to take the same advice."

Ken laughed. This was going to be interesting. "Job starts tomorrow. After the tour you can head back to town and get your things."

"No need. They're in the truck."

"You were that sure you'd get the job?"

"You said it yourself. Those not willing to take you at face value were out. Not too many men are going to put up with all your faults."

Anger stirred in Ken's chest, and he fisted his hands. "My family might damn well be a fault, a double-edge sword at best, but I don't apologize for being gay. It's who I am, not some damn disease I've been saddled with."

Andy nodded. "*I* didn't say it was, but there's plenty who think that way."

"Get your damn stuff now and put it up. Then we'll see the barn."

Andy grinned. "Sure thing, boss man."

He was playing with Ken with his sultry accent and cheeky grin. Andy enjoyed pushing his buttons as much as he enjoyed doing it to Andy. He was going to be a goddamn handful.

As he watched the man gather his meager belongings from a truck that had to be far older than either of them, he wondered what Andy really thought of his decision to give up his inheritance for shoveling horseshit. Ken didn't consider the ranch an indulgence, though most of his "friends" did, not that he gave a crap what those spoiled bastards thought.

He chuckled to himself. He supposed he was just as spoiled as they were, but goddammit he'd worked to make Carver Pharm what it was, a company focused on cutting-edge research, willing to take risks but stable enough to afford them. He was proud of it and letting it go hadn't been easy, but this life was what he wanted. Getting laughed at by those who doubted he could even ride a horse, much less muck out a stall, was probably good for him.

Andy was an indulgence, though. He wasn't who he said he was, and Ken intended to find out what he was hiding. Did he have a record, a drinking problem, drugs? Ken frowned. He couldn't see the man as an addict, but he knew firsthand it wasn't all that hard to hide. Ken's sister looked like an upstanding citizen when she was anything but. He bet she started doping herself up before she even got out of bed in the morning.

Andy was a mystery, and Ken wanted to peel back all his layers and find what was underneath. Would he dare to go that far? One accusation Andy had made rang true. Ken was used to getting what he wanted, and with the exception of making his parents love him, he'd never failed at anything he'd decided to go after.

Ken realized he was just standing around while Andy hauled his things from his truck, so he walked over and grabbed a box.

"I can get it," Andy assured him.

"No need to when I'm right here."

Andy gave him that unreadable look again. "Thanks."

Ken followed him into the guesthouse and set the box down. Andy turned to face him. Suddenly the fact that they were standing in what was now Andy's bedroom with a big, comfy bed right there went straight to Ken's cock. What would Andy do if Ken pushed him back onto the mattress and started stripping him?

Punch you in the face.
Probably. Might be worth it, though.
I thought you wanted this ranch to succeed.
Yeah. I do.

Andy was studying him. He didn't look pissed, so he must not know exactly where Ken's thoughts were headed, but his gaze was sharp, hawk-like, and Ken fought the urge to shiver under the scrutiny. Andy was a hell of a lot more than a country boy who'd grown up with horses. He'd spent four years in the army. Had his hard edge come from what he'd seen and done there?

"The barn?" Andy asked.

"Right. If that's all your stuff, let's check it out." Ken brushed a hand over his hair. He was actually nervous. What the fuck? He never acted like this. If being a Carver had taught him one thing, it was that you never let someone see you flustered. Giving Andy a tour of the ranch suddenly seemed like a bad idea. Maybe he'd find one of the hands in the barn and ask him to finish it up. Andy needed to get to know the other men anyway, and Ken could talk to him later, after a cold shower.

―――

ANDY TRIED NOT to let his awe show when he stepped into the barn. He didn't want to ruin the I-can-be-a-bigger-asshole-than-you act he had going. Ken liked it, just as Andy had known he would. Andy might be less than sane, but he could still read the fuck out of people. The barn was impressive, several times bigger than his uncle's, and the horses Andy saw poking their heads over the stalls were top quality.

"Beautiful, aren't they?" Ken asked.

Andy could hear the pride in his voice, but it sounded different from the arrogant banter they'd exchanged earlier. This time, Ken's tone was honest and real, and it was justified. The barn was clean and well-organized.

Andy already felt better about working here. Carver clearly had the place running smoothly even if it was understaffed. Maybe if Andy did what he was told, no one would catch on to the fact that he was completely unqualified. He watched Ken walk ahead of him, unable to tear his gaze away from the man's broad shoulders and the way his shirt stretched as he moved. He hoped Ken would go back to the main house before Andy gave into the desire to shove him against a wall and have at him. Did the great Kenneth Carver ever bottom? Or did he only put it to the adorable twinks he had on his arm during the media coverage of his coming out? Andy would show him a whole 'nother world if Ken let him.

"Rusty?" Ken's voice interrupted Andy's fantasy.

"In here, boss," someone—presumably Rusty—responded.

"Come out and meet the man I just hired."

A tall, skinny boy with longish blond hair stepped out of the tack room. He had smudges on his face, and he was wiping his hands on a rag. He didn't look much older than eighteen.

"Rusty, this is Andy. Rusty's been acting as barn manager."

Rusty grinned. "Finally found somebody who didn't care that you were a rich queer, huh?"

Ken narrowed his eyes at Rusty. "Could you at least try and act like you have some respect for me?"

Rusty laughed. "Anytime, Uncle Ken."

Andy frowned. "Uncle? I thought I wasn't allowed to discuss the ranch with any of your family."

"Aww. He ain't really my uncle. I mean, yeah, my momma married his brother, but she's like his fourth wife."

Ken held up five fingers.

"Fifth, then."

Andy nodded. "I see."

"I doubt it," Ken said. "Keep in mind he's the nicest of my siblings and the only one I can stand."

Andy whistled. "I guess the rich really do have their problems."

"Hell yes," Rusty said. "Not that I really know. Mama's not rich, just pretty."

Ken's many-times-married brother, Robert, was a doctor. If Rusty was his stepson and Robert was involved with the drug distribution ring, then Rusty could very well be the link to the farm. Based on the evidence they'd gathered, the drugs were coming straight from the manufacturer, not from a pharmacy, but Andy wasn't going to rule out the possibility of Robert Carver writing fake scripts.

"How did you end up here?" Andy asked.

"I'm merciful," Ken answered before Rusty could.

Rusty just grinned.

Andy would get the whole story later.

"Show Andy around the place, and let him know some of the basics," Ken ordered. "I've got some work I need to do up at the house."

"Sure. I guess those saddles will just polish themselves."

Ken narrowed his eyes. "I guess you'll have to go back and live with your new daddy."

"Nah, man, you know Mama doesn't want me there. Not that she ever wanted me anywhere. Besides, you need me."

Ken sighed. "Just don't run Andy off."

"Never."

Ken turned to Andy. "Settle in after you see the place. Dinner is at six thirty."

"Yep. Ramen noodles in the bunkhouse."

Ken scowled at his nephew. "He's joking. Renata feeds all the men here very well."

Rusty grinned. "She sure does. I think she loves how it pisses your mama off, her coming here."

Andy wanted that story too. Was the cook a potential lead? Unlikely, but anyone connected to Ken's family had to be looked into. "She used to cook for your family?"

Ken nodded. "Renata was our cook for most of my life. My mom was terrified of pissing her off because she was the only cook who'd ever been able to satisfy my dad. When I bought this place, they cut me off. She decided I deserved her cooking more than they did, so she came out here with me." He got a wistful look on his face. "Her chocolate cake is like heaven itself, and the things she can do to a steak... You'll love her."

Andy couldn't help but smile. Ken looked like a kid describing Renata's food. "If she's that good, I'm sure I will."

"Carry on, then." Ken put his business tycoon façade back on.

As he walked away, Andy pondered how easily Ken slipped from the corporate mogul to easygoing ranch owner to the uncertain man he'd been in Andy's bedroom.

Rusty clapped him on the shoulder, bringing him back to the moment. "I like to tease him, but he's really a good guy. I didn't have a lot of options about where to go due to my misspent youth. He asked me to move out here when he bought the place, taught me what I needed to know, and now he mostly trusts me to keep the barn running smoothly."

"Misspent youth?" Andy shook his head. "How old are you anyway, fifteen?"

Rusty sputtered. "Hell no. I'm twenty-one."

Andy glared at him until he looked away and muttered. "Okay, fine. I'm nineteen."

Andy would have to investigate Rusty, but he hoped he wouldn't find anything. For all his sass—or maybe because of it—Andy liked him, and obviously, Ken did too. Of course Ken could be the guilty one himself. Andy fucking hated thinking about that. He'd apparently lost his stomach for the deception and bullshit that went with UC work. If only Ken had been the asshole his family had groomed him to be. Then lying to him would have been much easier. "So... the tour?"

Rusty nodded. "Come on. You've seen the barn, let me show you the pastures. Then we'll circle around and see the other buildings. You want to ride one of these babies"—he gestured toward the horses—"or take the four-wheelers?"

Andy considered. He hadn't been on a horse in way too long. He didn't want to make a fool of himself in front of Rusty, but his next chance to ride might be in front of more of the hands. "Horses," he responded and Rusty smiled.

"That's what I was hoping you'd say. They're a hell of a lot more fun than four-wheelers, and we can talk while we ride."

AFTER VIEWING PASTURES, outbuildings, and a good bit of the perimeter fence, they rode back to the barn. Andy barely kept from wincing as he slid off his horse. Fuck, he was going to be sore the next day.

When they had untacked and groomed the horses, Rusty glanced at his phone as Andy shut the door to his horse's stall. "Dinner's in half an hour. We've just got time to get cleaned up. All the other guys should be there."

Andy had seen a few of the hands working horses in the corral, but he and Rusty had only waved to them. The last thing Andy wanted to do was socialize, but he wasn't going to figure out who was connected to the drug ring if he didn't get to know all the potential suspects. A shower wouldn't do much to improve his mood, but at least he wouldn't be covered in dust and sweat.

"Sounds good. Thanks for the tour."

"You bet. See ya in a few."

Rusty had done nothing to change Andy's initial opinion of him as they rode together. He was an interesting combination of tough guy and naive boy. He worshipped Ken no matter how much he snarked at him. Andy couldn't see him betraying his uncle by running drugs through his land.

CHAPTER FOUR

Andy had just finished a circuit of all the stalls in the barn when he heard the barn door creak. He'd been too restless to stay in his room after he'd unpacked his meager belongings, all things any ranch hand might own, nothing that might identify him as someone other than Andy Watson. He'd decided to check out the barn more thoroughly, not that he expected to find any evidence of drugs there. Anyone smart enough to elude the police for this long would have a much better hiding place, and the product wouldn't hang around for long. But he might get to talk to some of the other hands one on one as they wandered in and out, and he genuinely wanted to check out the horses.

He was petting a particularly beautiful Palomino when he heard someone approach. His skin prickled, and he knew it was Ken. How the hell had the man affected him on such a deep level so quickly?

Andy turned to face his new boss and tried to act casual when he felt anything but. His awareness of the man combined with his reaction to being undercover again kept him buzzing. He was finding it hard to keep still, but Andy

Watson was just a guy who liked working ranches. He had nothing to be fidgety about.

"How's it going?" Ken asked, his smooth voice sliding over Andy, making him want to luxuriate in it.

Sore as hell, but he wasn't about to admit how out of shape he was for riding. "Good. Rusty showed me around like you asked. I unpacked, but these horses really called to me."

Ken smiled. "They do that. Did Rusty treat you all right? He's a smartass, but he's damn good at what he does out here."

"He was great. He showed me some of the land and gave me a rundown of what needs to be done." Rusty hadn't been as forthcoming about himself or the other hands as Andy had hoped, but that would come with time. He'd forgotten how hard it was to be patient at the start of an assignment.

Ken nodded. "All right. You got any questions?"

Andy turned back to the horse he'd been petting to distract him from his desire to put Ken up against the stall door. "Not right now."

"Did Rusty tell you we've only got three other guys working out here now? I'd like to hire at least two more, but I'm picky."

Andy smiled. "You pay good. I wouldn't think many men would turn down a solid job just 'cause they don't like thinking about you having ass sex." Andy was glad his UC identity didn't prevent him from being a snarky asshole. That would be more than he could handle.

Ken narrowed his eyes. "I can see you're going to be as troublesome as Rusty."

"Can you now?"

Ken laughed and shook his head. "Remind me why I hired you?"

"I'm just that good." Fuck, he needed to stop flirting, but he couldn't help himself.

"Are you?"

Andy nodded. "Every bit as good as advertised." His background would show a man who had a knack for ranch work, even if he wasn't very good at following rules.

KEN WAS sweaty and flustered and fighting like hell not to show it. When he'd made the appointment with Andy, he'd expected another redneck asshole to show up in his office, one whose distaste for Ken's "lifestyle" was obvious no matter whether he was willing to swallow his slurs and take Ken's money or not. Ken had been prepared to grill the guy about his obviously doctored resume, but then he got Andy. Hot. Engaging. Intelligent. Gay?

He'd not thought so at first, and then holy hell, the man had flirted back. No way could he be misreading something so blatant, even considering he had limited experience with such things. When he'd lived in Houston and flaunted himself as one of the city's rich and powerful, men threw themselves at him, and he chose from those on offer. When he indulged his rougher needs, he went to places where sex was the only thing on the agenda and no questions were asked.

But this… whatever the hell it was with Andy made his heart race in a way nothing ever had. And it was fun, something else he didn't have a lot of experience with. He'd finally found a man who might fit in on the ranch as well as Rusty did, one who might have the potential to be a foreman if the secrets in his past weren't too dark, and now he might fuck up everything by trying to get Andy in bed. Risks were something he was used to, though. He'd never have gotten anywhere without jumping off a few cliffs.

He allowed himself a slow, careful perusal of Andy's toned body. His gaze lingered over Andy's crotch and then dropped lower to where the fabric of his jeans frayed at his inner thigh. There was a hole there at the seam, one big enough to see skin through, tanned, hair-dusted skin. Skin that would be soft, that would feel so good as Ken sank his teeth into it.

Stop. Don't go there.

Fuck. He couldn't help himself. That damn hole had him mesmerized. He might as well keep staring because he'd given himself away, and he wasn't going to apologize for what he wanted. He'd learned long ago that when you screwed up, the best thing to do was own it like it was what you'd meant all along. Bluster your way through and keep control. The technique had worked countless times before, and it would work now. Ken tore his gaze away from that damnably alluring skin and dared to look Andy in the eye.

"Looking at a man like that will get the shit beat out of you on most ranches," Andy said, his voice low and rough, not at all like he cared.

"You gonna try?" Ken's dick hardened just thinking about that.

"Try nothing. I'd have you on the ground in less than five seconds."

"You're awfully confident." Ken gave Andy his best CEO-to-underlings glare.

Andy pushed back his Stetson as his grin widened. "You wanna try me, City Boy?"

"That's Boss City Boy to you, and I don't think you'd fight all that hard." Because no matter how inexperienced Ken was in reading the cues, Ken was damn sure Andy wanted him as badly as he wanted Andy. Andy would fight, but only until the urge to fuck got stronger, and that wouldn't take long at all.

"Oh you don't, do you?" Andy's grin threatened to turn into a laugh.

Ken shook his head and took a step forward. "No, I don't."

Andy glanced side to side, looking down the barn aisle, the first sign he'd shown that he was nervous about anyone noticing their confrontation.

Ken imagined wrestling Andy to the ground, struggling, pressing up against his hard body, making Andy sweat even more than this Texas heat. It wouldn't be easy. The bulge of his biceps and the way his thin t-shirt stretched across his pecs showed how fit Andy was, and if he'd been doing ranch work for years, he'd know how to use that muscle. He looked back at Ken and grinned, shifting his stance. Andy was primed for a fight. That was for damn sure, but so was Ken. He'd spent far too many nights pretending the punching bag suspended in his city apartment was his father. And his gym wasn't the posh luxury affair most rich boys belonged to but one he attended under a fake name where no one questioned him. He could take Andy and enjoy every second of it. Fighting, fucking, he didn't care. He just wanted this man sweaty and underneath him.

He let his gaze rest on that damn hole in Andy's jeans again, that circle of tanned skin making his mouth water. He needed to see the power in those thighs.

Ken took a step closer to him. "Just me and you here. You gonna show me what you got?"

Andy laughed.

"Don't underestimate me."

"Never, but I thought you wanted everyone to think you could keep your hands off the men you hired."

"This is about you and me."

"I happen to be your employee."

"You also happen to be making quite an invitation."

Andy cocked his head. "I could charge you with harassment for that."

This time it was Ken's turn to laugh. "You gonna do that?"

"Hell no, but I am gonna tell you to stop this shit so I can shower and change before dinner."

Ken gave him a slow smile. "A shower, that's all you want?"

"That's all I'm gonna have."

"Maybe. Maybe not. The night's still young, and I've got a fifty-year-old scotch I've been waiting to open. You could come over and join me."

"Now you're gonna get me drunk?"

Ken smiled and took another step toward him. "I have far more interesting plans for you than that. The scotch will just make them more fun."

"Fuck. I should leave right now."

"You could. But I don't think that would make either one of us happy."

Without warning, Andy grabbed Ken by the front of his shirt, whirled him around, and slammed him into the stall door. His eyes burned with anger and desire.

Ken started to say something, but Andy crushed their mouths together, and Ken gave into the brutal kiss. He flattened his hands against the stall door and let Andy pin him there with the hand that was still splayed on his chest.

Andy's other hand speared through Ken's hair, jerking his head to the side, angling him just right for a kiss. Andy's tongue pushed against his lips, and Ken opened, letting him push inside and claim what he wanted.

Andy may have thought he had the upper hand, but Ken knew better. Ken was allowing this to happen. He could have fought it, shoved Andy off, given him the fight he was looking for. They both would have enjoyed it, but this was better, not only because—oh my fucking God Andy felt good pressed against him, tongue thrusting deep into his mouth, hard cock brushing his leg—but because Andy had shown his hand. He might not like Ken, might not like that he wanted him, but now there was no dispute, no pretending he didn't do men, no acting like he didn't understand what was burning between them.

Ken had been submissive long enough. He grabbed Andy's ass and pulled him in hard, slamming their bodies together. He held Andy there and rutted against him, sliding their denim-covered cocks against each other. Andy groaned and tightened his hold on Ken's hair. He sank his teeth into Ken's lower lip, making him curse. As he dug his fingers in harder, the kiss turned from rough to brutal. Their lips would be bruised and aching, but Ken loved the wildness he'd unleashed in Andy. The man was a mess, and Ken wanted it, on him, in him, all the fuck over him.

―――

ANDY COULDN'T BREATHE, couldn't think. He hadn't meant to do this, so how the fuck had Ken broken him? He'd meant to punish Ken when he started, but now he was punishing himself just as much. He couldn't let this go further. This was a crazy indulgence, a taste just so he'd have something to jerk off to when he went back to the guesthouse alone.

Ken's hands digging into him were driving him crazy. The man was so fucking hot. He'd let Andy manhandle him in a way Andy had never expected. Now Ken was thrusting against him, holding him at just the right angle. Andy might fucking come in his pants like a horny teenager. He hadn't felt this worked up over a man in fucking forever. Sure, he'd worked his way through more than his share of men after finally admitting women weren't what he really wanted, but this intensity, this was what he'd been looking for, even if it scared the fuck out of him.

With a groan, he let go of Ken's shirt and tore himself away.

Ken's hand came up to his mouth. He rubbed his fingers over his lips and gave Andy that knowing grin, the one that went right to his cock even as it pissed him off.

Then the damn man chuckled, a low sexy sound that had Andy's cock digging into his fly. "Fuck me. That was everything I thought it would be."

Andy glared at him. "That was a big mistake."

"Really?"

Major, possibly career-ending mistake. Andy had just lost all his objectivity. That line between fucking a suspect for information and involving yourself... He'd learned the hard way that it was way too thin. He couldn't even get near it, much less cross it. "You're the boss. I'm a ranch hand. This is not going to happen."

Ken pushed himself away from the wall, still smiling. His lips were swollen, his shirt askew, and damn it if he wasn't even sexier than he'd been before Andy had lost his mind.

"I'll see you around," Ken said, breath still ragged.

He turned and walked away without another word.

Andy balled his hands into fists. This assignment was going to make him lose what was left of his mind.

CHAPTER FIVE

Andy didn't even try to pretend he wasn't going to jerk off thinking about what it would have been like not to stop grinding against Ken in the barn. He'd barely gotten through the door before he was unzipping his pants, leaning back against the wall and stroking himself hard and fast, no stopping, no letting himself think too much, just reveling in the memory of Ken worked up and needy. In almost no time, Andy was coming, shooting again and again, sure Ken's scent still lingered in the air.

When he was done, he stumbled to the bathroom, turned the shower on, and stepped in, groaning as the hot water pounded his sore muscles. As he rubbed soap over his sweaty, dirt-covered body, he kept thinking about how Ken's hands would feel on him. His orgasm had barely taken the edge off. If Andy had met Ken under other circumstances, he'd have fucked that knowing smirk right off his face, but while he had to get close enough to find a connection to his case, he couldn't allow himself to feel anything for the man.

Andy wouldn't be able to fuck Ken once and get him out of his system. The man had a pull that could reel him in and turn him about until he didn't know up from down. The detective who'd mentored Andy before his first undercover assignment had told him again and again that he had to shut down all feelings or he wouldn't make it out. Andy had succeeded on mission after mission until Charlie. He'd slept with Charlie and felt something, not love or anything close, but they'd enjoyed each other, laughed together, cuddled after the sex. And that had been a huge mistake, because Andy had gotten the idea that he could save Charlie, get him out and keep him from going down with the rest of the gang he worked for. He'd been very, very wrong.

Andy tried to stop the memories, but they came on anyway. He was no longer standing in a shower stall. Instead he was crouched outside a barn in the driving rain, waiting for a chance to save his informant, the man he'd flirted with, seduced, conned. Yes, Charlie was part of the operation, but Andy knew every inch of his body, and as hardened as Andy had thought he was, he wasn't ready to watch a man who was still hardly more than a boy be gunned down.

He'd called for backup, begged for them to hurry, but he'd known no one would get there in time to save the young man he cared for. He knew that, and yet he pretended there was a way out, a way that didn't involve the assignment blowing up in his face. Someone had to help him rescue the man who was on his knees in front of the dealer because he couldn't do it on his own. If he stormed the place, he'd be dead before he got through the door.

"You sold us out." The gang leader's voice was calm and cold.

"Please. I didn't know he was a cop. I thought he wanted in. He said he wanted in. He—"

"Where do we find him?" The leader still acted unaf-

fected, as if they were discussing something of no consequence.

"I don't know." Charlie's voice was barely a whisper, but it echoed in Andy's head. He was lying for Andy, and Andy was going to watch him die.

The leader kicked Charlie in the gut. He doubled over, but he didn't make a sound.

Tears rolled down Andy's cheeks. How could he sit there and do nothing?

If you go in, you'll both die.

He couldn't save Charlie, not without more firepower and not without ruining the assignment he'd spent months on. They didn't have enough evidence yet. If they went in, guns blazing, and didn't find anything, they'd be fucked. From what Andy knew, this location was only used for meetings, too many of which were about killing those who had betrayed the men in charge.

"Where is he now?"

"I don't know," Charlie said, his voice louder now, more desperate. He knew he was going to die.

He knew exactly where to find Andy because Andy had lost his damn mind and risked bringing Charlie to his apartment. Charlie had been living on the streets, and Andy wanted him to have a decent night's sleep for once. He'd started seeing Charlie as a person rather than a tool for solving the case. Now he was going to be punished by watching him die trying to protect Andy.

"Tell me where to find him, you lying little shit."

"I don't know. He always found me. I—"

Another kick, this one accompanied by a rib-cracking crunch.

"Tell me his name."

"No names. He never—"

Bang. And like that, the man Andy had let past his barriers had a hole through his head. Andy knew he needed to get out of there before they found him. He'd managed to keep from being seen so far, but he was frozen in place, unable to stop looking at Charlie lying there on the dirt floor, the pool of blood under his head spreading wider. Andy imagined it continuing to grow until it touched him, ran over him, covered him.

He blinked, but he couldn't make the vision go away.

Blood dripped from his hands, and he screamed. Several men ran toward the door. They were coming for him, but his legs wouldn't move.

He slid down the wall and curled in on himself. Vehicles raced up the road. His backup. Too late. He started to laugh. Too late to save Charlie and right on time to ruin everything Andy had worked for.

The men who'd come out of the barn swung a light in his direction. When it shone on him, Andy finally remembered how to move. They started shooting, and Andy took off through the woods. There was little chance of losing them, but he had to try.

He turned to fire at them and tripped on a root. Something tore in his knee, and he crashed to the ground. A shot just missed him, raising dirt by his side. He forced himself up. The pain nearly sent him right back down, but he got himself under control. He headed off the trail, hoping he could disappear. Then he heard shouts and more gunfire. The men cursed and turned back. Andy sank to the ground, his knee throbbing.

He could hear the chaos at the barn, shouts, gunfire, vehicles taking off. He needed to get back there to see if he could salvage anything. He pulled himself to his feet with the aid of a tree trunk, but after a few steps, the pain from his knee and the pain inside him were more than he could take. He dropped back to the ground and vomited.

By the time he managed to stand again, the noise had died down. An FBI agent he recognized met him halfway back to the barn. "What happened?" Andy asked, his voice embarrassingly shaky.

The man shook his head. "Most of them got away and they didn't leave a damn thing behind to link them to the drugs."

"Fuck!" The world went dark around the edges.

Apparently, Andy had passed out because the next thing he knew he was in a hospital with Gomez sitting beside him.

He'd tried to quit the force, but Gomez convinced him to stay. She'd told him he had to put the case behind him and move on as if that was as simple as turning off a switch. He'd tried, but the despair and the conviction that he was a complete fuckup hadn't left him once since he'd watched Charlie die.

Andy shut the water off and stepped out of the shower. He dried off and started to get dressed while trying to shake off the sick feeling that delving back into the past always left him with. Now that he'd taken another UC assignment, he wasn't sure that feeling would go away until he closed the case, especially if he was right and the man he was after was the same one who'd killed Charlie.

He pictured the man in his mind again. He was the same height and build as Ken. No! Ken was not involved. The universe couldn't hate him that much.

But apparently it hated him a whole hell of a lot because he was already fucking up. He couldn't stay cold where Ken was concerned. The man made him feel way too damn much.

Anger rushed through him, and he picked up a lamp from the table by his bed and hurled it across the room. It slammed into the far wall. The shade bent, and the bulb shattered as it hit the ground.

He wondered if anyone had heard the crash. He supposed if they had, they'd just figure he had anger issues—which he sure as hell did. Those were too real to hide, no matter what identity he was using.

Andy ignored the mess and finished getting dressed. His breathing had slowed, and he'd found some semblance of composure before he pushed open the bunkhouse door and waved to the men who were already gathered at a table there.

"Hey!" Rusty called. "Grab a plate and come sit down."

Andy inhaled and almost swooned. He hadn't eaten since late morning and that had been a pack of doughnuts out of the machine at the precinct. He'd been so keyed up he hadn't even realized he was starving until then. He looked at the kitchen counter and saw macaroni and cheese with chunks of ham in it, a green bean casserole, and a big bowl of fruit salad. He filled a plate, grabbed a beer, and headed for the table.

When he sat, Rusty got everyone's attention. "This is Andy. He's staying in the guesthouse since there aren't any rooms here, but he's starting work with us tomorrow."

Luke, one of the guys he'd waved to as he and Rusty had taken their ride, was on his right. "Glad Ken's found someone. We could sure use the help."

Luke was tall and thin with dark hair. He looked about twenty. Based on the research he'd done before coming to the ranch, Ken had hired him soon after he'd bought the place.

Warren, a hulking, muscular man with graying hair, sat across the table. He was older, a little over fifty, and he'd been working on the ranch for close to fifteen years. He gave Rusty a gruff nod and continued shoveling his dinner into his mouth.

"Good to have you," said Rodrigo, who was seated next to Warren. He'd worked for the previous owner but only for a few years. Andy wondered what his real take on Ken was. Was he just here because it was hard to find another job, or was he indifferent to Ken's sexuality?

"So how do y'all like working here?" Andy asked in his best easygoing cowpoke tone.

"It's been great so far," Luke said. "Exhausting, but the boss works hard too, not like the guy at my last place. I don't think he even knew how to ride."

Andy snickered. "I wouldn't have much patience with that type."

"Carver's all right for a queer," Warren said.

Andy exchanged a glance with Rusty, but Rusty shook his head. Andy got it. This wasn't the time to make trouble.

"I try not to worry too much about bosses," Rodrigo said. "I do my work. I get paid."

Andy nodded. "I hear that."

They didn't talk much as they finished eating. Andy got the impression Luke and Rusty would be happy to chatter away, but Rodrigo was a quiet man, and Warren gave off a leave-me-the-hell-alone vibe that didn't make conversation easy. Warren had been acting as the de facto foreman since he had the most experience, even though technically Ken hadn't hired anyone for that position, having more or less run everything himself.

Warren had every right to be pissed at Ken, but that didn't make him a criminal. A lot of guys would pin their suspicions on Rodrigo just because he was Hispanic, but Andy had no reason to think he was anything other than the hard-working man he seemed to be. Luke could be the connection, but someone who'd been here longer fit better since drugs had been traveling this route since before Ken bought the ranch—

further evidence for his innocence. While there wasn't any reason Luke couldn't be the guy, there wasn't anything to link him to the drugs either.

Andy was going to have to watch and see what he could learn. At least he'd be well fed. Ken's cook was apparently as much of a goddess as he'd made her out to be. The macaroni melted in his mouth, and when Rusty revealed there was banana pudding for dessert, Andy forced himself to forgo a third helping of dinner so he had plenty of room.

When he finally headed back to the guesthouse, full and exhausted from his day, he felt better than he had in a long time, despite his misgivings about putting himself and everyone around him in danger with his instability. He could really like living here if only it weren't all a con.

He spent some time going over case notes, then went to bed early since he had to be up before dawn. After an hour or so of staring at the ceiling, he gave up and got out of bed. Sleep didn't come easily to him even in the best circumstances, not with the things he'd seen.

He unlocked the case where he kept his gun, checked the chamber, and stuck it into the back of his waistband. He hated foregoing his shoulder holster, but he didn't need anything making him look like a cop. He'd call Gomez, get her help following a few leads, and then poke around a bit to see if he could get lucky and find a trail to follow.

He glanced at his watch. Ten thirty. Knowing Gomez, she was likely still at her office. He left the guesthouse without making a sound and started walking away from the buildings. He didn't see anyone around, so he pulled out his phone and tapped the screen to call the number he was using to contact her while on assignment.

She answered by bitching at him. "This isn't a scheduled check-in time."

"I need some information."

"Where are you?"

Andy ignored her. Did she really think he was going to risk talking where the other men at the ranch could hear? "Ken has a… step-nephew I guess you'd call him, Rusty. His mom recently married Robert Carver. I need to know more about him."

"Where are you? Somewhere secure?"

"Goddammit, yes. I do remember how to do this. There's no one around. Ken put me in the guesthouse because part of the bunkhouse is being renovated. Since I can't be sure it's clean, I'm outside away from everyone."

"How's it going with him?"

"Not going at all yet. I've been here less than a day." Andy held his breath, waiting for her to realize he was lying, but if she did, she didn't call him on it.

"I'm sure you've gotten a read on him. I know you."

Andy exhaled. "It's not him."

"And your evidence for that is?"

Andy paced back and forth along the fence line. "You said I'd have a read on him, and I told you what it was."

"If I find out you're dismissing him because you're hot for him—"

"What the fuck, Maria? You really think that's how I run my investigations? That I ignore evidence because I want to get a guy in bed? Why the hell haven't you gotten rid of me before now if that's what you think? I've certainly given you plenty of opportunities."

"Yeah, you have. But that's not what I think of you, not really."

"Not really? What the hell does that mean? And you wouldn't have said it if you didn't mean it." He'd really thought Maria was the one person who believed in him.

"I know you better than that, but I'm not sure you're in the best frame of mind for this assignment."

He blew out a long breath. "I'm fine."

"Sure you are." The sarcasm in her voice made him want to hurl the phone into the woods on the other side of the fence. "You're not making any parallels with your last case or anything, are you?"

"Don't do this."

She sighed. "Be careful, and make sure you're seeing things clearly."

"Do you trust me or not?"

She paused for too long.

"Don't even answer that, but if you're going to pull me out, do it now."

"I'm not."

Some of the tension he was carrying drained from him. He stopped pacing and gazed up at the stars. "Get me the information I need. Please."

"I will. Just remember instincts are important, but they're not worth shit in court."

Did she really think he'd forgotten everything about being a cop? "If anyone knows that, it's me."

"No matter what you think right now, I do care about you, so stay safe."

She was gone before he could say any more.

He'd intended to do some snooping, but while he wasn't about to admit it to her, his conversation with Gomez had him second-guessing himself. Was he only seeing what he wanted to? Could he be objective, or was he just going to keep seeing Charlie die, keep wondering who was going to pull him in and mess with him, exploit that part of him that wasn't sure of himself anymore?

He stomped back to the guesthouse, jerked the door open,

and immediately saw the remains of the lamp he'd thrown and never cleaned up.

Gomez had every right to doubt him. He wanted to keep ignoring the evidence of his loss of control, but he wouldn't leave it for someone on Ken's staff to clean up. He sighed as he crossed the room. He crouched to gather the pieces so he could throw them in the trash. As he picked up one of the shards, it sliced into his finger. Blood welled up and dropped to the floor.

One drop. Two. And he was in the barn again, the sound of the shot that killed Charlie reverberating in his head. The pool of blood growing. Charlie's lifeless eyes looking his way. He dropped the shard again and sank to the floor.

CHAPTER SIX

Ken's phone buzzed as he walked toward the barn. Cursing under his breath, he checked the display. It was Samantha Alexander, the attorney he had on retainer. Sam was ruthless, calculating, and one of the best friends he'd ever had. She was also more than simply legal counsel. When he needed information of any sort, she was the one he went to. She had sources he knew better than to ask about, and sometimes she used them without asking him first. His instincts told him he wasn't going to enjoy this call. With a sigh, he swiped his finger across the screen to answer.

"What's up?" There was never a need for preliminary small talk with Sam.

"Two things."

"Shit, I didn't even want one."

Sam snorted. "No one ever does."

"Hey, I owe you a lot. I just don't want to deal with shit this morning, unless it's been made by horses."

"You're really into that now, aren't you?"

"Mucking stalls? Hell no, but you do what you have to, and it's still way better than mucking boardrooms."

She laughed. "Maybe I should try it some time."

Ken imagined Sam walking through the barnyard in stilettos and a perfectly tailored suit. Before he could respond, she said, "Or maybe not."

Ken laughed. "Yeah, I think not, but you're welcome to visit any time. I'd love to see you on a horse."

"I'm sure you would. I think I'll keep your image of me like it is now."

"Powerful. Controlled. Able to handle anything I throw your way."

He could imagine the satisfied smile on her face. "Exactly."

Ken loved that they could flirt without either of them being serious. Sam was as into women as he was into men. "So what are these two things I probably don't want to hear?"

"You were right to question Andy Watson's work history. The ranches he's worked for seem to exist on the surface, but when I dug for more, there weren't records of those ranches doing business with anyone."

"Fuck."

"I'd hold off on that until you figure out more about this guy."

Ken scowled even though she couldn't see him. "Cute. Do you think my dad sent him?"

"My instincts say no. Your father would be more likely to hit you from the business end."

"But if he wants someone watching me…"

"Why not just pay off one of your current employees or a ranch hand with real experience? Creating a fake background seems unnecessarily elaborate."

Ken had to agree. He considered what he'd learned about Andy so far—other than the fact that his ass was beautiful enough to worship. He was wary and watchful, but that could be explained by his army background, assuming that was real. Surely he hadn't been sent there to spy on Ken. Everything wasn't a goddamn conspiracy, no matter what his father thought.

"Keep digging and let me know what you find out. He's... I'd like to keep him."

"I've seen his photo. I'm sure you would."

Ken huffed. "He's good with the horses."

"Uh-uh. I don't even want to know what that's a euphemism for."

Ken ignored her. "And he doesn't give a fuck who I am."

"Smart-mouthed you from day one? Just like me?"

How did she always know shit like that? "Yeah."

"He does sound like a keeper. Maybe I won't find anything too sinister."

"And the second thing?" Ken needed to stop thinking too much about Andy. Otherwise, he'd be walking into the barn with a hard-on.

"Someone's been poking into Rusty's background."

Anger surged through Ken. "My dad is not going to use Rusty against me. I will—"

"I don't think it's him."

Ken frowned. "Who *do* you think it is?"

"I don't know, but it's not being done by any of your father's usual contacts."

"How'd you find out?"

"A friend who's a detective let me know."

"Detective as in Houston PD?"

"Yes."

Ken didn't like that at all. "So someone is after his arrest records?"

"That's what has me worried."

"They're supposed to be sealed."

"A lot of things are supposed to be off-limits."

"Yeah, right. I should know that as well as anyone. Do you think Rusty's gotten himself in more trouble?"

"I hope not. Keep an eye on him. And on Andy. I'll do what I can from this end."

Ken sighed. "Okay."

He ended the call and shoved his phone back into his pocket. Rusty damn well better not be fucking around with anything illegal. As far as Andy, he was going to willfully ignore that situation for the time being. That wasn't like him. He usually faced everything head on, but for just a little while, he was going to indulge himself and pretend Andy was exactly who Ken wanted him to be.

When Ken stepped into the barn, Andy was there, bent over, filling feed buckets. No one else was around so Ken let himself stare. He might not know what Andy was up to, but there weren't any rules that said he couldn't fuck him while investigating. It wasn't like he hadn't fucked men who were using him before, like the hot little twink his father sent to spy on him. Ken had used him thoroughly and then tossed him out with a message for his father. It had felt damn good too, making the traitorous little bastard pant and moan. He could do the same to Andy, although what he really wanted... No, he wouldn't go there until he knew more.

When Andy turned around, he didn't seem surprised to see Ken. Had he simply been ignoring him?

Andy tipped his hat. "Mornin', Mr. Carver. I didn't expect to see you this early."

"I already told you I work the ranch like everyone else." His response was snippier than he'd meant, but all he could think of was Andy kissing him the afternoon before, kissing him and then stopping right when things were really getting good. Ken hadn't stopped thinking about the feel of Andy's body against his since.

Andy nodded. "That you did. Don't let me get in your way."

Andy was more than in his way. He was under his skin like no man had been in a long time. "Sorry. Not enough coffee yet, I guess. I'm usually a morning person."

"Me too," Andy said, and when he smiled, Ken's heart sped up.

"How's everything this morning?" Ken asked, trying to focus on ranch business.

"Good. Jensen still doesn't seem to be eating enough, and Jekyll tried to bite me, which I hear is usual. Everything else is running smoothly."

Ken nodded. "Jekyll's probably meaner than usual because Jensen's not doing well, and we had to move him. They're inseparable. I'll give the vet a call and see if we need to try something else."

"Good. Once I've gotten everyone fed, I'm going to take Nelly out for a ride so she won't be too keyed up when the buyer comes to check on her."

"Thanks. If I didn't know better, I'd think you'd been here for weeks." *Almost like you'd been studying up on the ranch or you had an inside source.* Ken hated even having such suspicious thoughts.

Andy smiled. "Rusty told me a lot yesterday, and I've got a good memory."

Andy walked off to finish the feedings, and Ken checked on Jekyll. He was moody as hell and really only liked Warren, who was gruff and not much of a talker. Maybe that's what Jekyll preferred in a human.

Ken held out a carrot he'd brought with him from the house. Jekyll eyed him with suspicion but finally grabbed the treat. He snorted and jerked away when Ken tried to pet him, though, so Ken just stood there, letting Jekyll get used to Ken being in his space without trying to touch him.

A few minutes later, Andy led Nelly down the barn aisle. Nelly was nuzzling him, and Andy was smiling, looking more relaxed than Ken had yet seen him. He stopped next to Ken. "Anyplace I should or shouldn't take her?"

"No, go ahead and explore. She loves to move fast, so don't be afraid to let loose with her for a while. Just don't wear her out."

Ken realized how sexual his words sounded and heat rose to his face.

Andy grinned.

Damn it, he'd noticed. Kenneth Carver did not fucking blush. What was wrong with him? It was a good thing Andy hadn't worked for any of his competitors when Ken still owned Carver Pharm. No one had ever gotten to him like that in the boardroom.

He noticed a buckle on Nelly's bridle that hadn't been pushed all the way through its hook. He leaned over to fix it and his chest brushed against Andy's arm. Heat zinged through him, and his cock responded instantly. First blushing and now sporting wood from a brief touch. He should fire Andy now before he made a fool of himself and lost the ground he'd gained with the ranch workers.

When he leaned back, he caught Andy staring at him, his eyes darker than usual. So he *was* feeling something too. That soothed Ken's annoyance with himself a little. Ken moved back slowly, being sure to stay just out of touching range. He could feel the heat coming off the man, and he barely resisted the urge to look down and see if he was hard too.

"That's better. Be sure to check all the straps next time."

Andy scowled. "It wouldn't have come loose."

"Maybe. Maybe not." And maybe Andy shouldn't keep flirting with him if he wasn't going to follow through.

Andy watched him for a few more seconds, his eyes assessing. Knowing. Looking right into Ken. "I'll have her back in an hour."

Ken smiled. "Perfect."

Andy turned and walked out.

THAT NIGHT, Andy didn't even bother trying to go to sleep. If nerves about the case hadn't kept him awake, his dick would have. He'd spent every spare moment that day thinking of things he wanted to do to Kenneth Carver, and kissing him like a goddamn fool had only made it worse.

When he'd exercised Nelly earlier, he'd noticed a large shed near the fence that divided Carver's property from the neighboring ranch. There weren't any other structures away from the main barn and training facilities. If he were using the ranch as a distribution stop, that's exactly where he'd base his operation. Now, when the ranch was quiet, was the perfect time to check it out.

After arming himself in case he found trouble, he left the guesthouse and moved silently toward the barn. He listened carefully, but he didn't hear anyone moving around. Chances were good that all the hands were in the bunkhouse. They had several potential customers coming in the next day, and the workday would start sooner than Andy liked. He didn't want to make assumptions, though. If one of the men were involved, he could get lucky—or unlucky depending on how prepared he was—and catch them on a delivery night.

The shed he wanted to check out was too far across the property to walk. Andy didn't want to alert anyone to what he was doing with the sound of a four-wheeler. He didn't like the idea of saddling up one of the horses without permission, but he could always say he was having trouble sleeping and figured he'd get to know one of the animals better.

His body was still trying to adjust to hours of riding a day, and he was sore as hell. Another ride wasn't going to help, but if he walked, he wouldn't be back in time to even bother trying to sleep. He grabbed a hackamore and a saddle blanket. Much of the riding he'd done had been bareback, and not having to tack the horse up would be much faster and easier. Brandy, the gentle horse he'd chosen, seemed eager to escape into the night as he led her from the barn.

He thought again of each of the men who should be sleeping in the bunkhouse. Which one of them, if any, was part of the distribution ring? He was still convinced Ken wasn't part of it, but even if he was, one of the others was likely working with him. It would have been too much to expect to have his instincts lead him to the guilty party right away, but it would sure be better for his sanity. The longer he'd been here the more often he got pulled into the past, back to the night Charlie died and the days leading up to it.

He mounted the horse and rode out across the fields following as straight a path as he could toward the building he needed to check out. He didn't see or hear anyone, at least not any humans. He scared a few rabbits and saw a deer bound back into the woods.

Before he reached the shed, he put Brandy on a picket line. He didn't want her to be in any danger if he wasn't the only one prowling around.

The padlock on the shed door hung loose. The sight sent prickles down Andy's spine. Something was wrong. He pressed his back to the wall and raised his gun in a two-hand grip. His heart hammered. He didn't want to admit—even to himself—that his hands weren't as steady as they should be when holding a weapon.

After a slow breath, he shoved the door open with his shoulder and went in, sweeping the area.

"Who's there?" he called.

No one answered. The shed was dark, but Andy was certain he'd seen a flash of light coming from the back. It could have been moonlight shining through one of the cracks between the board walls, but he didn't think so. He listened carefully as he took out his flashlight and shined it around, keeping his gun in his other hand. There were old pieces of equipment, tractor parts, tools, and some saddles with dry, cracked leather. Nothing unusual. But when the light hit the back wall, he realized there was a door there. The shed had a second room.

His heart slammed against his ribs, and he inched toward the door. That's where the light must have come from. Someone was in there. He reached the door and took the loop of rope that served as a handle in his hand.

He eased it open. "Who's there?" he called again.

No answer.

He raised his gun, ready to fire if he needed to and shined the light into the room.

"Fuck, don't shoot."

Rusty. A lump rose in Andy's throat. He really hadn't wanted Rusty to be involved.

"What are you doing out here?" he asked, failing to keep the anger out of his voice.

"Umm."

Rusty was seated at a table with a clip-on light and what looked like boxes of art supplies.

"Drawing? You were out here drawing?"

Rusty still didn't say anything.

This made no fucking sense. "Turn that light on." He gestured toward the lamp with his flashlight.

A sound had Andy bringing his gun back up and shining the light toward the corner. There was another man there, lying on a blanket, naked. "Who the hell are you?"

The unknown man didn't answer. Andy grabbed his pants from a pile of clothes on the floor. "I'm going to toss these to you, and you're going to put them on." As he spoke, he worked his hand into the pockets. There was a bag there, filled with pills. He'd examine them more closely later. He palmed the bag and tossed the pants toward the boy who didn't look as scared to be naked with a gun pointed at him as he should be. He was going to have to talk to Rusty about his taste in men.

"Rusty, I said turn the damn light on."

Rusty stumbled backward. "O-okay."

Andy realized he was still pointing his gun at the young man, and he lowered it. "I'm not going to fucking shoot you. Just turn the light on so we can see."

Rusty did.

"What the hell are you doing out here?"

Rusty's cheeks got even redder, and Andy realized the obviousness of his question. Rusty rallied now that the gun wasn't pointing at him. "What are *you* doing here?"

"I couldn't sleep, so I went for a ride. I saw light coming from the shed and stopped to investigate."

Rusty nodded, apparently accepting the explanation.

"We needed a place to meet." Rusty gestured toward the young man who was now wearing jeans and a t-shirt and holding a pair of boots. "I knew about this place because I use it for my... uh... drawing."

Rusty looked more embarrassed about his art than he did

about being caught with a man. Andy would try to figure that out later.

He looked at the other boy. "Who are you?"

"I work over there." He pointed toward the neighboring ranch. "Please don't tell anyone about me and Rusty. If they find out I'm... you know. They'll kill me."

Andy sighed. He hadn't missed that the boy still hadn't said his name, but he could find it out if he needed to. He couldn't be sure the boys were involved in anything more than hooking up in an unused shed, not until he knew more about the pills he'd found. "I get it. Just get out of here."

The boy raced out the door, not even bothering to put his boots on.

Andy returned his attention to Rusty. "So the shed is your studio?"

Rusty shook his head. "No. I mean... Look, I don't talk to anyone about my art. Please don't say anything about it."

Andy frowned. "Why?

"The other guys. They wouldn't get it, okay? No one ever gets it."

Rusty looked so young, so vulnerable. Andy had been fooled before, but his instincts told him the boy was for real. He toyed with the baggie in his pocket. What the hell was really going on? "Can I see?" he asked.

Rusty nodded. He'd drawn pages of comics filled with brightly colored, wide-eyed animals. His ability to make his creations expressive with only a few sparse lines was incredible.

"These are amazing," Andy said.

Rusty frowned, obviously not taking Andy seriously. "My mom told me drawing comics was dumb. She threw away most of my stuff before our last move. Maybe she's right. It's not like I'm really going to make money doing this or anything, and—"

"Stop!" Andy said, loud enough that his voice echoed in the mostly empty room. "Nothing about this is stupid. It's... You're really talented."

Rusty shook his head. "Nah, it's just fun. But you... you don't think it's dumb?"

"No."

"And you really don't care that... you know... Ben and I were..."

Ben. He'd get Gomez to find out exactly who this little shit was. "I wasn't lying when I told your uncle I didn't care who he slept with, and I don't care about you being gay either."

"I wasn't sure. Warren and Rodrigo just pretended to be accepting so they could keep their jobs. Ken knows, but nobody else does. I wouldn't be comfortable staying in the bunkhouse if they did."

Andy nodded. "Does Ken know you come out here?"

Rusty shook his head. "Are you going to tell him?"

Andy pondered the question. "I don't suppose there's any reason to. How often are you here?" He needed to know because while his gut said Rusty wasn't involved, he had every intention of coming back to check things out. At the very least, Ben was using something. That didn't make him a dealer or part of the distribution ring, but Andy wasn't about to discount him yet.

Rusty shrugged. "Whenever I can't sleep."

"How often is that?"

"Too often."

Andy nodded in sympathy. "I know how that feels. Did you walk out here?"

"Yeah."

"You all right to walk back?"

Rusty nodded. "I'll be fine. I'm going to work a bit longer."

"All right."

"Thanks for keeping my secret."

Andy smiled. "Sure."

Andy didn't like riding away and leaving Rusty there alone. Even if he was innocent, that didn't mean the shed wasn't being used as a way station. Rusty could be in danger if the wrong person showed up. Now he had even more incentive to find the son of a bitch who was guilty as fast as he could.

CHAPTER SEVEN

Ken polished off the last of his coffee. He'd lost count of how many cups he'd had that day. Curse Andy and his cock teasing ways. Ken had been up half the night thinking about him and the other half he'd spent touching the man in his dreams. He entered the barn through the tack room, set his cup on a shelf, and grabbed Jensen's saddle off the hook, but he froze when he heard Rusty calling Warren's name with an edge of fear in his voice.

Ken rushed into the main part of the barn and saw Warren lying on the floor motionless.

"Warren? Warren, are you okay?" Rusty called, his voice almost a squeak. He laid a hand on the older man's back.

Warren gave no response.

Ken pulled out his phone and dialed 911. He knelt by Rusty and pressed a finger to Warren's neck, checking for a pulse. He couldn't find one. "Fuck."

"911, what is your emergency?" a woman said.

"This is Kenneth Carver at the KC Ranch. I just found one of my ranch hands lying on the floor in the barn. He has no pulse. I'm handing the phone to another employee so I can start CPR."

Rusty took the phone, and Ken started chest compressions even though he doubted he was going to be able to revive the man.

"Yes, we found him on the ground," he heard Rusty say. "651 Lancer Highway. The KC Ranch."

Ken checked for a pulse again, still nothing. He kept going with the compressions.

"My boss is starting CPR. Please hurry," Rusty said, his voice shaky. "Okay, okay, I… okay."

"The ambulance is on its way. I… Is it working?" Rusty asked, his voice shaking.

"I don't know, but I have to try."

Andy stepped into the barn. He looked at them and then down at Warren. "Oh my God, what happened?" he asked as he raced toward them.

"Warren collapsed, and he's… His heart stopped," Rusty said. He was starting to look distressingly green.

"Sit down," Andy ordered him before Ken had a chance. When Rusty didn't move, Andy took his arm and helped him settle on the floor against the wall of the tack room. "Take some deep breaths," he said as he stood and focused on Ken again. "Have you called 911?"

"Yeah, Ken did."

Ken was impressed by Andy's cool headedness. He didn't look nearly as surprised as someone might to find a dead man in the barn. Should Ken be worried by that?

"I heard Rusty calling Warren's name," he explained. "When I saw them, Warren was on the ground. He didn't have a pulse."

Sirens sounded in the distance.

"Do you need me to take over?" Andy asked Ken.

"No, I'm okay."

"I'll go meet them at the road," Andy said.

Ken nodded. "Yeah, go."

He wiped the sweat off his forehead. The heat in the barn seemed to be getting worse every second. Sweat ran down his back, and he wished he could take his shirt off, but he didn't want to stop in case Warren did have a chance.

Once Andy headed out the door, Ken turned to Rusty. "You don't have to stay."

"I don't want to leave you alone," Rusty said.

"I'm fine. Go outside and keep everyone else away."

"Are you sure?"

Ken nodded. "Yeah, but I'm going to need a drink or six as soon as we're done here."

Rusty nodded. "You and me both."

"Just go guard the door, okay?"

Rusty stood slowly and wiped the sweat off his face with the t-shirt he'd stuffed in his back pocket. Then he pulled the grimy shirt over his head and headed outside. Ken had been worried he might pass out, but he seemed to be walking steadily enough.

Andy and the EMTs arrived a few seconds later. Two men knelt by Ken. "We've got this now," one of them said.

Ken stood and stepped back, watching them as they checked Warren's vital signs and readied a defibrillator.

"Do you have any idea how long he'd been on the ground before you got to him?" the third man who'd come in with Andy asked.

"No. Rusty might have a better idea."

Andy stepped outside and returned a few seconds later. "Possibly as long as forty-five minutes. That's how long it had been since Rusty had seen him. He also said Warren was complaining of his chest hurting, but he thought he'd eaten something that had given him heartburn."

The man nodded. "Your foreman told us you began CPR as soon as you found him."

Had they just assumed Andy was the foreman? He certainly had the take-charge attitude needed for running a ranch. Ken nodded, not bothering to correct them. "That's right. He didn't have a pulse."

The man asked a few other questions that Ken barely remembered later. All he could recall was watching the men attempt to revive Warren with the defibrillator and more chest compressions. Finally, the paramedic who headed the team decided that Warren wasn't coming back.

"Was it a heart attack?" Ken asked.

"Very likely, but we can't say for certain," the paramedic said.

Warren had seemed perfectly healthy. He worked hard, and while older than the other hands, he was far from old. He'd turned fifty-two a few months before Ken bought the ranch. He'd been laughing and joking around with the other men earlier that morning, no sign that anything was wrong. Of course, it was hard to predict things like heart attacks. Ken was far more unsettled than he'd let on to Rusty, though he had a feeling Andy saw through his exterior calm.

As far as Ken could remember, Warren didn't have much family and not any he was close to, but he would've put someone down as his emergency contact. Ken would have to call them and let them know he was dead.

Ken had no idea what would happen now. Would Warren be taken to the hospital or a funeral home? If so, which one? Ken was more than willing to pay for the burial expenses, especially if he was right that Warren didn't have much family, but he had no idea how that worked. He was too used to having people handle things for him. Maybe he wasn't as independent now as he liked to think.

"Umm... what do we—"

Andy laid a hand on his shoulder. "I got this," he said, assured, confident, sexy. Ken shouldn't be thinking that with a dead man at his feet, but he lost all sense around Andy.

"Are you going to transport him to the hospital for the declaration of death?" Andy asked.

"Yes, sir."

Two other paramedics entered the barn, rolling a stretcher.

Andy spoke again. "We're going to contact his next of kin. Which hospital should we tell them to call?"

"We'll take him to the North Cypress Emergency Room."

"Okay, is there anything else we need to do?"

The man shook his head. "No, that's it."

That's it. A man's life has ended and there was nothing else to do. Ken suddenly felt as sick as Rusty had looked earlier.

Ken needed a moment to center himself. As the men loaded Warren's body onto the stretcher and then into the ambulance, he got a few peppermint treats from the tack room and walked over to Jensen's stall.

The bay mare smelled the treats and stuck her head over the door. "Hey there, girl," he said as he rubbed her nose.

Jensen snuffled his shirt pocket.

"Nope, not there." She snorted, and Ken smiled as he pulled a treat from his pants pocket. "Here you go."

Once the horse had her treats, Ken walked away from the stall and stood with Andy to watch the EMTs drive away.

"Go sit down and have a drink. I'll get the employee files and find out who we need to call," Andy said.

"You shouldn't have to—"

"You shouldn't have had to find a dead man in your barn. I can handle the calls."

"But he was my—"

"Ken, don't argue with me. I'll take care of it."

Andy's steely expression was not to be ignored, so Ken did the only thing he could, agreed to what Andy asked.

"Send Rusty to join me," he said.

Andy nodded. "Will do, boss."

ANDY PULLED the key Ken had given him out of his pocket. He'd been wondering how he was going to get a look at the employee files, and while he hated the circumstances, he was thrilled not to have to break in. Ken's security, when he actually turned it on, was damn good, and Andy was certain Ken had a sixth sense for trouble almost as keen as his own.

He'd need to be quick, but fortunately there weren't many employees, and he doubted Ken would come looking for him. He and Rusty had already started drinking when he'd headed toward the office.

Andy had to admit he was impressed with how well Ken had handled things. The EMTs wouldn't have known how ruffled he was by the end, but Andy had spent too much time studying people not to notice the telltale signs of an impending meltdown. Ken kept it together in public, but by the time the ambulance drove away, he was nearly as pale as Rusty had been.

Andy hoped he'd managed to look distressed enough to not raise suspicions. He'd seen his share of dead bodies on the job, and he handled it by turning cold and professional. He hoped Ken had been too distracted to worry about his lack of emotion.

Andy unlocked the drawer where the files were kept. He was glad they were still on paper. The previous owner had been an older man who refused to go digital, and Ken hadn't had a chance to convert everything over. Andy doubted Ken would have been as willing to give Andy access to his laptop, but Andy would have found a way no matter what. A healthy man in his fifties could die of a heart attack with no warning, but considering that someone on this ranch was connected to the drug ring, it made the death suspicious in his mind. A sudden death like Warren's wouldn't be difficult to arrange if he'd gotten reluctant about continuing to move the product through. It was also possible he'd been sampling the product and taken too much or that he'd seen something he shouldn't. Andy needed to find out fast, because if it was the latter, everyone at the ranch could be in danger.

There wasn't a file for Rusty, which wasn't too surprising since he was family, but it left Andy with no further information on what Rusty had meant about a "misspent youth." Luke's file held nothing outside of what Andy expected, but he used his phone to photograph the main information and he did the same with Rodrigo's even though he found nothing of interest.

His luck changed when he got to Warren's. As Andy looked back through vacation records from the year before, he noticed Warren had taken time off on the same dates that major drug shipments were thought to have been routed through the ranch. That and his sudden death were too much of a coincidence. Warren had been in on it, and that made sense because the drugs had been moving through since before Ken owned the ranch.

Andy's next move was to figure out who was responsible. Someone else at the ranch? Warren wasn't necessarily the only one involved. Ken or Rusty could have slipped him something to induce a heart attack without anyone noticing, but they'd been honestly shocked when he'd died. Andy would stake his badge on that. Rodrigo or Luke could have done it, but he had no reason to suspect them. He'd be watching his back, though, that was for sure.

Once he'd perused the file for any further clues, he found Warren's emergency contact information. A cousin in Oklahoma appeared to be the closest family he had. Taking a deep breath, Andy dialed the woman's number. He'd made these calls many times before, but it never got any easier. This time he didn't even have the professionalism of the badge to hide behind.

Many long minutes later, after patiently listening to Warren's cousin reminisce about him and sharing the contact details she would need to make arrangements for claiming the body, Andy slipped out of the office and over to the guesthouse. He needed to call Gomez and update her, but he couldn't risk being overheard in the house. In fact, after Warren's death, he had to be even more cautious about being caught. He pulled out his phone, tapped her number, and started walking across the yard to a place where the chances of anyone disturbing him were slim. He'd kept his phone with him the whole time he'd been on the ranch. Still, there was a chance the call was being intercepted, but he could only be so paranoid.

"This better be important," Gomez said. She obviously wasn't having a good day.

"One of the ranch hands just died."

Gomez didn't respond for several seconds. Andy waited patiently for her to process what he'd said.

"Naturally?"

"It appeared to be a heart attack that killed him instantly."

"You're not calling me because someone had a heart attack."

"No, I'm not. It was Warren. I just looked through his employee file. He had no medical conditions listed, and he took off every day last year that we know a major shipment left Houston."

"Where did they take the body?"

"North Cypress Emergency Room."

"You think he was the ranch contact?'

"Maybe, or maybe he learned something he shouldn't have."

"They would have taken him out immediately, then. These men do not hesitate to kill."

"True. He might not be the only one involved, though."

"There's also the chance someone made you, and they eliminated the link before you found them."

Andy winced. He'd thought of that but tried to push it aside. "Yeah, but by your logic, they would have killed me too."

"Just watch your back."

"I always do."

"Even when you're sure about someone?"

"I…" He started to say he had good instincts, but she wouldn't listen to that, and truthfully, he wasn't watching himself around Ken. The fucking kiss in the barn showed that. Would it make a difference if Ken weren't so damn beguiling? Maybe. Maybe not. Rusty was a hot little twink, but way too young for Andy, and he believed Rusty was innocent too.

"I've got some news you won't like," Gomez said.

"What?"

"We finally got access to Rusty's files. He was arrested for possession."

Fuck. "Okay, then I'll check him out better, see what I can get Ken to tell me."

"He was sixteen when he was arrested. It looks like he got in with bad people and couldn't get out, but that could have happened again. He's still young."

"Why, when he's got Ken looking after him?"

"I know you don't want to hear this, but Ken could still be involved. Rusty's stepdad could be too."

"Rusty doesn't want a damn thing to do with his stepdad or his mom, and Ken—"

"Is a fine-looking man and very good at persuasion. How do you think he got where he is?"

"Because he was born to it."

"Carver Pharm was all his. He built it from scratch and owned it outright. He knows how to manipulate people. It's a survival skill for him."

That didn't make him the one running drugs, but arguing further on that with Gomez was likely to get Andy pulled from the case. He couldn't let that happen. He wanted justice, and he was going to get it.

Even if that meant arresting Ken?

Andy took a deep breath. "I get it, okay? I'm looking at everyone no matter what my instincts say."

"Look harder at Rusty."

Andy rolled his eyes, glad he wasn't having the conversation face to face. "I will. Let me know what you find on Warren."

She started to say something, but he hung up because if she were about to give him another warning, he wasn't going to take it well. Better to pretend he thought they were done or that someone walked up to him than yell at her. She'd taken a chance on him. No one thought he was stable enough to do this, and they were most likely right.

CHAPTER EIGHT

Ken poured himself and Rusty another drink. The kid was going to have a hell of a hangover the next day. Ken would have to get some water in him and get him to bed soon. Hopefully, Rusty would just pass out and not see Warren's body in his dreams. Ken figured he'd have to crack open another bottle of Jack to get himself to that point.

Unless... No, this wasn't the night to decide to forego all sanity and throw himself into a full-out seduction of his employee. He figured at this point it was inevitable he was going to sleep with Andy, hopefully more than once. After Andy had kissed him, the tension between them every time they were in the barn together was thick enough to choke them. But not tonight with all this alcohol in him. Ken wanted to be fully aware, especially the first time. He wasn't sure he'd survive the experience if he wasn't.

Andy had said he'd check back in with him, and Ken wished he'd hurry up. Hopefully, he wasn't having trouble contacting Warren's family. "Maybe I should go check on Andy."

Rusty shook his head. "Hell no."

"'Cause he's a big boy and can handle himself?" Ken asked, trying not to laugh at Rusty's slurred words.

Rusty laughed. "No, 'cause you won't come back, and I don't wanna be alone. I might puke on your carpet."

"Oh God, are you that bad off already?"

Rusty laid his head back and looked up at the ceiling. "Nope. I'm good, or I would be if the damn room would stop spinning."

Ken rolled his eyes. "I'd come back. I'm not even drunk yet."

Rusty started giggling. "Nah, you'd fuck him."

Ken laid a hand over his eyes. So much for no one having noticed his attraction to Andy. "Is it that obvious?"

Rusty's laughter turned hysterical. When he'd finally calmed down enough to speak, he said. "Only as obvious as his hard-on for you."

Ken rolled his eyes. "You're a fucking idiot."

"Not as big a one as you're going to be."

Ken narrowed his eyes. Rusty shouldn't be that perceptive, especially not when he was drunk. "I can handle myself."

"Not with that one. There's something dangerous about him."

Ken didn't like the slightly wistful sound of Rusty's voice. "You damn well better stay away from him."

"He's outta my league." The giggles started again just as Andy walked in.

Ken was just drunk enough not to be able to keep from staring. Despite the hell he'd been through, Andy looked like sin poured into tight jeans. He was wearing Ken's favorite pair, the ones with the hole along the seam on the inner thigh. Tanned skin showed through, and Ken wanted to taste it, to bite and suck until that little circle of skin was marked as his.

"Ken? You okay?" Andy asked

Holy fuck. Obviously not. "More than he is." He gestured to Rusty, which only served to intensify the giggles.

"He's drunk as a skunk, but you're brooding. That worries me more."

Brooding because I can't beg you to help me forget this whole day by driving me through the wall. "I'm fine. I just never…" He didn't want to talk about Warren.

"Yeah, it doesn't really get easier."

Fuck. Ken hadn't meant to make it sound like he thought death wouldn't mean anything to Andy. He wished he could take the words back. Would saying more just make that worse? He threw back the rest of his drink. "I didn't mean…"

―――

ANDY SHOOK HIS HEAD. "It's okay. I saw a hell of a lotta shit in the desert. And…" Out of nowhere, images from that night came to mind. What the hell was happening to him? He'd had this under control. Before taking this assignment, memories only swamped him in his dreams. He'd served four years in the army. That wasn't a lie, and he'd seen numerous men die in Afghanistan, but when he thought too long about death, he watched through a crack in the wall as Charlie was shot and then—

"Andy?" Ken was on his feet standing right in front of him. "Andy? Are you okay?"

He managed to nod, but he couldn't move. He was frozen in place.

"Drink?"

He nodded again.

Ken grabbed a glass and poured him some whiskey. He was probably meant to sip it, but he swallowed it all at once.

The vicious burn as it went down sent away the last of the demons.

Ken watched him, a wary expression on his face.

"Long day," he said, hoping Ken didn't question him.

He took a step back and settled into his chair again. "Sit down, then. You want another one?"

"Yeah." He held out his glass. At least he'd managed a word, and he was no longer seeing ghosts.

Rusty was watching him carefully, and he took the opportunity to shift the focus from himself. "How are you handling things, or is the whiskey handling it for you?"

Rusty studied him for a few seconds. "Not sure. I'm not drunk enough yet."

Ken shook his head. "He's more than drunk enough."

Andy nodded. "As long as he's feeling good, that's all that matters right now."

"He won't be feeling good tomorrow."

Andy smiled and looked at Rusty as the boy lay back once more and smiled up at the ceiling. "He sure won't, but he needed this. I wish I'd been there from the start."

Ken studied him like he hadn't expected him to say that.

"I know you could have handled it. Hell, you ran a company, so you can deal with whatever shit comes your way, but…" Andy looked away, afraid emotions he didn't want to reveal would show on his face.

"Thank you." Andy looked back at Ken then, the simple words like a magnet. He knew his eyes were wide and his surprise obvious.

"I can appreciate help, you know," Ken said, a sexy-as-hell grin on his face.

"Sometimes." Andy was certain Ken didn't let anyone else take charge often.

"I hired you, didn't I?"

The reminder that he worked for Ken threw him off balance for a few seconds. At first, he wasn't sure why, and then he got it. For a brief time, he'd forgotten he was a ranch hand and not a cop—Andy not Andrew. It was a subtle shift, not something he'd been conscious of until Ken had spoken. He'd done nothing to give himself away, so it shouldn't really matter. Except it did. One of the most important rules about a UC assignment was to never forget who you were, not even in your sleep.

Rusty was staring at him, and Andy started to wonder if Rusty suspected something about him after all. Then he started giggling maniacally again, and Andy knew better.

"You should go to bed before you pass out," Ken said.

Rusty shook his head. "Hell no. I'm not done."

He reached for the bottle, but Ken grabbed it and held it away from him.

Rusty frowned. "Gimme."

"No," Andy and Ken said at the same time.

"Yes," Rusty yelled. He tried to leap up, but he swayed and grabbed onto a table, nearly turning it over. Andy took hold of his waist and hauled him up. "I'm putting you to bed."

"No, 'm fine."

Ken rolled his eyes. "Rusty, do what he says."

"Fine. I got more in my room. I'm gonna keep drinking there. Maybe I'll…" His words trailed off, and he leaned against Andy's shoulder. "Damn, you feel like you're made of rock. You're strong, ain't ya?"

Andy grinned. "That I am." He spun Rusty around and tossed him over his shoulder in a fireman's carry.

"Whoa. The world is like upside down."

"Try not to puke on him," Ken said.

"Whee! The world is spinning so fast."

Ken stood and took a step toward them. "Are you sure—"

"I'm fine. I got this." Andy hated that he was being such a manipulative bastard, but in his current state Rusty would say anything, and he was unlikely to remember having been questioned. If Andy got him into his room before he lost consciousness, he could interrogate him for a while.

"Will you still be soberish when I get back?" he asked Ken.

"You're coming back?"

Andy frowned. "I don't have to, but I thought maybe you didn't want to be alone."

Ken focused on his drink. "I don't guess I do."

"Then I'll be back." If nothing else, Andy would have known how off balance the man was from his uncertainty. He'd always at least appeared to be in control. Maybe it was the alcohol, but Andy doubted it. He suspected Ken was acting drunker than he really was.

"I'm not sober now, though," Ken asserted.

"You gonna be worse later?"

"Not like that," he said, waving his hand toward Rusty.

"Good. I'd hate to have to put you to bed too." The words were out before Andy thought them through. He was lying of course. He'd love to put Ken to bed unless he did get as drunk as Rusty. Although then he might let Andy do any fucking thing he wanted to him, and there were some very dirty things that Andy wanted to do.

Ken's eyes widened, and he licked his lips as if he'd read Andy's mind. Right now, Ken was not at all the suave man he'd pretended to be when they'd met or the cold hard-ass who ordered everyone around and pretended he always knew the answer. He was vulnerable, and if Andy had any sense, he'd go right back to the guesthouse because like this, Ken was even more devastating. But Andy couldn't walk away.

He needed info, and this would be a great time to ask questions. Ken's guard was down. Andy needed to exploit that, even if he didn't want to.

You're on a case.
Shut the fuck up. I'm going to take care of it.
Without questioning the suspects?
He's not a suspect, not to me.
You're not fit for this.
Tell me something I don't know.

Finally shutting down his infuriating inner voice with a growl, he carried Rusty to his room in the bunkhouse. Miraculously, he didn't get vomited on, and when he got Rusty settled in bed, the young man was still slightly conscious. "Another one," he mumbled.

"You've had enough." Since when did Andy act like a parent?

"Not enough in the world," Rusty argued.

Andy patted his leg. "You think that now, but it'll fade." Maybe. He hoped so.

"Don't wanna dream about it."

"At this point, I don't think you will." *Or if you do, you won't remember.*

"Really?"

"Yeah."

"'Kay."

Andy headed toward the bathroom Rusty shared with Luke. "I'm going to get you some water and ibuprofen."

When he got back, Rusty grabbed his arm and pulled him down. "Take care of him for me."

"Who?"

"Uncle Ken. He's not like he seems. He's a mess."

Andy frowned. "How?"

"He can't do it all, not by himself, and he misses his

family or what his family should have been for him."

"Is he... mixed up in anything bad?" Andy asked.

Rusty frowned. "No. Ken's the only Carver who's a decent human being. I'd be in prison now if it weren't for him. He'd never... Don't listen to what people say. He's not what he shows people. He needs someone to take care of him."

Andy didn't want to think about the hell Ken's family put him through and the walls he'd built up to help him deal with it. And he sure as hell didn't want to think about taking care of the man.

"What happened that put you in prison? You wanna talk about it?"

Rusty frowned. "Only if I get another drink."

Andy weighed the consequences of that. "One."

Rusty lay back then and looked up at the ceiling. He grabbed on to the headboard as if trying to steady himself.

"Or maybe not."

"The fucking drugs were easier on me. Lance got me hooked on them—son of a bitch—then got me dealing and left me to rot for it. Ken got my sentence reduced, and I ain't never fucked up that bad again. I don't even drink usually, maybe a beer or two, but not like this and... Oh fuck!"

Andy grabbed the trashcan just in time as Rusty shot up off the bed and hung over it, his body letting go of what had to be most of the alcohol he'd poured into himself to help him deal with finding Warren. Anyone working with the crew who'd been doing those drug runs wouldn't be that squeamish about a corpse. No way was Rusty involved with them.

When Rusty's body quieted, he wiped his mouth on his sleeve and lay on his back on the floor. "I'm sorry, man. Oh God, I feel like shit."

"Think you can drink some water?" Andy asked.

Rusty made a face. "Maybe."

"Try. Slow sips and then see if you think these might stay down." He held up the ibuprofen.

After Rusty had swallowed a few sips of water, Andy said, "Let me help you get back in bed."

"Don't make me move," Rusty whined.

Andy considered Rusty's position on the floor. He was lying on a rug, not a thick one, but at least he wasn't on the bare floor. He'd survive. He was going to feel like shit in the morning no matter where he slept. Andy yanked a blanket off the bed and laid it beside him. "You can cover up with this if you want."

Rusty took a few more tentative sips of water and grimaced.

Andy set the ibuprofen bottle down beside him. "I'll leave the pills here in case you decide to take them."

Rusty made a noncommittal sound, and Andy focused on cleaning up and returning the trashcan to a place where Rusty could easily grab it if he needed it again.

Rusty was curled on his side, sleeping, by the time he finished. Andy would check on him again later, but for now, he'd be okay.

Andy closed Rusty's door and left the bunkhouse. He looked toward Ken's office and wished he hadn't promised to come back. He didn't want Ken to be alone, but he'd done about all the babying he could do for the day. He really needed to go think through this fucking case, maybe poke around the farm a bit, call Gomez back about Warren, follow some leads on the computer. Anything but sit there with a hard-on ignoring the fact that Ken could be involved, longing to get on his knees and show Ken the very best way to forget something you wished you'd never seen.

But he wouldn't leave Ken sitting alone in the dark. He

walked back to the main house and entered through the kitchen. The door was unlocked. Ken needed to be more careful. Anyone could walk in and... An image of Warren lying on the barn floor flashed in front of him. The room wavered. Andy held up his hand like he could literally push the vision back. There weren't any other bodies here, he told himself. There weren't *any* bodies here now at all. Yet there it was, the familiar vision. No matter how hard he tried, he couldn't stop it. Except this time there was one important change. Instead of Charlie lying there bleeding out, his eyes pleading for mercy, it was Ken.

No! That was never going to happen. No matter how much of his sanity he had to compromise to stop it.

"Ken!" he called, heart racing. He'd never gotten premonitions before, but suddenly he felt like Ken was in danger.

"Still right here," Ken called, his words slightly slurred. He'd definitely been drinking more while Andy was gone.

Andy told himself he was being an idiot. He locked the door behind him, but the damn house had five more doors and any number of easily accessible windows. If the men he was investigating wanted to get to Ken, a locked door, even an alarmed one, wasn't going to stop them.

There weren't any lights on in the house, but Andy didn't need them. He made his way to the room where he'd left Ken. Ken was still sitting in the same chair, and the level of whiskey in the bottle was a lot lower.

"Looks like I may have to put you to bed after all."

Ken looked him up and down. "That you may."

"Or I could just let you stay right here."

Ken smiled. "Might be safer."

"For who?"

He frowned and seemed to be pondering that. Andy had given up on getting an answer when he said, "I don't know."

Andy didn't know either. For both of them probably because he really wanted to put his hands on Ken.

"Maybe I should go."

"Have a drink," Ken insisted, his voice unsteady.

Andy shook his head. "Someone's got to be capable of work in the morning."

"I'll be fine. I'm a Carver. We can hold our liquor."

"I'm sure you can."

"We're good at other things too," Ken assured him.

"Are you coming on to me?" *Why the hell did he just say that?*

Ken closed his eyes and let his head rest back like Rusty had done, but he wasn't drunk enough for the world to tilt around him, at least Andy didn't think he was. "I... Yeah."

Andy's heart pounded. "This is a terrible idea."

"Yeah, it is."

"Should I go?" Andy asked, not sure what he wanted Ken's answer to be.

Ken chewed his lip for a few seconds and then said, "You were right."

"About what?"

"I don't want to be alone."

Andy took a deep breath. "Okay. I'll stay, but I'm not fucking you. Not tonight."

Ken took a sip of whiskey and smiled. "Another night?"

"I can't say what's going to happen any other night, but right now you're not thinking straight, and I'm not either."

Ken nodded. "Did Rusty pass out?"

"After throwing up most of his insides."

Ken grimaced and set his drink down. "You sure you don't want anything?"

"I am. You were right too, you know."

Ken frowned. "About what?"

"About this not bothering me so much because of what I saw in the army." *And as a cop.* "I've seen a lot of people die in much worse ways. It's not like it doesn't mean anything but... Fuck. Apparently, I don't need a drink to say shit I shouldn't."

"You haven't said anything wrong. Talk to me. I asked you for company. The least I can do is listen."

"You don't want to hear about this shit," Andy insisted.

"Please."

Andy was moving into dangerous territory, but that raw word from Ken, his need for someone else to be vulnerable, was something Andy couldn't deny. "I served four years. I needed to pay for college, and one of my buddies was going in, so I went too. It was pure hell from almost the get-go. Boot camp and then the desert. My first day over there I saw a group of men get blown up with a grenade launcher. Days were either boring as hell as we sat around in the heat waiting for orders or a run of pure, shit-yourself terror. I still don't sleep soundly." He shouldn't have admitted how scared he'd been. Never let them see the soft side when you're UC, or really, any fucking time. That was what he'd been taught, but with Ken, his judgment was blown. It had been from the first moment they met.

You're not fit for this.

He should call Gomez and have her get him out, but then he would have failed not only himself but her too, and Ken, and Rusty, and anyone else on the ranch who didn't need this bullshit threatening them. He had to finish this. Then maybe he would disappear, become someone else, get work at a ranch, stop thinking about anything but horses and sun, and work himself until he was so exhausted he couldn't lie awake seeing death and failure.

Could he walk away from police work? What about from

Ken? *Whoa*. Where the hell had that come from? He might give in and fuck the guy, sure, but there wasn't going to be some goddamn relationship. That was ridiculous.

He looked up at Ken, realizing he'd been staring at the floor for a long time. "I really can't talk about this anymore."

"Sorry. I shouldn't have pushed."

Andy closed his eyes, but he started to see Charlie. He hoped to God Ken couldn't see the depth of his fear.

If he did, he ignored it and simply said, "I'm sorry you had to deal with everything today."

"Don't be. I volunteered, remember?"

"I let you take over when it was my job." Ken looked disgusted with himself.

"Yeah, I get it. You like to run everything, control everything. You want everyone to know you can, but sometimes you've got to let people help you." Andy was great at giving advice he'd never follow.

"And you don't?"

"Don't what?"

"Like to control everything?"

Andy tilted his head and studied Ken. "I'm good at control." They were back to flirting, but at least that was safer than him slipping into the past.

Ken grinned and finished off another drink. "I just bet you are. Do you want to take charge here?"

Andy tried not to react, but his dick pressed against his jeans, wanting out. Hell yes, he wanted to take control of Ken, drag him on the floor and fuck him until he didn't remember a damn thing that had happened that day.

Ken grinned. "Of the ranch, I mean."

"What?"

"I need a foreman. You like to be in charge, and you're damn good at ordering people around—"

"I'm not—"

Ken raised a brow and Andy laughed.

"Okay, yeah, I am."

"And you enjoy it."

Andy gave him an assessing look. "So do you."

"I do. Very much."

The low tone of those words had Andy sucking in his breath. He didn't submit to anyone. It wasn't in his nature, but Ken made him think about crouching on his hands and knees, Ken behind him ordering him not to move, Ken's cock breaching him.

He was sweating, even in the air conditioning. So not good. He wasn't qualified to run a ranch. He'd blustered his way through playing ranch hand, but running the place would put him at greater risk for revealing his lack of experience.

You'd have access to the files all the time. You could have a legitimate reason to ask Ken details about all the employees, about suppliers, about nearly anything.

He had to be honest, or as honest as he was allowed to be. "I know horses, that's all. This business shit—"

"Can be taught to someone who already knows how to lead."

Why the hell did Andy's chest get tight hearing those words. He'd been told he was a good leader before, even believed it until losing Charlie got him so fucked-up he wasn't trustworthy anymore. But even now—plagued by visions of the past and wanting to run—he still had an instinct to take care of his people.

"Then I guess I'm your man."

Ken licked his lips, and Andy's heart stopped. "That sounds perfect."

It could be, if they were in an alternate universe. "I should head to bed now. I've got a ranch to run tomorrow."

"I might just pass out right here."

Andy frowned. "You're not really that drunk, are you?"

Ken shrugged. "I'm not as drunk as I'd like to be."

Andy wanted to help him forget with something much better than alcohol, but his heart was thundering against his chest. He didn't need to get any closer. This man had the potential to wreck him. He wasn't sure how he knew that, but it was a certainty.

"Call me if things get bad. I can actually be a decent listener."

Ken looked like he wanted to say something else, but he simply nodded.

Andy started to walk away. He paused at the door, so tempted to look back he ached. Just a few steps and Ken would be his to do with as he wished. The man was having a moment of vulnerability, and for some reason he trusted Andy enough not to cover it up. But Andy kept going. He turned the knob, pulled the door open, and started to step into the night.

"Let's have dinner tomorrow," Ken said.

Andy made a choked sound. His heart might have actually stopped. "Wh-what?" Ken pushing to take him to bed he'd expected but a date? No way.

"We need to discuss the ranch and all the 'business shit,' don't we?"

Heat rushed to Andy's cheeks. Why had he thought Ken meant it to be a date? Still not turning around, he replied. "Fine. I'll see you tomorrow."

He left then, and Ken's laugh followed him out as if the man knew what he'd assumed. Goddamn him for getting the upper hand even when he was off balance.

Andy collapsed as soon as he reached the guesthouse couch. After five days at the ranch, he was just getting over the worst of his aches. The combination of working hard and not sleeping was going to do him in very soon, but possibly not as quickly as watching Ken saunter through the barn in his perfectly fitted jeans, wearing a Stetson like he was born to it, like a wet dream come true.

Andy was quickly losing the strength to fight it. He wanted Ken, and so far he'd found nothing to implicate him in the case. But he wouldn't sleep with him to get information, no matter how much he needed it. If he fucked Kenneth Carver, it would be because he wanted to, because he couldn't walk away without tasting him. Once this ended and he went back to being Andrew Wofford, Ken wouldn't want a damn thing to do with him. One way or another this case was bound to bring a shitstorm down on the ranch.

He pulled out the bag of drugs he'd found on Ben, the boy Rusty was fucking. Gomez had gotten him the boy's cell number, but Andy had wanted him to sweat a bit after realizing the pills were gone. He'd managed to hand one off to be analyzed at a meeting with a contact in town. They were in fact the superpowered Vicodin laced with what amounted to poison that he'd feared they were.

The time had come to take some action and hopefully scare the fuck out of Ben. Andy intended to make sure he stayed away from Rusty as part of their bargain.

He dialed the number from a phone the contact had passed him. When the voicemail picked up, he left a message. "We met the other night. I picked up something of yours. I'm interested in more of it. Let's talk."

Knowing sleep would be as elusive as always, he grabbed a beer from the guesthouse fridge and settled on the bed with his laptop. It was time to dig a little deeper into Carver Pharm, the hospital, Ken's brother, and any possible connection to Warren or anyone else at the ranch.

CHAPTER NINE

Andy walked quickly to the guesthouse when he finished the last of his barn chores. He'd thought of nothing but the dinner with Ken and what might happen after —or hell, during it—if his dick had its way.

He turned the shower to cold and stepped in, but as he soaped up his shivering body, fantasies about where the night could lead only got worse so he gave up, changed the water temperature, and slicked his cock with soap. As he jacked himself off, he imagined pinning Ken to the wall and fucking him until he begged, screamed, fought, and then took everything Andy had to give. He spent the rest of the shower replaying the moment from his fantasy when Ken had come all over his hand as Andy pumped his cock and thrust deep in his ass. Great. That image was going to make dinner so much more awkward.

He tried not to let himself think about what he should wear. No way in hell was he going to start worrying about what Ken thought of his fucking clothes. Besides, he liked Andy well enough covered in dirt and horseshit. Andy finally chose a pair of jeans with no stains on them and a green t-shirt with a rattlesnake on it, a gag gift from Gomez after he'd had a run-in that could have gone far worse than it had.

He took a deep breath and tried to put himself in the right headspace for this role. He was already frustrated with trying to tease out information. He'd gotten too used to running an investigation where he simply brought the suspect into an interrogation room and had at him. Even that had started to wear thin. Should he even be a cop anymore?

As far as he was concerned, this was it. If he fucked this up, he was walking, and if he didn't... he'd see what happened then. If there was any chance of this going right, he had to question everyone. That meant that tonight, he needed to forget what his instincts told him about Ken, forget that he didn't want him to be guilty, and push for information on Carver Pharm. How hard could it be to ask some questions and see how much Ken squirmed?

Pretty fucking hard if you're too focused on getting in his pants.

Andy would pretend that first afternoon in the barn was nothing but a deluded fantasy. It was as unreal as the chance of him and Ken having a relationship. Tonight, Andy would behave like a good UC detective, push for information, evade questions about himself, and remember who he was.

A fuckup.

He sighed. Not this time. He'd bring these assholes down and move on to the next case. No involvement. No fucking Ken against the door of a stall.

What if he's involved and fucking him gets you a confession or an invitation to join him?

No. Andy would not go there.

You fuck for nothing but a pleasure high all the time, no names, no connection beyond your cock in some guy's ass. Why do you care who your partner is now?

He shouldn't care. But ever since he'd watched Charlie die after sleeping with him for weeks, he hadn't been able to think about sex the same way. He'd hardly been able to handle hooking up at all.

Charlie was working for a vicious dealer.

He was also a decent human being, especially compared to most of the assholes that walked when the operation went ass up.

That wasn't your fault.

The hell it wasn't.

Andy glanced at the clock and realized he was going to be late if he didn't walk over now.

He shoved his feet into his boots and grabbed his keys so he could lock up. The ranch seemed like the kind of place where people didn't lock doors, but the last thing Andy needed was someone going through his stuff. Someone with even rudimentary hacker abilities would make him easily, and he had more weapons than a ranch hand really needed, even for a Texan.

When he entered the big house from the side door, he stepped into a kitchen that was nearly as warm as the outside but smelled like heaven. A dark-haired woman was sliding a Bundt pan into one of two massive wall-mounted ovens. When she'd closed the door, she turned around and smiled at him.

"You must be Andy."

He smiled. His instincts told him immediately that he was going to like this woman as much as Ken did.

"I'm Renata."

"I'm very pleased to make your acquaintance, ma'am."

"None of that. Just Renata will do. And I hope you'll be as pleased to get acquainted with the dinner I've made. I made some of Ken's favorites, hoping you'd like them too. If there's anything you need in your cottage, just let me know, okay?"

Andy smiled. "Thanks. Most of my meals lately have come out of a little blue box or from the pizza delivery guy, so I'm sure whatever smells so amazing is going to be perfect."

Renata shook her head and made the sign of the cross. "No more talk about such things. You are going to be well fed here. I will make my special pancakes tomorrow just for you."

"Please don't go to—"

Ken walked up behind Renata and made a slashing motion across his throat.

"I mean thank you."

Renata beamed. "Much better." She turned to Ken. "Show this man into the dining room like a good host."

Andy started to protest. "But he's—"

Ken shook his head, once again telling Andy to shut up. "Of course. Would you like a drink, Andy?"

The right answer was no, but he heard himself say, "I wouldn't say no to a beer."

Ken opened the fridge, grabbed two beers, and motioned for Andy to follow him. They stepped into the sunroom that was located off the kitchen and dining room. "Renata will let us know when dinner's ready."

Andy grinned. "Apparently your mother isn't the only one who's scared of her."

"She's… I don't know how to explain it. I'd rather say I respect her and her feelings."

"And you're also fucking scared of her, but in a good way."

"You've tasted her food. Would you really want to anger someone who is such a creative genius?"

"So what about your family? Do they miss her cooking?"

Ken shrugged. "My parents assuredly do, but none of my siblings live at home, and honestly, as much as I was the outcast, I ate there more than anyone. Robert has his own cook, and the younger of my sisters is in Europe fucking her way through minor royalty. My other sister is too much like my mother to be able to be under the same roof with her for long. She doesn't eat much anyway, too fixated on being as big around as a toothpick."

A clanging bell interrupted their conversation. Ken motioned for Andy to head into the dining room through the French doors at the far end of the sunroom.

The dining room lights were off and there were candles on the beautiful antique table. The polished wood gleamed and the gold band around the white china glistened. The room was perfectly arranged for a seduction. Had Ken ordered this? Or had Renata done it on her own?

"Renata?"

"Yes, Kenneth."

"Did you forget this was a business meeting?" Ken asked, his voice more tentative than Andy would have guessed it could be.

"No business while you eat. A beautiful atmosphere accentuates the taste of the food. You'll have plenty of time to talk business later."

Andy bit his lip trying not to laugh. He could only imagine what Ken's former colleagues would think if they saw the formidable Kenneth Carver being berated by his cook. It ought to make him ridiculous in Andy's eyes, but it only made him sexier.

"Have a seat, and I'll bring your food," Renata ordered.

There was a bottle of wine on the table, and Ken poured them each a glass. Andy had never been into wine, but he'd learned to tolerate it when he needed to. It wasn't like Andy Watson, ranch hand, would be a wine connoisseur.

When he looked up, Ken was smiling. "Try it with the food. If you don't like it, I'll get you another beer."

"That obvious, huh?"

Ken nodded.

Andy didn't make a retort because Renata walked in carrying two plates, and his mouth started watering.

Andy looked down at the plate Renata set in front of him and saw steak, thinly sliced with a creamy sauce over it that smelled like garlic and an herb he couldn't identify. The mashed potatoes were so smooth and creamy he bet they would melt in his mouth. There were also green beans with diced onions mixed in. He wasn't much of a vegetable eater, but he thought he might fall in love with them anyway just because someone had made him a beautiful meal. Not that Renata had really done if for him, but he hadn't had anything like that in years.

Ken shook out the perfectly pressed cloth napkin that looked too nice to wipe his mouth with and placed it in his lap. Andy had been about to grab his fork and start shoveling it in, but he guessed that wasn't how things were done in Ken's world. So he followed suit.

"I'm not the etiquette police," Ken said, grinning. "I don't give a fuck if you want to break all the rules. I just can't break habits that were enforced by my mother and numerous governesses charged with grooming me for Carver greatness."

"I can eat like a decent human being," Andy said, trying to decide if he should be offended.

Ken waved his hand. "Do as you like and don't be shy about seconds. Not like Renata would let you anyway. There'll be dessert too."

"I saw the cake." His voice sounded dreamy. He would have been embarrassed except that Ken replied with equal rapture.

"It'll come with homemade ice cream."

Ken looked young and innocent when he talked about dessert. Andy wanted to reach across the table and eat him.

When Andy took his first bite of steak, he tried to keep from moaning as he chewed. When he'd swallowed, he went right for another bite. After that one he was able to pause long enough to say. "I'll do anything she asks. No matter what. Anything for more of this."

Ken laughed. "Try the potatoes."

"I'm almost afraid to."

"Do it." The command in Ken's voice had Andy's cock paying attention. That voice in bed would be deadly.

He scooped up a bite of mashed potatoes and sighed as he tasted them, buttery, creamy, garlicky, and something else, some kind of fancy cheese? "Incredible," he murmured.

"This is just the beginning."

"She said she'd make her special pancakes tomorrow morning."

"Wow, she really does like you."

"She just met me," Andy protested.

"She's got this… sixth sense about people. She knew from the get-go that my mom was… unsavory, but she stayed for me and Robert."

Please don't let him be connected to the dealers. Please. Andy prayed.

They didn't talk much as they ate, but when Andy was nearly done with his second plate, he said, "I know I can't talk to anyone else about your family, but am I allowed to ask you questions?"

Ken studied him for several seconds. He looked like he was about to say no, but instead, he nodded.

"What was it like growing up as a Carver?"

Ken rolled his eyes. "Great in some ways, if I'm being honest. I mean it's not like having money sucks or anything. It's just that it would have been nice to have parents who cared about more than what I could do for the family image. They could never accept that I wasn't going to be a clone of my dad."

"Did they treat all your siblings like that?"

Ken nodded. "Yeah, it didn't really work for any of us except Catherine. Her husband works for Carver Corp, and she's a cold bitch just like my mom."

Andy winced. "The rest of you rebelled?"

Ken frowned and appeared to be considering his answer. "Anna, yes. She's the very image of the youngest-child-in-a-rich-family stereotype—drugs, bad boys, public scenes, you name it. You can't really call being a surgeon an act of rebellion, but Robert did refuse his place in the company. I was their last hope until I told them I fuck men. They almost decided they could stand it, but I couldn't stand them. I was suffocating, and I had to get out. This is who I am—this ranch, the horses, the barn, shoveling shit out of stalls, getting sweaty and dirty not having to smile when I don't want to, or kiss anyone's ass.

"As CEO of your own company you still had to do that?"

"It doesn't matter who you are. If you own a business, you're always kissing someone's ass even if it's so you can own them later. Horseshit ain't nothing compared to the stuff they sling at merger meetings."

"You said your brother was the only one of your siblings you could stand. Are you close?"

KEN NARROWED his eyes at Andy. Why was Andy so curious? A natural desire to understand a family like Ken's or something else? He still hadn't figured out why Andy had lied on his resume. If he found out Andy was a reporter or someone sent to spy on him, he would destroy him, no matter how hard he made Ken's cock. He might fuck him first. Fuck him, own him, and then tear him apart. He realized he was snarling. Why did he always fail at self-control around Andy?

"Sorry. My family. They piss me off. Trust me. None of them are worth worrying about. Robert is far from amiable, but I can get through a dinner with him without needing to be rip-roaring drunk."

Andy didn't ask any more questions. Either he realized Ken was getting suspicious or he really was just curious—as most people were—but decided not to push. Ken hated having to question people's motives even out here at the ranch. He'd known he couldn't really escape his family, though.

A few years ago, he'd checked out completely, spending a month in a retreat center in the Alps while leaving Carver Pharm in the hands of his—thank God—honest and capable VPs. Even there, someone had recognized him from the headlines he'd made when he'd come out. Normally, the rest of the country, much less the world, wasn't all that interested in Houston business tycoons, but when one of them turned out to have a gay son, suddenly they were major news. His father should have paid him for the extra press.

"Ready for cake?" Renata asked as she swept in to check on them.

"Yes, please," Andy answered enthusiastically.

"Dinner was good, yes?"

"Best I ever had, ma'am," Andy replied.

Renata beamed. "I like this one. I think he's a keeper."

Ken laughed. "We'll see about that. He is good with the horses."

"Bah!" she waved her hand. "Horses. There are plenty of people out there who can take care of horses. You need someone who can take care of you. That is much harder to find."

Heat crept up Ken's neck into his face. "Renata, please."

She sniffed. "Fine. I'll bring you cake, but I didn't leave your mother to see you run yourself into the ground."

"I promoted Andy to foreman so I don't have to, remember?"

She threw her hands up in the air and walked out. If she wasn't so good to him, he'd never put up with her embarrassing him like this.

"I'm sorry. She—"

The laugh Andy had obviously been holding in burst out. "It's well worth the entertainment. Trust me."

"You know, when I ran Carver Pharm, my employees actually respected me."

"Really? Did they know how to treat a colicky horse or how to fix a tractor when it overheats?"

"Hell no, but it's not like the guys here could deal with the shit we did at Carver Pharm either."

"No, they'd be bored to death and grow pale and weak locked up inside all day."

Ken laughed. As much as he might bitch about it, he found it refreshing not to have everyone simply agree with his wishes. He decided to ignore his instincts that something serious was up with Andy for just a little longer. "Fine, but you would do well not to push me too far."

Andy grinned, obviously not cowed. "Did you hire me

because I know what I'm doing or because you wanted someone to kiss your ass?"

Ken tilted his head and gave Andy a grin that would have unnerved most men. "What do you think?"

Andy narrowed his eyes. "You better not have hired me for my body."

Ken laughed. "Of course not Mr. Shove-Me-Up-Against-A-Stall. There are no strings attached, just opportunities."

Andy opened his mouth to reply, but Renata entered with plates of cake and ice cream. The chocolate Bundt cake was gooey in the center, and the ice cream melted over it. She'd even drizzled chocolate syrup over the ice cream. Ken sighed. "Thank you."

Renata patted his shoulder. "I love spoiling you."

"Don't ever stop."

Renata tilted her head toward Andy, not at all subtly. "Take my advice, and you'll get more cake."

Renata had gotten one look at Andy and declared he was the man Ken was destined to be with. Forever. Ken had rolled his eyes and changed the subject, but Renata was obviously not letting go of the idea. Andy didn't strike him as the happily-ever-after type. More the work-here-until-he-got-bored-then-move-on type. His resume showed that clearly. Ken hoped to alter his plans if things worked out—the leaving the ranch part, not the happily-ever-after part. The ranch was enough to love for now. He wasn't going to turn down a chance to fuck Andy, to be fucked by him, to burn through whatever was sizzling between them, but he wasn't going all-in. He'd hold enough of himself back. He always did.

Andy devoured his cake and Ken found himself watching the man. He had a fuck-you exterior, but underneath was a man who loved cake and comforts as much as Ken did, and he was ready to worship Renata for trying to take care of him. Was the softer man the real Andy and the harsher exterior something he put on to deal with being gay on a ranch, or were there other reasons he usually showed only his arrogant asshole side?

You know all about ways to armor up.

Fuck off. His issues aren't the same as mine.

Control. Hiding. Don't you think maybe he would understand what it's like for you?

Ken ignored his conscience. He would not start down that road. He didn't need to understand Andy, just to enjoy him.

Andy looked like he was considering licking his plate, but he pushed it away instead and looked up at Ken. "Business now?"

Ken frowned. He'd been enjoying how much this evening was like a... Fuck no, this was not a date. Damn Renata for planting notions in his head when he'd said he wouldn't go there. "Sure."

"Is there anything I need to know about the other hands? I haven't had much of a chance to get to know anyone but Rusty."

"Rusty would talk to you all day if you let him."

Andy smiled and nodded in agreement.

"You probably know that Warren and Rodrigo both worked for the previous owner. Warren never liked me, but he liked his steady job, and he loved the horses. Rodrigo is harder to read, but he's not been openly hostile."

"So you haven't had any problems with them?"

Ken grinned. "You mean like back talking me or assaulting me when we're in the barn alone? Nope, nothing like that."

Andy narrowed his eyes. "Assaulting you, huh?"

Ken nodded. "My virtue will never recover."

Andy snorted. "You'll never recover, but it sure as hell has nothing to do with virtue."

"You could make me all better," Ken said, almost wishing he could take it back but knowing he was kidding himself if he thought they weren't going to go there.

Andy shook his head. "We both know how stupid that would be."

"Speaking of stupid, you want to talk business over scotch?"

"Hell yeah."

"No longer afraid I'm going to get you drunk and take advantage of you?"

"Not afraid you will, certain of it, although it remains to be seen who's going to take advantage of who, and what's to say I won't get you drunk first?"

Anticipation zinged through Ken. "Don't challenge me. You have no idea how much alcohol a good Carver has to put away to survive."

―――――

KEN DOUBTED Andy had ever tasted a fifty-year-old scotch, and he couldn't wait to see his reaction. He'd been saving this particular bottle, a present from Sam when he closed on the ranch, for months. Maybe he was crazy to break it open now, but he had to drink it sometime.

When he handed Andy a glass, Andy stared at the amber liquid looking very uncertain. The bottle cost more than several months of Andy's salary. Ken didn't like thinking of that. It made him both embarrassed about their differences and eager to spoil Andy every chance he got.

Finally, Andy brought the glass up to his nose and

breathed deeply. His gaze rose to Ken's over the rim of the glass, and the power he saw there made Ken shiver.

"Try it."

Andy took a careful sip. His eyes widened. "Wow."

"Good, right?"

He nodded and took another sip. "That's fucking amazing."

"You haven't really had scotch until you've had one like this," Ken said, realizing his voice had taken on that dreamy quality he used when he talked about good food and alcohol.

"I guess this is just normal for you."

Ken rolled his eyes. "Oh, don't start bashing the rich boy. Just enjoy it."

Andy sighed. "As long as you don't start any patronize-the-country-boy shit."

"I get the feeling you aren't just a country boy."

Andy looked unsettled for a few seconds, then he schooled his features. "You'd be wrong there. I reckon I'm a little more educated than most, but horses are all I really know."

"You don't have to tell me any more about your history if you don't want to, but don't lie to me."

Andy sucked in his breath ever so slightly. If Ken hadn't honed his skills watching the opposition during business deals, he would never have noticed, but he was certain of it. Andy was unsettled, and he was lying. What he was less certain of was why he wasn't calling Andy on it?

Because he's the one.

Renata had never been wrong. Her hunches were legendary in his family, and he'd just made one come true, one she'd been repeating since he was a teenager. *You'll only thrive when you're on your own.* He'd never felt better than he had since he'd walked away, but now she was pushing him to jump into a relationship with a man who wasn't who he said he was.

He took a sip of scotch and tried to focus on business. "Luke applied for the job shortly after I posted it. He's young, and he doesn't seem to give a damn who I am or what I do. He just wanted a chance to get away from home and work with horses. He doesn't have much experience, but so far he's reliable."

Andy nodded. "We need more help."

"Yeah, I've been working on that."

"Any chance of working faster?"

"I do the hiring. You make the ranch run. Got it?" Ken sure as hell wasn't going to tell him Renata had encouraged him to turn away several men who looked like perfect prospects. She hadn't liked Warren, but Ken had refused to fire him without a solid reason.

Andy frowned. "Well, I see how it is. Don't question the hiring policy."

Ken should apologize for acting like an ass, but he didn't.

"Would it be too much for us to go over the basic routines and what you want me to focus on this week?"

Ken described the details of the schedule that Andy wouldn't yet have picked up on with the duties he'd been assigned and the breeding program, especially concerns about a few of the mares who were pregnant for the first time. "Once the morning chores are done tomorrow, I'll show you some of the stuff in the office: ordering spreadsheets, suppliers, accounting."

Andy nodded. "Sounds like a plan."

Ken took another sip of his scotch, letting it warm him. If it wasn't so fine, he'd down the rest of the glass and pour himself another, but he couldn't bear to mistreat it like that.

"More?" He raised the glass, noticing Andy had nearly finished his.

Andy shook his head. "I think it would be wiser for me to go."

What had Ken expected after snapping at him? "Wiser?"

Andy nodded.

"Do you always make the smart choice?"

"Almost never. But I'm doing it tonight."

Ken nodded. "That's too bad."

"You want a foreman who's unwise? I guess he'd be easier to control."

Ken tightened his fists but managed to stop the angry response he wanted to make.

"Good night, Mr. Carver." Andy set his glass down and rose.

Back to last names, then. "Good night, Mr. Watson. Sleep well."

Andy mumbled something that might have been 'fat chance of that.' Ken smiled as he watched the man walk out. Andy wasn't as unaffected as he was trying to act. There was no way in hell they'd keep their hands off each other much longer. Ken could wait. The anticipation just sweetened the deal.

CHAPTER TEN

Andy closed the door of the guesthouse and leaned against it. As he'd feared—hoped?—the night had felt like a date rather than a meeting. Ken slid right under his skin and did things to him that would make him weak. Wanting to fuck the man was one thing, but Andy wanted more than just a rough fuck. He wanted to run his hands all over Ken, to kiss him, to taste him. Those things were dangerous.

Reveling in a sensual fantasy was a sure way to forget how cold he had to be. The assholes running drugs through the ranch sure as hell weren't shy about killing anyone they saw as a threat. If he was wrong and Ken was in charge, he'd see through Andy if he didn't figure out how to toughen up around him.

He should have punched him instead of kissing him that day in the barn. Maybe then Ken would have backed off. But in reality, hitting him would have been just as bad. Anger, lust, both were signs he wasn't in control. Control was the only thing that would get him through this assignment—control of his identity, of himself, of the information.

He needed to call Gomez and check in, but he wasn't in

the right frame of mind to do it. She was too perceptive not to sense that he was unsure of himself. Sadly, not calling in would be worse.

He grabbed his phone and made the call, not even bothering to leave the guesthouse, another sign he wasn't thinking straight.

"Gomez."

"You got anything for me?"

"Nothing substantial to connect Warren to this operation. Are you getting anywhere with Ken or Rusty?"

He closed his eyes and fought to keep his voice calm. "It's not them."

"Andy, you've got to be objective."

"I'm not going after someone who isn't guilty just because it would be convenient if they were."

He could hear the echo of her shoes hitting the floor as she paced. "You like them. That doesn't make them innocent."

"I'm handling this investigation. If you didn't think I was capable, you shouldn't have sent me in."

"Do you remember our conversation when you volunteered for this?" She was shouting now. "I know you've never gotten over your last run-in with this man. I know how often you think about Charlie—"

Anger surged through Andy, making him hot and cold at the same time. "Don't. I warned you last time. Do not go there."

"Somebody has to go there. Better me than someone else. I've got to know this assignment is being carried out properly. Do I need to get you out?"

"No. I'm fine."

"Then get your head out of your ass and figure out who

the bastard is who's responsible for these tainted drugs. People are dying."

Like he didn't already know that. "Leave me the hell alone and let me work." He jabbed at his phone, ending the call with only the slightest guilt tightening his gut. Gomez had put up with a hell of a lot from him, but he didn't need to be reminded that he was a fuckup, that he had been since Charlie died.

Blood. So damn much blood. The memories started to pull him under, but he caught himself.

Only one thing was going to make him feel better and keep the demons at bay. If Gomez wanted him to fuck the answers out of Ken, then that's what he'd do. He'd betray the last of his dignity, Ken's decency, and everything else he held on to, but it would feel so damn good. He wanted Ken like he hadn't wanted anything in years. That desire almost made him believe he was really alive after all.

He would've gotten into the main house any way he had to, even if it meant picking the lock, but there was a light on in Ken's office so he walked up to the French doors that opened onto the patio and looked in. Ken was bent over his desk, looking tense and stressed and hot as hell. If figured that even after a few glasses of scotch the man wouldn't just give in and go to bed. Andy had a feeling Ken was as poor a sleeper as he was.

Ken ran a hand through his hair and Andy watched his long fingers. How could hands be so sexy? He wanted Ken's fingers wrapped around his cock, stroking him. He wanted to make the man beg. Tonight, he was going to be the boss, and Ken was going to submit to him in every possible way.

Not bothering to knock, he tried the knob. Ken looked up at the sound. When he saw Andy, he raised a brow. Andy stood his ground and waited for Ken to make a move.

A few seconds later, Ken stood and stalked to the door, his movements fluid and graceful. Andy imagined him moving like that in bed, his body arching up, taking Andy deep, undulating with that sexy rhythm that made everyone turn when he walked by.

When Ken opened the door, Andy took a step toward him, not bothering to wait for an invitation, not giving a damn that Ken was his boss. After the way he'd reacted to his kiss in the barn, no way in hell was Ken going to turn him away. He was just as anxious for a hard fuck as Andy was. But Andy hoped Ken gave some resistance because he was more than ready for a fight.

"What—" That was as far as Ken got. Andy grabbed him by the back of the neck and crushed their lips together, taking, possessing. Ken struggled, but Andy held him tight. Eventually, Ken's tongue stroked his and pushed into his mouth as Ken tried to gain the upper hand.

Andy shoved at him, walking him toward the wall as they fought with tongues and teeth and grasping hands. Ken bit his lip so hard Andy tasted blood. He yanked Ken's hair, forcing his head back and sank his teeth into Ken's neck. He worked the skin between his teeth and sucked at it, desperate to mark Ken. The man was his, and in that moment, he didn't give a fuck about the case or the job or anything else. His cock was in total control.

"Fuck!" Ken shouted when Andy slammed him against the wall. Ken slid his hands between them and pushed, trying to free himself, but Andy grabbed his wrist, spun him around, and pushed his arm up his back.

"Holy God, you're a bastard when you're horny," Ken said.

Andy chuckled against his ear. "You act like you control everything, but you like to be fucked, don't you?"

KEN bit his lip to hold in a groan as Andy punctuated the question by thrusting against his ass. Finally, he answered, "Yes, but I don't give in easily."

Andy chuckled, his breath warm against Ken's ear, raising goose bumps down his neck. "What would be the fun in that?"

Ken didn't know what had made Andy change his mind and come back, but he wasn't going to question it. Especially when it was just as good as he'd imagined it would be. He tilted his hips back, letting Andy's cock settle between his ass cheeks. Then he rubbed himself up and down.

"Be still," Andy growled.

Ken looked over his shoulder and grinned. "Make me."

"Don't try my patience," Andy said, twisting Ken's arm harder.

Ken hissed. His shoulder ached from the strain, but his cock was harder than ever. He fucking loved Andy in this dominant mood. "What are you going to do to stop me? Tie me up?"

"You'd like that wouldn't you, you kinky bastard?"

"Fuck yeah. I like just about everything."

Andy squeezed Ken's wrist harder. "Even this?"

"Only because I'm going to get loose and make you pay."

"The hell you will. You're going to turn around and get on your knees because you can't wait to have my dick down your throat."

Andy eased up the pressure on Ken's arm. He couldn't really think Ken would just do what he said which must mean he wanted a fight. Ken was more than happy to give it to him. There was almost nothing as good as tussling with a man, then making it up to him by letting him have your ass.

The second Andy's grip was loose enough, Ken spun around and drove his knee into Andy's abdomen.

Andy's eyes widened in shock. He doubled over and stayed there for a second. Then he roared and ran at Ken, but Ken was ready. He feinted to the side and used Andy's momentum to shove him against the wall. He circled Andy's wrists and pinned them at his sides as he brought their bodies into full contact, rubbing their still-clothed cocks against each other. "You like it rough, Andy?"

"Fuck, yeah, just like you enjoy bending over and taking a big hard cock up your ass. That's exactly what I'm going to give you."

Ken grinned. "Control issues?

"You're one to talk."

Ken gave a hard thrust, and Andy groaned, tipping his head back and closing his eyes. Ken should have known it was an act, but he got lost in seeing Andy's pleasure.

Andy used the moment to break free and shove at Ken's shoulders, knocking him off balance. He stumbled, and Andy lunged for him, grabbing him around the waist and dragging him to the floor.

He wrapped a leg around Andy's and flipped them, spearing his hands into Andy's hair and using the leverage to slam him against the floor.

Andy roared and arched up, nearly bucking Ken off.

They tussled, rolling over until they hit the edge of Ken's desk. Andy ended up on top, and he managed to get hold of Ken's wrists and pin them over his head. Andy hung over him, looking like he was trying to decide if he was ready to stop fighting and fuck.

"Fighting is excellent foreplay, but maybe it's time for more. What do you think?" Ken asked.

"Fuck you," Andy said, shoving at him and standing up.

Ken watched Andy as he loomed over him. The man was pissed that he'd given up on self-control and come back for what he wanted.

Andy turned like he was going to walk away, but Ken wasn't about to let that happen. "Andy."

Andy froze and slowly turned. Ken pressed his palm against his cock and rubbed back and forth along his length. Andy watched, mesmerized. Then Ken unzipped his jeans, pulled his cock out, and kept stroking. "I thought you were here to do something about this."

"Hands off," Andy ordered.

Ken grinned at him. "Make me."

Andy took a step toward him. "I'm going to tear you up."

Ken grinned. "You were right, you know?"

"About what?"

"I love a man who's got what it takes to hold me down and shove his cock up my ass. Do *you* have what it takes?"

Andy growled. "Hands and knees. Now."

"You're awful high-handed considering our positions."

Andy's glare would have scared the fuck out of most men. "Our only position right now is you under me, begging to be fucked."

Ken smiled. "Is that how it is?"

"Damn fucking right."

"Okay," Ken said, studying Andy for his reaction. "Here, in this office, that's how it can be. You try this shit anywhere else, and I will take you down, hogtie you, and kick you right the fuck off this ranch, got that?"

Andy laughed. "Might be fun to see you try."

Now it was Ken's turn to glare. "I could have taken you anytime tonight."

"Keep talking. Your ass is going to pay for every word."

Ken laughed as he pushed his pants over his hips and

down his legs. Then he sat up so he could get out of his shirt. Andy watched, heat burning in his eyes.

"You going to get naked too?" Ken asked.

"Maybe," Andy answered. Ken imagined himself bent over his desk, Andy behind him, his jeans open enough to pull his cock out but the rest of his clothes in place, even his boots. It was hot as hell. "I get to see you naked eventually, no matter how you do me right now."

"Deal. I'm glad you understand this is going to be more than a one-time thing, because once you've had my dick in you, you're going to be begging for more."

When Ken was completely naked, he caressed himself, stroking his neck with his right hand and then running his fingers across his collarbone, down his sternum, over his abs, and toward the thatch of dark hair framing his cock.

Andy's mouth dropped open as he watched Ken drag his thumb through the drop of precum that had beaded at his slit. He brought it to his mouth and licked, his gaze never leaving Andy's.

"On your knees now," Andy commanded, his voice less certain than it had been before Ken's little show.

Ken turned over, done with resistance. He was more than ready to let Andy take over.

Danger. Danger.

Ken had no intention of listening to his inner warning system. For years, he'd shut himself off from what he liked, what he needed, the way he wanted to live. Maybe he was being an idiot. Maybe he was full-on insane. Andy could be there to spy on him, sent by his father or someone hoping to con him, but he didn't fucking care. He hadn't gotten where he was by being stupid like this, but he deserved a chance to let go and feel.

Andy dropped to his knees behind Ken and laid a heavy hand at the base of his spine.

Yes. This was what he needed. He'd deal with the consequences later.

Andy slid his hand up and down Ken's spine and Ken flexed, reaching for more, loving the feel of his callused fingers. Andy's hand might as well have been wrapped around Ken's dick for the way it responded. He hung his head, trying to keep his breathing even so Andy wouldn't realize just how much those simple touches turned him on.

When Andy stopped, Ken bit his lip to stifle the pleas that threatened to spill out. Then Andy gripped Ken's ass cheeks and pulled them apart, exposing him. He brushed a thumb over Ken's hole, and Ken let a whimper escape.

Andy teased him, slowly, back and forth. Then he pushed just the tip of his thumb past the tight muscle. Ken couldn't breathe, couldn't think. He needed Andy to fuck him right that second.

"Lube? Condoms?" The words came out strained. He wasn't sure he was comprehensible.

"Brought 'em."

Thank God. Ken wasn't sure he was capable of finding his own. "So get on with it, then."

Andy swatted his ass hard and Ken groaned. "Hmm. I think you like that?"

Ken shook his head, but he was lying. Oh, how he was lying.

Andy spanked him again, and Ken arched, sticking his ass out to beg for more.

Andy chuckled. "No more for now. I'm in control here, remember?"

"You're fucking me, but you don't control me."

Andy grabbed Ken's hair and yanked his head back. "Yeah, I do."

Ken hadn't thought his cock could get harder, but apparently, he was wrong. How the fuck did Andy know exactly what to say to drive him crazy?

Andy pushed his head down until it rested on his arms. "Don't fucking move."

Ken wasn't sure he could even breathe. He heard Andy tearing a condom packet. He wanted to turn around, watch him roll it on, and see if his cock was as big as it felt when it was trapped in his jeans. But he didn't. Because no matter how much he might fight or protest, he liked Andy controlling him. The man was going to drive him out of his fucking mind.

Slick fingers pressed against him, pushing deep and making him gasp. Andy wasn't going to go slow with this, and that was just how Ken liked it.

ANDY PUSHED IN AGAIN, scissoring his fingers and loving the way Ken pushed back, trying to take him deeper. His surrender was so fucking hot—the way his back arched, the catch of his breath, the curl of his feet every time Andy pushed into him.

He leaned over Ken and ran his tongue along his spine, the same path his hand had taken earlier. His skin was soft, salty with sweat, and if Andy hadn't needed to get inside him so damn bad, he could have licked him for hours.

Usually, he got down to business, got off, and walked away. What the fuck kind of spell had Ken put on him? This desire to rub himself all over Ken, to kiss every inch of him, taste him, inhale him, absorb him, it wasn't natural. He shook his head. Maybe he was just really damn horny because it had been too long since he'd had anything other than his own hand wrapped around his dick. That had to be it.

He bit down on the back of Ken's neck as he drove three fingers deep. Ken hissed and struggled under him. He bit harder and then sucked at the wound.

"That fucking hurts," Ken yelled.

"You love it, just like you're going to love having my cock inside you. Are you ready?"

"I've been ready. What the hell are you waiting for? Afraid you won't measure up to my standards?"

Andy's cock twitched. Ken was baiting him, trying to push him into an angry fuck, but he was going to hang on to his control, because that's what really got to Ken, not the fight or the roughness, but being totally taken over. That's what would make him writhe.

Andy grabbed Ken's hair again. It was just long enough to get his hands into, and it was so fucking soft. He probably used some product that cost as much as Andy made in a week. He used his grip on the silky strands to turn Ken's head to the side. "You've never had anything as good as what I'm going to give you… when and if I choose to."

"If you don't get your cock in my ass right this fucking second, I'm going to flip you over, and we'll see who hasn't had anything this good."

Andy nearly snapped, shoved him down, and gave him exactly what he wanted as hard and fast as he could just to prove himself. The only thing stopping him was the need to hear Ken lose it.

He reached underneath Ken and wrapped a hand around his cock, stroking him slowly.

"Fuck you," Ken shouted. "This isn't what—" Andy's

hand moved faster as he held Ken tight with an arm around his chest.

Ken groaned and started thrusting into his hand. When he was sure Ken was really close to the edge, Andy clamped his hand around the base of Ken's cock and held on.

Ken struggled. "Get the fuck off me."

"Hell no. I told you I was in control, and I'm going to stay right here until I'm ready to give you the ride of your life."

Ken bucked, trying to knock him off, but Andy just tightened his hand around his cock.

"I can't decide if that hurts like hell or if it's the hottest thing I've ever felt."

Andy laughed. "I hope it's both. Let's do it again."

"N—" Andy yanked his head around and kissed him as he started stroking his cock again, slowly and carefully twisting his hand over the head, loving that Ken tensed every time he did.

Andy increased his pace and Ken whimpered. "Oh, yeah. Let me hear what this is doing to you."

Ken shook his head, and Andy stopped moving his hand. "Beg me."

"No."

He slid his hand along Ken's shaft so slowly it was barely moving. Sweat coated Ken's back and ran down his face. Ken looked over his shoulder and glared at Andy.

"Give in," Andy ordered.

Ken closed his eyes and let his head hang again.

"Yeah, that's it." Andy stroked him slowly. "Now tell me what you want."

"Your cock in my ass."

Andy stroked faster. In seconds, Ken was close again, muscles tense, his balls high and tight.

"Please," Ken begged. "Want you inside me. Want you to take me hard. Use me. Own me."

"Oh God, yes." This was better than Andy had dreamed. Ken was so far gone, so open, more than Andy had ever had the courage to be.

And you're going to betray him.

He's never going to know the real you.

Andy shut those thoughts down, because worse ones were right around the corner, and he would not spiral into hell, not now with Ken begging him for more.

He let go of Ken's cock and rose onto his knees. He positioned himself and thrust hard enough to go almost all the way in on one stroke.

Ken hissed. "Fuck, yeah."

Andy smiled as he pulled out, the heat and tightness of Ken's ass making him insane with need. He drove back in, rocking Ken forward. Ken pushed back into him, and he grabbed Ken's hips to hold him still and find an angle where his cock slid over Ken's prostate.

He knew he'd succeeded when Ken made the most exquisite keening sound. It vibrated through Andy, making him realize he wasn't going to last long.

"Again, Andy. Please, God, do that again."

Andy thrust deep, and Ken cried out, "More."

Andy kept it up, hitting Ken's sweet spot on almost every stroke. Ken panted and struggled, bucking into him and reaching back to try to grab his hip and pull him deeper. He was totally abandoned to his needs.

Andy was close. He wanted to make this last, but he couldn't. He needed Ken to come soon. "Touch yourself," he ordered.

Ken slipped as he tried to balance himself and reach a

hand between his legs. He groaned as he wrapped his hand around his dick.

"Hard and fast. And don't hold back when you come. I want to hear every sound. I want you to make me feel it too," Andy ordered.

"Fuck yes. You're gonna feel it. You're gonna blow your load inside me and lose your fucking mind, you bastard."

Andy growled and tightened his grip on Ken's hips, wanting to leave bruises. He wanted Ken marked all over so he would never forget who owned him.

That thought made Andy lose his rhythm. What the fuck was he doing? Ken wasn't his. He was just something to distract Andy, to help him forget for just a little while.

"Andy, don't stop. Don't—"

Ken cried out, loud and long. His ass tightened around Andy, and then he jerked, slamming himself back. Andy's mind went blank. There was nothing in his world but Ken's tight, hot ass. Heat scorched his spine, and his balls drew up. He tried to fight it because he needed more, but he couldn't hold back. With Ken's body still shaking from his orgasm, Andy started coming too. He held onto Ken as his body was wracked with spasm after spasm. He wasn't sure he would survive the ride. He'd never… No one had ever…

"Holy fucking shit!" Ken exclaimed as Andy collapsed on him.

Andy would have voiced his agreement, but he couldn't speak. He was nothing but a throbbing husk. His weight forced Ken flat against the floor, but Ken didn't seem to mind.

"You're fucking hot as hell," Ken said. "They might have heard us in the bunkhouse."

"Um…" Andy's attempt to speak failed. His mouth was devoid of all moisture. If he could've moved, he would've fixed his problem by licking the cum off Ken's hand. What was wrong with him? Now was the time when he usually got up and walked away.

You should question him first. He'd tell you anything right now.

No.

He rolled off Ken onto his back and scrubbed his hands over his face.

Ken laughed. "Told you it would be like nothing else."

"Fuck off."

"Stay there. I'll be right back," Ken said. The smirk on his face made Andy want to punch him, but as annoying as Ken was, Andy couldn't question him now. Holy hell, what had just happened? He'd had some damn good sex, but comparing any previous experience to what he'd felt with Ken was like comparing a cherry bomb to a nuclear explosion.

He's not guilty. Was that conviction based on instinct or on wishful thinking? How could he ever be sure now? He should call Gomez and tell her to get him out. Or better yet, he should just walk away. Disappear. Go somewhere no one knew him and find a ranch that would hire him. Maybe then he'd never have to face another blood-soaked night again.

Blood. On his hands. On his clothes. On the walls. Andy saw it. He knew it wasn't there and yet it was, right in front of him. His heart slammed against his chest. He couldn't draw in air. He was going to pass out. He clutched at the carpet and squeezed his eyes shut.

"Andy? Andy, are you okay?" Ken knelt next to him and laid a hand on his chest. "What's wrong?"

Andy opened his mouth, but no sound came out.

"Here, sit up." Ken helped him.

Now Ken would know how weak he was. He wouldn't

want—

"Do I need to take you to the ER?"

Andy shook his head. "Army. Desert." Admitting to PTSD was embarrassing as hell, but at least he could make Ken think it came from his army days. He used to get flashbacks to the desert occasionally, but never as strong as the ones of that night, of Charlie looking at him as he bled out. Ken's soothing touch on his back helped slow Andy's heart rate. The panic began to fade. When he opened his eyes, he no longer saw blood on his hands.

"I'll be right back," Ken said. He laid a towel on Andy's lap and walked toward the kitchen. He returned with a the scotch and two glasses. Ken held up a glass. "Will this help?"

Andy nodded. Getting drunk with Ken was probably an even worse idea than fucking him.

"Don't ask me about it," he said, defensive about falling apart.

"I wasn't going to. Figured you'd talk about it if you wanted to. Suit yourself."

Fuck. Ken being understanding was worse than him asking questions. Questions Andy could blow off, or he could use them as an excuse to storm out and go back to the guesthouse where he could finish falling apart.

"I…" He shook his head. "Just pour me a drink."

When he reached for the glass Ken held out, Andy expected to see pity in his expression, instead he saw desire. "My freaking out turns you on? You are a kinky bastard."

Ken smiled. "Apparently, you being you turns me on."

Oh fuck. That was way too real. Andy didn't do real. Not ever.

"Would another round of sex help more than the alcohol?" Ken asked. "Because I'm fine with that."

Andy's heart sped up again, but not from the flashbacks.

He tipped the glass back, downed the contents, and held it out to Ken. "I should go."

Ken raised a brow. "You sure about that?"

Andy looked at him. His eyes. His long fingers wrapped around the glass, sliding up and down the slick surface. He was mesmerizing, and suddenly Andy wanted him again so badly he'd be the one begging if he didn't watch out.

"Suck me," he said, giving Ken a hard look, the look of a man who knew exactly what he wanted and expected to get it, not like the messed-up son of a bitch he really was.

Ken studied him for a few seconds, then he set Andy's glass down on the table with his own unused one.

"Strip," Ken said.

Andy started to protest, but something made him stand up and do exactly as Ken said. Ken knelt in front of him and assessed him with his sexy hazel eyes, obviously liking what he saw too much for Andy's comfort. A rough scar ran across Andy's ribs, and Ken traced his fingers over it before caressing it with his tongue. Andy stared, wide-eyed, as Ken continued to explore his chest, teasing him.

"My cock. In your mouth. Now," Andy said through gritted teeth.

Ken laughed, then pressed a last kiss to his abdomen before taking Andy deep into his mouth with no warning and no warm-up. When he started sucking, Andy worried Ken might be pulling his soul—or what was left of it—right out of him. Ken pulled back and teased Andy's slit. Then he rolled his eyes up and looked at Andy. Something caught in Andy's chest. There was so much emotion in that gaze, things he didn't want to see.

Andy took hold of Ken's head and held on while Ken tore apart all the barricades Andy had built around himself and sent him hurtling off a cliff.

CHAPTER ELEVEN

Late the next morning, Ken heard someone enter through the kitchen and head toward the office. He expected it to be Andy, and his body took a decided interest despite the fact that his ass was almost too sore to let him sit at his desk.

He took a deep breath, determined to act normal when Andy came in. Of course, he'd given away just how damn infatuated he was the night before. Andy had loved every second of conquering him, and Ken was more okay with that than he would have expected. Andy wasn't fucking him because he wanted something from him, like the hangers-on in Houston who'd hoped for a generous reward for warming his bed. They'd never really satisfied him. It was worth a little humility to come as hard as Andy had made him.

A tentative knock startled him. Andy was more the charge-in-already-talking type.

"Come in." He looked up and saw Rusty poking his head in the door. He'd been working in the heat for hours, but his face was pale instead of red like Ken would expect, and he gripped his hat so tightly Ken wondered if he was going to rip it in two. "What's wrong?"

"H-have you got a minute?"

Ken nodded. "Close the door and come sit."

Rusty did as he asked, practically falling into one of the chairs by Ken's desk.

"You need something to drink?" Ken asked.

Rusty shook his head.

"Let me at least get you some water." Ken reached into the mini fridge, grabbed a bottle, and tossed it to him. Rusty pressed it to his pale face. "I don't know where to start."

Ken frowned. "How about at the beginning?"

"Andy knows I'm gay."

Ken tensed. "How?"

"He caught me with a guy."

"How is this the beginning of a story?"

Rusty ran a hand through his hair. "It's… Fuck if I know."

"Where'd he catch you?"

"I was out at that old shed close to the border with Lawson's place."

Ken exhaled. "You need to be careful. I wish you'd just take a room here in the house…" Did he really want Rusty bringing his hookups here? No, but at least he'd be safe.

"I told you I don't want to be the kiss-ass who lives in the big house and lets his uncle pamper him."

"No, you just like to come here and take my food and beer."

Rusty rolled his eyes. "And seriously, you think I want to bring guys back here where you might be listening in?"

Ken huffed. "What kind of pervert do you think I am?"

Rusty grinned, looking more like himself.

"Can you just get on with the story?"

Rusty's smile faded, and he dropped his head into his hands. "You're not going to like it."

Ken's stomach knotted. He really hoped Rusty hadn't gotten into trouble again. "Talk to me."

"I haven't broken my promise to you, I swear it."

Ken drew in a breath and prayed for calm. "Why would I think you had?"

"Because of what I've got to tell you. I have to tell because otherwise someone will think it's me when it's not."

Ken braced himself. "Just tell me."

"Someone's hiding drugs in that shed."

Ken forced himself not to react. "How do you know that?"

"Because I found them."

Please don't be lying. Rusty wouldn't have come to Ken in the first place if he were guilty. He'd gotten in with some real bastards in high school, but he wasn't devious. That was part of how he'd gotten caught, by refusing to hurt people. "Go on."

"I've been meeting a guy out there kind of regularly, a guy who works at Lawson's."

Ken frowned. "Do you think the drugs are his?"

Rusty shrugged.

"If you think they're his, you need to tell me."

"Maybe. He's offered me pills before."

Ken fought to stay calm. Before he had a chance to respond, Rusty spoke again.

"He might be involved, but I don't think it's just him. There were several crates."

"Crates? Full of drugs?"

"I think. I mean, at least one of them had pills in it. I didn't open the others. I was scared to, but I've been going out there for a while, and I've never seen these crates before."

"There's something else." Ken was certain he was still holding back.

"Yeah, but it's not related."

"Rusty."

"Okay. I've been going out there to draw. I used to do art a lot, and my mom… Well, she didn't really like it, so I quit, but I missed it, and I didn't want the other guys to see."

Ken wanted to take Rusty's mom and wring her neck. Thank God Rusty was here now where he could be himself if he learned to stop expecting judgment for it. "You can have any room in this house for a studio. You just tell me where and what you need, and I'll get it set up."

"Uncle Ken, you don't have to—"

"I'm going to. Now talk to me about these crates. You think there were drugs in them? You think this guy you've been seeing is a dealer?"

"I don't know, and I can't be sure what was in them. I could see into one a little, and I saw pills in plastic bags. I didn't open anything. I was scared to."

"Have you seen anyone else around the shed?"

Rusty nodded. Whatever was coming, Ken wasn't going to like it. "Who?"

"Andy."

There are holes in his resume. Things I can't confirm. "When did you see him?"

"He showed up once when I was meeting Ben, and then another time when I was just out there drawing, I heard something and saw him creeping around. He never came in that time, though."

Ken's heart pounded. He did not want to be hearing this, especially after the full-on nuclear meltdown he'd experienced with Andy inside him the night before. "Did you ask him what he was doing?"

Rusty nodded. "The first time, yeah. He said he couldn't sleep, and he decided to take a ride. He saw a light in the shed and decided to check it out. He scared the hell out of me and Ben, but at that point I believed him. Then I saw him again another night, and now I can't help but wonder…"

"Stay away from there. If your guy wants to meet again, he's going to have to come here."

"He won't. He doesn't want anyone to know."

"That he's a drug dealer? No, I guess not."

Rusty rolled his eyes. "That he's gay."

"Lawson's foreman is gay. It's not like he'd—"

"Ben said his mom would kill him."

Ken sighed. At least he'd only had to worry about being disinherited. His mother would never stoop to physical violence. "Right now, we can't prove he's not the one who left the pills. It would be best if you stayed away from him."

Rusty shook his head. "I know. I just… Fuck! How do I manage to find trouble everywhere?"

"Because you've got a really big heart, and you believe in people."

"Too big." He spat out the words in disgust.

Ken looked away and ran his hand through his hair. Rusty wasn't the only one putting his trust where he shouldn't. If Renata hadn't endorsed Andy, Ken would have already decided he was full-on crazy.

"You really like him, don't you?"

"Andy?"

"Yeah."

"I don't want to talk about that."

Rusty frowned. "I like him too, and I don't want to think…"

"Neither do I. Get back to work now. I'm going to head out to that shed and poke around." After that, Ken planned to talk to Lawson's foreman. Lawson was an asshole, but Blake was a good man as far as he could tell. Blake would want to know if one of his hands was running drugs.

Rusty stood. "I'll come with you."

"The hell you will. I need you in the barn. And tonight, I expect you to show me some of these drawings of yours."

Rusty chewed his lip. "I'm not sure about that."

Ken raised his brows and glared.

"Fine."

"I've seen your doodles on the records in the barn. You're talented. I like helping people with talent."

"Ken, I don't want—"

"Just bring them."

Rusty blew out a harsh breath. "Fine. Are you sure it's safe for you to go out there by yourself?"

Ken unlocked his desk drawer, pulled out his pistol, and motioned for Rusty to follow him.

He opened the French doors to the patio, the ones Andy had appeared at the night before. *Don't think about that. Not now. Not until you figure this out.*

"See the longest branch of that pecan tree?" Ken asked.

Rusty nodded.

"See the pecan there close to the end?"

"Damn, your eyes are sharp for an old guy."

"Watch it, kid." Ken raised the gun and shot, knocking the nut down without taking out any of the branch.

He looked at Rusty. "Still worried?"

"Impressive, but being a good shot won't always save you."

"I'll be fine." Rusty was right, but Ken wasn't going to risk him, nor was he going to alert anyone else about the trouble until he checked it out himself.

Luke came charging out of the barn. "What the hell was that for?"

"Fuckin' squirrels," Ken called across to him.

He stared at Ken, openmouthed. Then he shook his head and went back into the barn.

"Were you always this crazy?" Rusty asked.

Ken laughed. "Yeah. I just hid it better in the city."

Rusty shook his head as he walked toward the barn.

Ken thought about how his friends in Houston would laugh at him playing badass, but goddammit, he wasn't going to let someone fuck up his ranch. If Andy was storing drugs in his shed, the man would fucking pay. And if the asshole from Lawson's place was in on it, he'd go down too. If either of them hurt Rusty, Ken would personally send them straight to hell.

He grabbed a set of keys for one of the four-wheelers. He'd rather be on horseback, but he didn't want to have to worry about the safety of an animal if he ran into someone at the shed. As he walked across the barnyard, he pulled out his phone and tapped on Sam's name.

When she answered, he got right to business. "Those holes you found in Andy's resume. Go after them. Hard. And get information on my neighbors at Lawson's Ranch, especially an employee there named Ben."

He hung up before she even had a chance to respond, sure she'd do as he asked without needing clarification.

He stuffed his phone into his pocket, straddled the four-wheeler, and started the engine. As he drove toward the boundary of his land where the shed sat, he tried to let his mind go blank, but he failed miserably. He'd started to believe there was a chance for something more than just sex with Andy. Fuck that bastard.

He laughed, wild and hysterical.

Maybe that's exactly what he'd do. That would wipe the smug, knowing smile off his face.

Rusty could be wrong, though. There was no evidence to link Andy to whatever Rusty had seen at the shed. But why else would Andy be sneaking around a remote outbuilding? Unless he was meeting someone there too. Ken would put a stop to that if he had to burn the place to the ground. Andy was his.

Unless, of course, he's using your land as a drug depot.

Against his will, Ken remembered the feeling of Andy sliding into him. The man had tormented him and made him beg. He'd never felt so out of control. He'd craved that feeling, but Andy took it beyond his wildest dreams.

He swallowed hard and revved the engine, pushing the four-wheeler harder.

When he reached the building, he jumped off as he cut the engine and headed for the door. If anyone was there, they'd better run. He wasn't in any kind of mood to be merciful.

Gun in hand, Ken pulled the broken padlock off the door and pushed it open. Nothing met him but emptiness and suffocating heat. How the hell did Rusty fuck in here without dying of heatstroke? He chuckled. Maybe Ben wasn't all that good.

He poked around and lifted several bales of straw, but the crates Rusty had seen were gone. Either someone knew Rusty had found them, in which case Rusty might be in danger, or the owners had only been storing them there for a short time. He needed to find out how often Rusty had been out there.

Ken pondered calling the police, but he had nothing to go on except Rusty's word, and the police weren't about to trust a nineteen-year-old who'd done time. The last thing Ken wanted was to hurt Rusty and get bad publicity for his ranch.

He'd handle this himself at least until he had enough evidence for the police to catch the bastards.

What if Andy was in on it? Could Ken keep fucking the man not knowing? Maybe. Maybe not. He could always hope Sam would turn up something quickly.

ANDY'S PHONE BUZZED, and he looked at the screen.

Meet me. You know where. Half an hour.

The message had to be from Ben or someone associated with him. Andy should be excited that things were moving forward. Instead, his chest was tight and his stomach unhappy. If this connection led where Andy hoped, he wouldn't be at the ranch much longer. He thought about Ken, about the look of ecstasy on his face the night before. He wanted to see that look again and he wanted so much more he wouldn't even let himself name.

But that wasn't going to happen. Either he'd find out Ken was guilty and arrest him, or he'd disappear and never see him again. Gomez would insist he preserve his UC identity if there was any way to. Even if Ken did find out who he was, he'd never believe Andy hadn't fucked him to get information out of him. He'd think everything between them was about the case and that Andy was a lying sack of shit.

Andy didn't bother to respond to the text. Instead he found Rusty and said, "I'm going to ride out and check on the border fence. I need you to make sure Desiree is ready for the buyer who's coming in today. Can you do that?"

"Yeah, sure. I'd love to." Rusty grinned, obviously glad to be trusted with something important. Andy was going to disappoint the hell out of him too, when he disappeared.

Andy started up a four-wheeler and took off, wanting to

get to the outbuilding first and be prepared to get the hell out of there if it was an ambush. He thought about checking in with Gomez and letting her know about this development, but there wasn't much point until he pulled the meeting off. It wasn't like anyone could help him without blowing his cover.

When he reached his destination, he sat on the ATV and surveyed the area. He had a knife and his own gun, a Smith & Wesson instead of the Glock he carried as a service weapon. But if Ben brought company, he'd be outgunned quickly.

Are you fit for this?

Gomez's question echoed in his mind. Hell no, he wasn't. He wasn't fit for jack shit, and yet here he was. The landscape wavered, threatening to become a very different place with a very different hidden warehouse. He could feel the rough wood against his cheek.

No. Not now.

He considered turning around and getting the hell out of there. Then he heard the rumble of an engine and realized it was too late.

Ben rode up to the fence that separated the KC from Lawson's. He cut the engine, slipped under the barbed wire, and walked across the field looking like a punk-ass kid. Andy could have dropped him before he even blinked. The kid had no business playing with the big boys who were in charge of this operation. Andy almost felt sorry for him, but Ben had toyed with Rusty, and that lost him any chance of Andy's sympathy.

"I want my shit back," he demanded.

Andy raised a brow. Damn the boy was green. Whatever fool had brought him into the operation was going to regret it, and then Ben was going to die. "You were the idiot who lost it."

The kid reached behind him. Andy had his gun out in a flash. "You don't want to go there," he said.

The kid dropped his hands to his sides looking even more pissed off than he had at first.

"That's better," Andy said. "Now let's talk business. I've got experience, and I'd rather help you than make trouble for you, but I need to know there's someone in charge here who's less careless than you."

"Look, man, I can't get you in. I don't have that kind of authority."

"You're in, so you must know someone."

He shook his head.

"How about you pass on my number and give me a character reference."

Ben looked like he might throw up. Maybe he'd realized how much trouble he was in. "You don't understand what you're fucking around with."

"Oh, I think I do." He held up the bag of pills. "These little guys are potent and potentially deadly, but they make you feel really good. They remind me of something I heard about on the market a year ago or so."

The boy's eyes widened. So it was the same man or at least a close associate.

"I've done my research, kid. You, on the other hand, are an ignorant underling who is about to become a liability when your boss finds out how easily you gave yourself away."

"Fine. I'll see what I can do."

"Damn right you will. You've got forty-eight hours."

To his credit the kid glared at Andy, and then he turned and stalked off, though he was probably about to piss himself wondering if Andy would change his mind and shoot him in the back. Fortunately for him, Andy hadn't sunk that low yet. Besides the kid was his way in. Right into hell.

CHAPTER TWELVE

The next afternoon, Andy's phone rang as he was heading back to the barn from a remote pasture. He didn't recognize the number, but he answered anyway, hoping Ben had found a way to get him in.

"Yes," he answered.

"I understand you're interested in a business venture."

A shiver ran over him. That voice. It was the man who'd killed Charlie. "I am."

"We've got some product coming to a drop-off tomorrow night. Problem is, the driver is unaware it belongs to us. I need someone to take care of that, so I thought of you. A little initiation if you're truly interested in joining us."

"That sounds like a problem I can solve." Because offing innocent truck drivers was his favorite thing.

"Good. I'll have eyes on you. If I don't get results, our relationship will be terminated." He emphasized the last word like a cheesy-ass movie villain. Fucking asshole.

"When I work, there are always results," Andy replied.

"You'll get the location an hour before you're expected there."

"Fine, but after this, no more playing around. I want a meet." *And I want to watch you die.*

"We'll see."

"Yeah, we will." Andy ended the call.

He took a slow breath and headed toward the kitchenette. Getting really drunk sounded like a fine idea. Fuck the need to stay alert. Fuck the whole operation. Of course, what he'd really like to fuck was Ken's sexy ass. Ken had ignored him all day. Not that Andy had necessarily expected him to acknowledge what had happened between them, but that had been one hell of an intense night. Was he embarrassed? Was he game for more?

Andy pulled a bottle of Jack from the cabinet and considered whether or not to bother with a glass. He looked out the window toward the main house as he opened the bottle. The light was on in Ken's office again. Ken was there, sitting at his desk.

No glass. He brought the bottle to his lips. As the whiskey burned down his throat, he wondered how many times he'd have to fuck Ken before he reached the same oblivion he could get from finishing the bottle.

Once if it's like the other night.

He remembered Ken moving under him, his lithe body shoving back and demanding more. Ken only pretended to surrender; he'd still believed himself in control the whole damn time. What if Andy could make him actually give in completely? How amazing would it be to have a man like that under his control?

He set the whiskey bottle down with a bang, grabbed a few things from his bag and stalked over to the main house. This time he didn't bother knocking; he just let himself in.

Ken didn't flinch when Andy banged the door open. He

kept staring at his laptop screen for a few moments before glancing up.

"Did you decide you wanted company?"

Andy held up a pair of cuffs. "I want to restrain you."

Ken's eyes widened, and he swallowed visibly. The sight made Andy's cock swell.

"Letting me top you isn't enough. I want you utterly helpless."

"Andy, I—"

He looked down. Ken's cock was straining his jeans. "Don't argue with me. You want it too."

Ken growled. "I don't do submissive. I made that very clear."

"You like to fight, and I like that too, but tonight, I... Fuck. I need this, and I think you do too."

Ken looked uncertain. "I'm not sure I can."

"Do you trust me?" The moment he said the words, Andy regretted them. Why the hell should Ken trust him? No one should trust him.

Ken hesitated. "Honestly, I don't know."

Andy nodded. "You shouldn't, not for most things. I'm not good at being trustworthy, but for this, I swear to you, I'll take care of you."

Ken licked his lips and swallowed again. Then he held out his arms, bringing his wrists close together. "Cuff me."

Andy sucked in his breath. "Fuck."

Ken gave him a cheeky look over his shoulder. "You sure you can maintain control?"

"Seductive bastard," he grumbled.

"What are you going to do about it?" Ken asked, his voice low and rough.

"Make you cry for me. Watch you give in like you never have before."

"We'll see about that."

Andy snarled. "Don't fucking challenge me."

"Isn't that what this is all about? You meeting my challenge. I'm not going to make it easy for you."

It would be so much simpler if that was all Andy wanted. "Shut the fuck up."

"What are you going to do, gag me as well?" Ken asked, grinning.

"No, because then I wouldn't be able to hear you scream."

"I'm not—"

Andy laid his hand on the back of Ken's neck. "Please. Do this for me?"

Ken shuddered under his hand. "Yes."

He didn't say anything else. Andy grabbed the hem of his shirt and tugged. "Arms up." Ken held his arms still so Andy could get the shirt off. He threw it down and then spun Ken around and pulled his wrists together at the base of his spine far more roughly than he needed to. He had to pause and try to force air into his lungs before he could work the cuffs. He said he'd stay in control, but he was fooling himself. Ken messed him up. All he had to do was look at Andy and Andy began longing for things he could never have.

Ken didn't struggle or fight or speak. He kept his head down and let Andy hold him in position. Andy wished to God he knew what he was thinking, but he wasn't about to ask. He pulled the cuffs from his pocket and snapped them over Ken's wrists.

Ken tugged on them, testing their strength. His breath caught, and he jerked away from Andy. These were real police-issue, not a toy he was going to be able to break out of.

Andy grabbed Ken's arm and held on. "I won't hurt you. If you need me to, I'll take them off."

Ken shook his head. "If you want me like this, restrained for you, I'll do it, but don't fucking toy with me."

Andy wrapped a hand around Ken's throat and hauled him back. "You need me pushing you. You need it to be about this"—he thrust against Ken's ass—"and nothing else."

Ken nodded. "Yeah."

His voice shook, and Andy closed his eyes, needing a moment to keep from taking things way too fast.

Andy forced Ken's head back and kissed his neck. Ken's hands were trapped between their bodies, but he could reach Andy's cock. He stroked Andy too lightly to be anything but a tease, and Andy bit down on the tight muscle where Ken's neck and shoulder met. Ken cried out as Andy sucked at the skin, not giving a damn who might see his mark when Ken took his shirt off while working. Ken could fucking explain it any way he wanted to, not that Kenneth Carver needed to explain anything to anyone. The fucking bastard.

"Andy. Fuck. No."

Andy squeezed harder on Ken's throat. "Yes," he said against Ken's ear. "I want to watch you fall apart. I want you desperate."

———

"ANDY, I HAVE... I... JESUS."

Ken's voice came out low and cracked. He was going to have bruises on his throat from Andy's fingers. That should worry him, but it was the hottest damn thing he'd ever felt.

"Fuck me, Andy. Right fucking now."

Andy laughed. "I intended to torment you, to make this hard for you, but, goddammit, what have you done to me?"

Andy was angry at more than just Ken, not that Ken really understood where the anger came from. Just how unbalanced was Andy? Ken should never have let the man cuff him. But his dick was so hard, and he wanted this so bad, no matter how crazy Andy got, no matter how rough. "You think owning my ass will solve things for you?"

"Yes." The word came out as a hiss, like Andy was in pain. "Opening you up until there's nothing more you can give, going so deep you'll never get me out of your fucking head, that's what I need."

"God, Andy."

Andy put his hands on Ken's shoulders and pushed. Ken fell to his knees, almost pitching over onto his face. He tugged on the cuffs again to test them. They weren't flimsy play cuffs, and they weren't going anywhere. For a second, a spike of fear raced through him. His goddamn cock didn't care, though. The uncertainty made it even more interested.

Andy knelt behind him. "You're fucking killing me."

Ken grinned, hoping Andy wouldn't see. "It's not like this is easy for me." There was nothing easy about the things he felt every time he caught a glimpse of Andy.

"The fuck it's not. Spread your legs." Andy shoved one of his thighs between Ken's legs to separate them. "Now lie down."

Somehow Ken managed to do so without tumbling over. He pressed his cheek into the carpet and tried to remember to breathe, still wondering if he'd lost his mind to let Andy do this to him. Probably. Andy was so fucking wrong to think Ken wasn't as affected as he was. What did Andy really want? Ken had been as open with him as he'd been with anyone. He didn't think he could drop the rest of his walls. Ken didn't think anyone could make him do that.

"I want to see you, the real you."

Could Andy read his mind? "You have."

"No. I've gone deeper than most, maybe, but not all the way."

Ken hated how right Andy was. "I can't give you more. I just can't."

"Try."

The plea in Andy's voice made Ken want to.

He took as deep a breath as he could and tried to sink into the carpet, widening his legs even more and letting his cuffed hands rest at the base of his spine.

"Fuck." The word whooshed from Andy as a whisper.

Ken wanted to look at him, but he stayed like he was, knowing that was what Andy needed.

Andy leaned forward, and Ken held his breath, nearly toppling off balance when Andy licked his wrists right below where the cuffs were. He kissed Ken's bound hands gently. "You're gorgeous like this."

Ken's chest tightened, and he bit his lip to hold in a whimper. Andy had him off balance, literally and figuratively, and he wasn't sure how much more he could take.

Andy shifted position and pulled Ken's ass cheeks apart. Ken held his breath, not sure what to hope for next. When Andy ran his tongue across Ken's hole, the needy sounds he'd been holding back spilled over.

Andy chuckled, his warm breath tickling Ken's crack. "Like that?"

"Goddammit, Andy."

"Think I can make you come apart like this?"

Almost certainly. He'd sure as hell never expected this from Andy.

Andy tightened his grip on Ken's ass, spreading him wider. Ken resisted the urge to fight. "Andy. I can't—"

Andy licked him then, and Ken no longer cared what happened. He was lost to sensation. He tried to push back, needing Andy's tongue buried deep inside him, but Andy teased him, circling his entrance with the tip of his tongue.

"Do it."

Andy slapped Ken's ass hard, and the sting made his cock jerk.

"I'm in charge here. You got that?"

"Fuck no. If you were in charge, I'd be writhing under you, not waiting for you to make up your mind what to do."

"No, because that's not what I need. What I need is you begging, whimpering, crying."

Ken lost it then. He fought, sliding forward and trying to free himself from Andy's grip. He couldn't give anymore. He needed to turn the tables. To make Andy beg.

Andy tightened his grip on Ken's hip. "Stop. You're going to hurt yourself."

"Take these off," Ken said, jerking at the cuffs.

Andy laid a hand on his back and tried to push him back to the floor, but Ken struggled, panic consuming him.

"Ken? Calm down. Ken! Are you with me?"

Ken stopped, slowly getting a grip on himself, not sure why he was so freaked out. "Yeah, I'm okay."

"Do you really want me to let you go?"

Ken nodded, frantically. "I've got to get my hands on you."

"To fight me?"

Ken shook his head. "No, to... Fuck, I don't know."

———

ANDY UNDERSTOOD EVEN though Ken couldn't explain with words. He'd thought he wanted to punish Ken. He'd been so angry, at the world, at himself, but he'd channeled it all into keeping Ken from holding back.

If he kept pushing Ken, he wouldn't be able to hold back either. Everything he felt for the man was spilling out like he'd been stabbed, ripped apart, opened up. Nothing could staunch the wound. What had he done? Why had he come here? With shaking hands, he reached into his pocket for the handcuff key.

When the cuffs were off, Ken turned over and sat up. He started rubbing his wrist, but Andy grabbed his hand.

"Let me." He stroked Ken's wrists with his thumbs and then kissed them. As his lips brushed Ken's skin, Andy's panic subsided. He rubbed his face against Ken's wrists and palms. Part of him still wanted to run, because if he didn't, Ken was going to see too much. But the rest of him knew he'd never have anything this good again. He couldn't walk away.

"Lie down on your back," he said, his voice barely audible.

"Andy—"

"Do it."

Ken lay back and dropped his legs open. For several moments, Andy looked at him. Ken's body had been honed to perfection, and he knew just how to use it. Andy had seen him slinging hay bales, dripping sweat as he worked to pry loose the old board of a fence, gripping a stallion's side with his legs while he leaned out to grab hold of a runaway horse. Maybe he was playing cowboy, maybe it was a phase, but it was a damn fine one to watch.

He brushed his fingertips over Ken's ribs. Ken closed his eyes, and Andy felt him relax.

"Hands over your head," he said. "I won't cuff you again, but I want you to keep them there."

When Ken reached up, Andy slid his hands down Ken's sides, letting his thumbs rub over the hard ridges of his abs.

Then he curved his hands over the top of his thighs. Ken arched into his touch, and Andy swallowed back a groan. How could anyone be so fucking sexy?

He kissed the soft skin of Ken's inner thigh, then he bit down and was rewarded with a yelp. He smiled as he sucked at the wound. When he'd left his mark, he shoved Ken's legs apart and returned to what he'd been doing before Ken had freaked out. Except now he no longer needed to wrest cries and confessions from Ken. He just wanted to pleasure him.

He still longed to open Ken up until he couldn't hide, but he didn't want to hurt him to do it. He was a bastard to be so insistent when he'd never exposed himself, never even let Ken know who he really was. Maybe when the case ended… but not unless his cover was blown.

You could quit. Right now.

No, the man he'd hunted for long after Charlie died was using this ranch to further his trade in deadly pills. He couldn't let that go, couldn't let the man kill even more people. Charlie deserved justice and someone had to protect Ken and the others on the ranch.

Andy looked at the man under him, saw the ecstasy on his face, and thought about how he treated Rusty and the men who worked for him, even those who didn't like him. He was not a cold, murdering bastard.

Ken would never really know who Andy was. Yet in a way, Andy had been more honest with him than he'd ever been with anyone.

He stretched out on the floor and settled between Ken's legs.

"Andy, you don't have to—"

"I want to."

Ken sucked in his breath when Andy once again touched the tip of his tongue to Ken's hole.

IF WISHES WERE HORSES

He blew warm breath across the wet skin, and a choked groan escaped Ken.

"Let it out. Don't hold back with me."

"Fuck, Andy. I—"

Andy teased him a bit more before pushing into him, opening him up, and reveling in the sound of raw need it pulled from him. He pushed in more, tormenting Ken with his tongue before finally tongue-fucking him as deep as he could.

Ken strained under him, muttering, making those sounds that shot straight to Andy's cock. Desperate to hear more, Andy added a finger alongside his tongue.

Ken gasped. "Fuck."

Andy's only response was to keep going, stretching him, getting him ready to be fucked senseless.

Finally, he pulled back and looked at Ken.

His eyes were wide, his cock red and straining, a puddle of precum on his belly. Andy wanted to lick it up.

He swiped his tongue across his lips, and Ken chuckled. As he studied Ken, he realized he wanted this man to be his, truly his, more than he'd ever wanted that with anyone. Andy didn't just want him to be someone he fucked until they begged or someone he conquered, but someone who... No, he couldn't go there.

"Tell me you're going to fuck me now," Ken said, interrupting Andy's dangerous thoughts.

Andy's cock was so hard he thought he would come before he could even get inside Ken. He couldn't wait anymore. "Hell yes."

Ken started to turn over, but Andy grabbed his hips and shoved him back to the floor. "No, like this."

Ken's eyes widened.

"Scared?" Andy taunted.

"Fuck no. You think you're going to break me?"

"I know I am. You won't walk right for days."

Ken growled. "Andy."

"You'll love it."

Ken watched him as he rolled on a condom and lubed up. The hunger in his eyes told Andy he was as deeply affected as Andy was.

Andy stroked himself slowly, biting back a groan. "Is this what you want?"

"You fucking know it is."

He smiled. "Remember that."

"Outside this office, *you* obey *me*, remember that."

Andy leaned over him and closed his hands around Ken's wrists, pinning them to the floor. "What I remember is how you sounded begging for more as I tongued your ass and the way you react when I drive my cock into you."

"Andy."

"We're not out there. We're here, and there's nothing but you and me and what is between us."

"What do you think that is?"

That was not a question he intended to answer. He growled and let go of Ken, rising up so he could position his cock at Ken's entrance. Then he thrust, going balls-deep in one powerful stroke.

Ken arched up and gasped. "Holy fuck."

Andy smiled. "You love that."

"Fuck you."

"Damn right you will."

He pulled out slowly, almost all the way, and then slammed back in.

Ken bucked under him. "Fucking bastard!"

"Oh yeah, you love it."

Andy fucked Ken hard and deep, over and over until they were both dripping with sweat. Ken kept his hands over his head, but Andy could see he was fighting the urge to grab hold of him, and Andy needed to feel him. "You said you wanted to touch me, so do it."

KEN SEIZED Andy's biceps and wrapped his legs around his lover's back, using his heels to try to force him deeper. Andy fought him until Ken pulled him down for a kiss. When their lips touched, all the passion inside Ken exploded. He drove his tongue into Andy's mouth and writhed, desperately trying to get Andy to fill him, to drive into him in just the right way to put him all the way over the fucking edge.

Andy ended the kiss and shifted so he was at the perfect angle for driving Ken insane.

"Fuck!" Ken cried out as Andy sent pleasure zinging through him. The intensity threatened to burn him up, to render him incapable of thought.

"Let go, Ken. Let me see you."

"Fuck you, Andy." Andy was even more closed off than Ken. Why was he demanding this, and why was Ken unable to stop himself from giving Andy what he wanted? It scared Ken half to death.

Andy's cock slid over his gland again, and Ken thrust upward, wanting more, feeling like he was going to come apart. Andy fucked him at just the right angle. Right there, face to face. If Ken opened his eyes, Andy would see into his soul. He locked his legs around Andy's back and held on for the ride that was wrecking him.

"Look at me," Andy demanded.

Ken shook his head.

Andy pulled out. Ken reached for his hips, trying to pull him back in, but he couldn't get enough leverage.

"Open your eyes. Now."

If he did, then Andy would get everything he wanted because all of Ken's barriers were down. Andy would see that, see how naked Ken really was.

"Ken."

Andy's voice was softer, frantic. He was about to lose it himself. If Ken could just hold out until Andy came, then…

He opened his eyes and looked right at Andy.

Both men gasped.

Andy was as wide open as Ken. Ken saw emotion in his eyes so deep it made Ken shudder. He was more certain than ever that Andy wasn't who he said he was, and when Ken learned his real identity, it was going to crush him.

"Ken. Ken! I can't—"

Andy threw his head back and shouted as he jerked his hips frantically against Ken. Ken held on and fought his own orgasm, needing to see Andy as he let go.

Seconds later, Andy looked down at him, shock on his face. Ken was sure he hadn't been prepared to lose control so utterly. He pulled out of Ken and repositioned himself so he could take Ken's cock into his mouth.

Ken sucked in his breath, glad he didn't shoot off at the first touch of Andy's lips. Andy took him deep, and Ken couldn't help thrusting against Andy's mouth. Andy didn't fight him. Ken came much too fast, emptying himself down Andy's throat. Andy swallowed again and again, not letting go until Ken stilled completely. Only then did he pull off and wipe at the cum that dripped from his mouth.

"Kiss me," Ken begged, his voice barely more than a whisper.

Andy did, and Ken groaned as he tasted himself on Andy's tongue. He wrapped his arms around Andy's neck and pulled him down, needing to feel his weight.

Andy rolled them as they kissed so Ken was on top, and even after all they'd done, Ken's body was considering round two. Andy was fucking killing him, and he couldn't make himself care.

When he pulled back from the kiss and looked down at Andy, Andy was the one who'd closed his eyes, trying to hide himself.

"I should go," Andy said.

Ken's chest tightened. He knew a relationship with Andy was impossible, but it still hurt that the man was willing to walk away so soon after physically and emotionally devastating him. Andy was the one who'd pushed things between them.

But Ken wasn't going to stop him. He rolled over onto his back, and Andy reached for his clothes. Neither of them spoke while Andy disposed of the condom, used his boxers to wipe himself off, and then pulled on his pants and shirt.

Andy ran a hand through his hair and started out the door. Ken wasn't sure if he wanted Andy to look at him or not. If he looked and still walked away, it would hurt even more. And yet...

"Andy?"

Andy turned, and the corner of his mouth quirked up in a reluctant smile. "Yeah?"

"You're wrong. It's not easy for me. Not any easier than it is for you. I... Just know that, okay?"

"Okay."

He lifted his hand like he might reach out to Ken, like the need to touch him was too much to deny, but then he dropped his arm back to his side and walked out the patio door.

CHAPTER THIRTEEN

Andy waited for the truck to approach. His stomach threatened to revolt, and sweat dripped from his face. He'd sworn he'd never let himself get put in this position again, where some asshole expected him to kill an innocent man so he could complete his assignment.

He saw the headlights of a large truck down the road. He was certain the asshole in charge had someone watching like he'd said he would, and Andy was unnerved by just how good the guy must be. He'd heard rustling a few times, but he hadn't seen anyone or gotten any proof it was more than the wind.

The truck was getting close. Andy moved into position. He'd parked his truck so it looked like it had run off the road and waved a white t-shirt to flag the driver down. The man wasn't supposed to stop, not with the shipment he was carrying. There were strict rules for dealing with his cargo, but Andy was hoping compassion for a stranded, injured man would override his need to follow the rules. It was a gamble, but it was the best he'd come up with. He'd splattered dirt and fake blood on his shirt, hoping to make himself look bad off. The truck slowed, and Andy moved right in front of it, risking his life if the man didn't have good reflexes. The brakes hissed and creaked. The truck fishtailed, but the man brought it to a stop.

"What the hell are you doing?" the driver yelled out the window.

Andy couldn't assume the man would be a Good Samaritan and stick around to help him. Standing on the runner board, he grabbed the handle on the passenger door, smashed the window, and pointed his gun at the driver, all before the driver had time to react.

"Get out of the truck."

"You have no idea how much trouble you're starting," the man said.

"Not nearly as much as you're going to be in if you don't do what I say."

The man stared him down. Why the fuck did he have to get all heroic? "Cut the engine and get the fuck out of this truck now."

When the man still didn't move, Andy fired a shot that sailed past the man's head and shattered the window behind him.

The man cut the engine, and Andy jerked the passenger door open and grabbed his shirt to pull him across the seat. Andy sensed that the man wasn't done fighting, so he was ready for him to try something. When he did, Andy effortlessly rolled with the man as he lunged and brought him to his knees with Andy's arm around his throat and the gun to his head.

He bent close to the man's ear, hoping the truck wasn't bugged, at least not well enough for anyone to hear a conversation taking place outside. "I'm a cop. I'm going to shoot you and miss. You're going to go down and play dead. There

IF WISHES WERE HORSES

are others watching, and they will kill you if they think I didn't."

Andy started to loosen his grip, but the man struggled so he tightened it again. "I will shoot you if I have to. Don't forget that." He shot into the dirt, praying he was right about the location of the men who were watching him. If the truck didn't hide what he was doing, he and the driver were both dead.

Andy heard movement in the trees, more than one man if he guessed right.

"Don't move," he whispered. The man was shaking now, his bravado gone. Andy was thankful it was dark and that he wasn't yet shaking himself. That would start after all this was done. Andy dragged the man toward the truck he'd parked on the side of the road, then tossed him in the back, grunting to cover any sound he might make. Thank God the man lay still.

Andy turned back to see a man hopping into the cab on the passenger side. Another had already taken the wheel. "Take care of that before you meet us," the man on the passenger side said, gesturing toward the driver. Hopefully he believed the man was dead.

Andy nodded. He couldn't let his guard down yet, so he tried to act casual as he got into his truck. He prayed the driver wouldn't sit up or do something else to give them away. Andy had left some things in the truck bed that he could hold onto, but still it was going to be a bumpy ride. He pulled out his phone and called the number Gomez had given him when he'd let her know what was going down.

"I'm on my way," he said when a man answered. He cut the call after that, trusting that someone would show up and take the driver to safety.

When he turned off the main road, he contemplated letting the man come into the cab, but he decided against it.

He hadn't heard anyone following him, but he was paranoid as shit. He stopped close to the river at an abandoned fishing camp. After surveying the area, he walked around to the truck bed. "I'm going to leave you here. Someone's coming for you. Soon."

The man sat up and looked around. "What the hell is going on?"

"Just do what I say," Andy ordered, wishing he could give more of an explanation. He saw car lights in the distance. "You need to get out of the truck now. I've got to go, but I promise someone is coming to help you."

After a few seconds, the man jumped down from the truck bed, apparently willing to take his chances if it meant getting away from the crazy man who'd abducted him. Andy hopped back in the truck and took off. He hoped the man wouldn't run before help arrived, but if Andy had been him, he would have taken off the second his feet hit the ground.

KEN'S PHONE RANG, waking him up. He glanced at it. Sam. Was it an emergency or had she just forgotten that ranchers go to bed much earlier than citified lawyers?

Hell, he was awake, he might as well answer it. "Hello, Sam."

"Hear me out. Promise to do that."

"Fuck. This is bad, isn't it?"

"Yes. You'll think so. I mean it is bad. Yes."

Sam was flustered. That was a very bad sign. Ken's heart pounded against his chest. "Tell me my father hasn't done something more asinine than usual."

"No, this is about Andy."

He pushed a hand through his hair and braced himself.

He'd known better than to get involved with Andy, certainly he'd known not to let it go beyond fucking, but the man did things no one should be able to do to him.

"Just tell me."

Sam's exhausted sigh made him shiver. "I had to dig deep. He's using a false identity, probably because he's been arrested several times."

"Arrested?" Ken knew what was coming, but it still hurt.

"For possession, dealing, DUI. Every time he got off with nothing more than a slap on the wrist, which means he's got powerful friends."

"Or maybe he got in trouble like Rusty." As soon as the words left his mouth, he knew how ridiculous he sounded. If it had been anyone but Sam, the shame of his attempt to make Andy into the man Ken wanted to be would have humiliated him.

"He wasn't a kid when this happened, Ken." Sam didn't even have the heart to mock him. Was he really that pathetic?

"There's more," Sam said.

How much worse could it get?

"I had him followed."

Great. She probably knew how deeply Ken had gotten involved, possibly even with photographic evidence.

"That's an invasion of privacy, mine and his. I never asked you—"

"He has the potential to hurt both you and the ranch, and you're not thinking clearly right now."

He wasn't, but it didn't stop him from being furious. One of the things he loved about being out at the ranch was not having the press or his family or anyone else following him around. "You don't make that call. How dare you intrude in my private business?"

"I don't give a damn who you fuck, Ken, but if this man

is engaged in criminal activities on your property, you've got to turn him in."

"Of course, I would turn him in if he... I don't want any shit going down on my ranch. I didn't keep myself clean when my father was willing to do anything to further himself just to be complacent about someone running drugs on my own fucking ranch."

"Rusty could be in danger too. He'd at least be questioned, if not implicated."

"Goddammit, Sam. What kind of asshole do you think I am? And Rusty is not involved. He's already come to me to tell me about—" Ken froze. If he told Sam any more she'd push for him to go ahead and call the police. He didn't want to do that until he had some proof. He'd bring down a media circus on himself and the cops would go after Rusty as hard as they could.

"Told you about what?"

"Nothing. Now's not the time."

"Ken, what are you keeping from me?"

"I'll tell you once I know more."

Sam made a noise like a growl. Most men would be terrified. "I believe Rusty just like you do, but our opinions won't stop the police from putting him through hell if we aren't proactive on this."

"Do you have any evidence Andy's done something illegal while he's been here?"

Sam blew out a long breath. "Not really."

Ken's heart pounded. "What does that mean?"

"Andy left the ranch tonight alone. My man lost him for a while, but when he located him again—"

"Wait. How the hell did Andy slip past him? I thought you only used the best."

"I do. That should tell you something right there. Andy is

not just a ranch hand, or he wouldn't know how to throw off a tail like that."

Ken bit back the urge to argue. Maybe her guy had simply slacked off. "There's no crime in leaving the ranch. He probably needed to blow off steam." With a fucking man? With someone other than Ken? Oh hell no.

"On an unmarked back road?"

Ken had met men in stranger places. "What happened after your guy caught up to him again?"

"He was out in the middle of nowhere by the river. There was a guy passed out in the bed of his truck, and he shoved him out of the truck at gunpoint and left."

"And?"

"He came back to the ranch."

Son of a fucking bitch. Ken would have given Andy whatever he needed, no matter how kinky.

Everything except for a chance to run from what is between the two of you.

This man is using you. You've got to stop thinking about him like that.

Renata says he's a good man, and she's never wrong.

"So he met a guy, fucked him, dumped him, and walked away. That's still not a crime."

"You really think that's all this was about? Sex? The guy looked half-dead."

"But he wasn't dead?" Ken bit his lip, scared to hear the answer. There'd been times he'd looked dead too when he'd headed to those dark places where he lost himself to anonymous pleasure.

"No, he wasn't dead, but—"

Ken lay back on the bed and stared at the ceiling, wanting all of this to go away. Why they hell couldn't he indulge himself just this once and get away with it? Why did the man he wanted have to be mixed up in something dangerous? "I want a straight answer. Did you see Andy do anything illegal?"

"Illegal, no. Suspicious? Hell yes. You've got to stop thinking with your dick on this."

"Sam, don't push me too far."

"I care about you, and you're not acting like yourself."

Ken closed his eyes and took a slow breath. Sam did care, and she didn't deserve his anger. "I know. I just wanted…"

"Not to have to be responsible," Sam responded. She'd always read him easily.

"Yeah." He sounded like a fucking idiot, a defeated idiot. Ken didn't do defeated. He pulled himself together. "I'm going to do some investigating on my own. I'll figure out what is going on, and no matter what, I'll deal with it."

"There's something off here that I'm not seeing. You need to be careful."

Ken had always trusted Sam's instincts. "I think you're right, but I don't know what's going on either."

"Don't you think it's time to send Andy packing?"

Ken laid a hand over his face. "I just made him foreman."

"Fuck, Ken. That is a terrible idea. He'll have access to—"

"Exactly what I want him to. Keep your enemies close. You've always preached that. Don't try to back down now."

Sam sighed. "For that strategy to work, you have to acknowledge that the person is an enemy, not keep them around because they're good in bed."

If Andy was merely good in bed, Ken would have kicked him off the ranch at the first sign of trouble. It was the fluttery feeling he got in his chest every time he was around Andy that had Ken hesitating even with evidence piling up against him. That feeling Ken was afraid to name coupled with Renata's insistence that Andy was meant to be here.

"Even if Andy is involved in something illegal, something tied to this ranch—and I admit there's a real possibility of that—he's not working alone. What Rusty talked to me about wouldn't be run by one person. We need to figure out who else is involved."

"Are you sure Warren's death was an accident?"

Ken sat up, his stomach churning. "Now you think Andy's a murderer too?"

"Not necessarily, though you did say he was quite cool about it. But as you just pointed out, more than one person is likely involved."

Ken thought about the day Warren died. Could someone have poisoned him? He'd never have imagined it, but was he simply being naive? Apparently despite him being a wolf in the boardroom, he was a lamb in the outside world. "I really think he just had a heart attack. It happens."

"It does, even to fit men with no known heart problems, but…"

"Push harder. Find out everything you can about Andy or whatever the hell name he used to go by. Dig into Rusty's old associates too."

"I'm on it." Sam sounded relieved.

"I'm on things from here too, but no more spying on me."

"What about spying on Andy?"

"Only if he leaves the ranch. I do not want anyone peering into my fucking house, you got that? I've had enough of being watched by my family, and I can take care of myself."

"Fine, but you can only take care of yourself if you're looking out for threats."

"I'm looking."

"Okay. I really do care about you and Rusty."

"I know you do." Ken ended the call.

Ken wasn't going to be able to fall asleep anytime soon, so he headed for the kitchen. He was in serious need of a huge bowl of ice cream.

As he walked down the hall, he noticed a light on in the kitchen. Sometimes Renata didn't sleep well, and she swore by a glass of buttermilk to help her fall back asleep. Ken almost turned back, not sure he could handle even Renata's company, but she walked out of the kitchen before he could escape.

"Ken?" she asked, peering down the dark hallway.

"It's me. I couldn't sleep."

"Come on. Let me get something for you."

"No, you go on back to bed. I can take care of myself," Ken insisted.

She snorted and turned back toward the kitchen. Ken had no choice but to follow.

"Strawberry or butter pecan?" Renata asked as Ken sat down at the eating shelf in the kitchen.

"How did you know I wanted ice cream?"

She narrowed her eyes at him. "You think I've forgotten what you like? You think I don't know you now because you've grown up?"

"I've been a grownup for a long time," Ken said.

"Hmpf."

"Butter pecan."

"I thought so." She got a large bowl and filled it with at least four scoops of ice cream. Then she set it in front of Ken along with a spoon. "Now, tell me what's wrong."

"I'm fine," Ken said through his first bite.

She raised her brows. "You think I am stupid? When have you ever eaten ice cream at midnight because you were fine?"

"I woke up, and I'm hungry."

"Kenneth Worthington Carver, do not lie to me."

How did she manage to make him feel like he was five years old? "I got some news I didn't like."

"And that was?"

Ken scowled. "You won't like it either."

"I lived with your family. I'm used to disappointment. Now talk."

Ken took a few more bites of ice cream. "Sam, my attorney—"

"She's your friend too."

He nodded. "Yes, she is. She checked up on Andy because his resume was sketchy. He's using a fake name, probably to hide the fact that he's been arrested for dealing drugs."

Renata frowned. "So was our Rusty, but you know what a good man he is."

"This isn't like what happened with Rusty."

She didn't say anything for several moments. "Andy needs you. I know. I dreamed it, and one day you will see it too."

Ken closed his eyes and took a deep breath. When he opened them again, Renata was gazing at him with so much love in her eyes, he couldn't help but feel better. "You truly believe that?"

"My dreams are never wrong."

Ken wished he had the same conviction Renata did.

―――

ANDY'S PHONE chimed with a text alert right after he'd tucked himself into bed. It wasn't like he was going to sleep anyway, not as pissed off and jittery as he was. He could go over to the main house, seek Ken out, push until he got what he wanted. Ken would give in; he was sure of it. But something—maybe whatever was left of his self-preservation—held him back.

He reached out blindly and found his phone on the table by his bed.

Meeting in twenty.

No more information, not even a location. He had to assume it was the shed. No way to know if the mysterious asshole would be there, and Andy wasn't any closer to figuring out if it was the same man he'd tried to take down before. The voice and attitude matched. Andy's instincts screamed that the men were one and the same, but he needed to see the son of a bitch.

Getting to the shed would take him nearly twenty minutes. Fucking bastard. He wanted Andy to screw up. Was that because he'd been made or just because he was a bastard to everyone?

He'd have to take his truck and pray it didn't fall apart. He didn't want someone hearing one of the four-wheelers start up and wondering what he was doing using one this late. If anyone saw him head out in his truck, they'd assume he was going out to get drunk or laid or both. Maybe after this meeting, he'd do just that. He fitted a knife into an ankle sheath and checked his gun. They'd probably try to confiscate it, but he wasn't going in without it. He grabbed his keys and stuffed the phone into his pocket.

When he crossed the yard to the side of the barn where his truck was parked, he noticed a light on in the main house's kitchen. Was it Ken, or had Rusty snuck over to steal a midnight snack? Whoever it was, Andy prayed they didn't see him.

He battled flashbacks as he drove. *Turn back*, the sensible side of him chanted, but he didn't listen.

Call this in. No. There was no hard evidence.

They've probably already moved the shipment I helped them divert.

If he stopped now, all the work he'd done would be for nothing, just like before.

You don't want it to end because then Ken will know you've been lying to him.

Ken would hate him, and Andy would walk away even more fucking broken than he had been when he'd arrived.

That thought was enough to send him into hell. The road wavered, and he skidded off the side, barely missing a tree.

Can't be late. Can't do this now. Holy fuck.

A shot echoed, and he flinched. But there was nothing out there in the night. Everything was happening in his head.

He rubbed his eyes like that would help and wished to God Ken was there. He was the only thing that could push the visions away, and if Andy found out who the leader was tonight, if he got enough evidence to bring them down, Ken would never be there to soothe him again.

His stomach flip-flopped. This time Charlie's image only wavered in front of him for a few seconds. Then he was frozen in place, unable to run, as men shot at him. *Run! Goddammit, Run!*

He just sat there, waiting to die. *No!* Andy was fairly certain he actually screamed out loud. At least he was far from the main house, the bunkhouse, and anyone who would care.

He flexed his hands on the steering wheel, once more marginally in control of his body. What if he flipped out in the middle of this meet-up? The deeper he got into this assignment, the worse the flashbacks got. What if he stopped being able to send those images away and lost contact with reality all together?

For a few seconds, he thought he was going to have to stop the truck again so he could throw up, but he managed to keep going. He was going to bring these men down and clear Ken and Rusty. They'd treated him more decently than anyone had in years. If he died doing it, then fine, but he'd bring these bastards down with him.

He sped up, flying over the dirt paths that led to the shed on the edge of the property. He skidded to a stop and grabbed his gun as he jumped from the truck, tucking it into his waistband.

A man stood by the door. He looked Andy up and down.

"I was summoned," Andy said, trying to sound bored.

The man glared at him. "Hand your weapons over."

Andy shook his head.

"You're not going in with weapons on you, and if you don't go in, I'm supposed to kill you right here."

Andy pulled his gun and pointed it at the guy's face. "I've got no reason to trust any of you."

The man drew a knife from a wrist sheath. "I can have this through your neck before you fire."

"You're that fucking confident? Good for you."

Sweat poured down Andy's back as he fought not to show how uncertain he was of the situation. *Stay grounded. Stay here.*

"I do like your spirit." The voice came from the doorway. Andy fought the urge to turn away from the man at the door. The asshole might just stab him the second he did.

"He refused to lose the gun and whatever else he's got on him," the guard said, his tone almost whining.

"Yes, I see. Send him in anyway."

"But, sir," the guard protested.

"Don't argue with me. You know better."

"Yes, sir." The man put his knife away and gestured toward the door. "Go on, then."

Andy lowered his gun and turned to see the man who had spoken. His face was covered with a ski mask so Andy couldn't make out any of his features, but he was a few inches shorter than Andy. The tight t-shirt he wore revealed that he was fit but not bulky. He wore jeans and boots like nearly everyone else, Ariats like Ken's. He was about Ken's size. *No. Don't think that way.*

His voice was different, lower and rough like a heavy smoker's, like the man who had killed Charlie, not like Ken's smooth voice that slid right over him. Of course, voices could easily be altered. *Do not go there.*

This wasn't Ken. It couldn't be. And yet there was plenty of evidence that Ken could be a deceptive bastard. That was how he'd taken Carver Pharm as far as he had. *No.* Andy was the deceptive one. Unless Ken had been playing him the whole time. If this was a mindfuck that deep, Andy was never coming out of it.

"Come on in," the man said, clapping Andy on the shoulder with a firm possessive grip so much like Ken's.

Stop comparing. Just do your fucking job.

As they stepped through the doorway, Andy observed four other men in the room, Ben was the only one he recognized. None of them wore masks like the man who was obviously in charge. Even without the display outside or the mask, Andy would have known he was expected to defer to this man whose body was so like Ken's. He held himself in a way that said he expected to be worshipped.

The fact that the rest of the men were exposed meant they were likely no more important than he was. He had an urge to just shoot them all, drive away, and disappear.

"I was so glad when you called. Dear Warren had grown tiresome. He was questioning everything. We needed a replacement, and as you pointed out, you have the right background. Thank you for coming to Ben before I had to bother making contact."

So they'd checked his background as soon as he started at the ranch and killed Warren because they decided to bring him in. His meeting with Ben hadn't mattered. He'd have ended up here anyway. "You did get lucky," Andy said, his voice steady, even though he wasn't sure he could hold on to sanity long enough to get through the meeting. "I'm not usually an easy recruit."

Was the man fucking with him or had he actually bought Andy's cover? Andy kept smiling, but his stomach threatened to betray him. A man Andy was supposed to protect was dead because of him. Charlie had voluntarily gotten mixed up with these bastards, but his death was on Andy's head. He willed his heart rate to slow. He could not lose it here.

"You're cocky. I like that," the leader said. "But you also know when to do as you're told. I hope to see that continue."

Andy nodded; now wasn't the time to push. "I can follow orders, sir. And I can be an asset to your business."

"I see you've done so before and managed never to serve any serious time."

"Yes, sir."

"You get caught now and you won't live to see jail."

Andy inclined his head toward the man. "I wouldn't expect to."

"Good. We've had to move up the next shipment date. The fucking police are sniffing around us again, so we've got to change our route. I want you here to take delivery and see that the goods are stored correctly. You'll also need to ensure that we aren't interrupted. If we have to kill too many more people at this ranch, it will start to look odd."

"Yes, sir. I'll take care of it."

"Good. Ben will be helping you."

Helping him or spying on him? The kid was no match for Andy, and he was unpredictable and had an overinflated notion of his own importance. The leader was probably setting Ben up to take a fall. Andy wanted to send the kid away, but he knew he couldn't risk it.

He was probably going to have to watch another kid die. How would he ever recover from that?

CHAPTER FOURTEEN

"Where the hell have you been?" Ken was waiting for him. Andy had been so focused on fighting the flashbacks threatening to swallow him up that he hadn't noticed Ken sitting in the rocking chair on the guesthouse porch. Ken rocked back and forth slowly, but he didn't look like a man wiling the evening hours away. He was a jungle cat, quivering with power, ready to spring and tear Andy apart right when all of Andy's defenses were down. He toyed with simply telling Ken where he'd been. He might have if he hadn't thought it would put the man in greater danger.

"Out," he said, grabbing onto his anger instead of letting his devastation show.

"Out with whom?" Ken snarled.

"Why do you assume I was with someone?"

"You've been disappearing a lot at night. What the hell else is there to do around here but drink and fuck? And you ain't been drinking, least not tonight and probably not any other nights based on how damnably wide awake you are at dawn."

So Ken assumed he'd been meeting a man. Well, that was

a hell of a lot better than the other things he could think, and it meant that they were more likely headed toward a hard, angry fuck than him getting his ass fired or Ken nosing around in things that could get him killed.

"I didn't realize we were exclusive." He threw the words out, intentionally goading Ken, because while they surely hadn't made any commitments, he had no need to go elsewhere when he had someone as hot as Ken to pin underneath him.

"Get in here," Ken yelled. "I don't need the whole damn ranch listening to this."

Like Ken hadn't given them away by sitting there waiting for Andy like a jealous husband. Andy had no desire to protest, though, so he sauntered into the guesthouse. Ken crowded behind him, slammed the door, and flipped the lock.

"Locking me in? Have I been a bad boy?" Andy asked.

"You're a fucking irritating son of a bitch!"

"Are you going to punish me?" Andy asked, walking toward the kitchenette. He pulled two beers from the fridge as if he thought he and Ken were going to sit down and have a chat.

Ken didn't say a word. Andy could feel the tension. His dick hardened as he imagined Ken coming at him. He needed to either punch Ken or kiss him, and he didn't think he could wait. He set the open bottles down and turned, ready to do one or the other, but something in Ken's eyes stopped him.

The man was watching him like he wasn't sure he knew him. *Uh-oh*. Things might get ugly after all.

"Who are you, really?"

Andy shrugged. "A son of a bitch who likes men and working with horses."

KEN CLENCHED his fists and tensed. He started to take a step forward, but he stopped and opened his hands as he blew out a breath.

Damn it. He knew Andy was trying to push him to violence, and he wasn't sure he could resist. Andy was obviously a hell of a lot better equipped to defend himself against a punch than against questions that had no good answer.

"Fine. Don't tell me who you really are. You know what? I don't even give a damn right now. I don't want to know your fucking secrets. I want to pretend you're exactly who I'd like you to be: a hot cowboy who likes walking around the ranch, looking like sin in skintight jeans that were made to drive a man fucking insane. You're just the man who's been fucking me six ways from Sunday, and that's all I want you to be. But tonight, I'll be the one topping."

"Oh really?" Andy stood, legs slightly apart, arms at his sides, ready to meet Ken's challenge.

Ken moved toward him, never dropping his gaze from Andy's. "Yes, really."

"And what if that's not what I want?"

Ken raised a brow and hoped Andy couldn't hear his heart pounding. "You saying it's not? You saying you don't want me to pin you against the counter, drag that skin-hugging denim down your legs, and plow your ass until you're crying like a little girl?" Ken stared at the hard ridge of Andy's cock, which threatened to split the worn seams of his jeans. "Don't even try to deny it."

"What are you going to do if I refuse? Think you can take me?"

"I won't have to. You might be a cagey bastard about everything else but not this. This you have no power to resist."

His chest rose and fell rapidly as he stared at Ken. "I—"

"Turn around," Ken demanded.

"No."

Andy's voice held less conviction than it had before. Ken was getting to him. "Turn around. I'm going to show you who's boss here. I'm going to make sure you remember who's running this ranch. I may be from the city, but I won't take shit off my men."

"You took my cock well enough."

"And now you're going to take mine."

Andy licked his lips, nearly mesmerizing Ken with his tongue. "You seem so sure about that."

Ken moved forward until he was right in front of Andy. He lifted his hand and ran his thumb over Andy's lip, reveling in the feel of his soft skin.

Andy didn't move, so Ken crowded into his space. His eyes went wide, like he hadn't really believed Ken would be the aggressor. Ken leaned into him, putting him off balance, and Andy stepped back, exhaling hard when he hit the counter.

"Mine," Ken whispered.

Andy started to protest, but Ken put a finger on his lips.

"Let me pretend that's true for just a little longer."

Something clouded Andy's eyes—fear, longing? Ken wasn't sure, but it softened Andy for a moment, and that's when Ken swooped in and captured his mouth in a kiss that made Ken's head swim. He'd almost lost his focus and let Andy take over. It would be so easy to fall under his spell, but this time, Ken wanted to devastate him the way he'd wrecked Ken every day since they'd first kissed in the barn.

Ken pressed his lips to Andy's, and Andy tensed. Ken had to force his mouth open with his tongue. After several seconds of fighting what he needed, Andy relaxed and let Ken thoroughly tongue-fuck him. He kissed Andy's throat, gently at first, letting his lips slide over corded muscle. Andy groaned and grabbed his ass, pulling him in tighter. Ken smiled against him, then used his teeth, biting hard enough to draw a hiss from Andy and worrying the skin between his teeth.

"Damn you, Ken," Andy hissed.

"This is nothing," he whispered in Andy's ear before tracing the outside of it with his tongue. "I'm going to do this to your whole body, and you're going to lie there and let me. Then maybe I'll give you what you want."

"You won't last," Andy taunted.

Ken wrapped a hand around his throat and squeezed. Andy's eyes widened. Was he shocked at just how strong Ken really was? "I don't make promises I can't keep." Andy's eyes darkened, and he glared at Ken as he swallowed against Ken's fingers. "You're going to do exactly what I say tonight because I've had enough of your games."

Something flashed in Andy's eyes, and Ken thought it might be fear. What was Andy afraid of? The intensity between them or something worse? Ken had told himself he was going to confront Andy when he returned from wherever he'd gone. Then he'd seen him and lost his mind.

He needed this first. They both did. Before he interrogated him, Ken was going to blow his fucking mind. He let Andy go and pushed away from him. "Strip."

Andy held his gaze for a few moments before his hands went to the button of his pants. They were shaking so badly, he couldn't get it open.

Ken's heart thundered. *Keep pretending everything's all right. He's just a hot guy, and this is just fucking.*

Ken watched Andy struggle with his task for a few more seconds before he broke. "Change of plan. Grab the counter and keep your hands there."

Andy reached back and took hold of the cold marble as Ken dropped to his knees in front of him. This was going to be so good. Fuck all the consequences. Ken deserved this moment. He leaned forward and pressed his lips to the skin Andy had exposed when he'd finally popped the button of his jeans. Ken flicked out his tongue, tasting the saltiness of Andy's sweat.

Instead of opening his pants enough to expose his cock, Ken pushed Andy's shirt up and ran his tongue over the firm ridges of his abs and up across his breastbone. Andy leaned into him, encouraging him to keep going. Ken grabbed his shoulder and pulled him forward until he could flick his tongue over one of Andy's nipples. "Hang on," he whispered. Andy shuddered as he hung there, anchored by his grip on the counter.

Ken sucked on the hard bud, making Andy howl. The sound shot straight to Ken's cock, and it was all he could do not to touch himself. He soothed Andy's nipple with the flat of his tongue and then blew on it until Andy shivered. "Good?" he asked.

"Fuck you," Andy growled.

"Not a chance." Ken looked up at him and smiled. He put a hand on Andy's chest and pushed, urging him to stand up straight again. Andy watched him, eyes huge, mouth slightly open. He might be protesting out of habit, but he was slowly giving in, recognizing that he wanted to go where Ken wanted to take him.

Ken still didn't touch Andy's cock. He pushed at his thighs until Andy opened them wider, and then Ken flicked his tongue over the skin exposed by the hole along the seam of Andy's jeans, the one that had tormented him so many times before. Andy sucked in his breath when Ken sucked at the tender skin, loving the feel of coarse hair over softness as much as he'd known he would.

When he'd sucked long enough to leave a mark, he finally turned his attention to Andy's cock, which strained against his pants trying to push its way through the fabric. He lowered the zipper slowly. Andy remained so still Ken reached up and laid a hand on his chest. "Breathe," he ordered.

On command, Andy drew in a shuddery breath.

"Better," Ken said as he slipped his hands under the waistband of Andy's pants, teased the top of his ass, then pushed his pants over his hips. Andy wiggled just enough to help him. Ken looked up. Andy's teeth were sunk into his lower lip, and the muscles in his neck strained. He was right where Ken wanted him.

He pulled Andy's boxer briefs down slowly, giving a quick lick to his cockhead when it came free. "Fuck," Andy said, the word more an exhale than speech. Ken pushed pants and underwear farther down, letting them trap Andy's ankles.

As he worked his way back up, he nibbled Andy's inner thighs, loving how his quadriceps twitched and tensed. He used his hand to push Andy's thighs apart, forcing him to spread them as much as he could.

"Perfect," Ken murmured as he licked Andy's balls and then drew one into his mouth. A glance toward Andy's hand told him he might be replacing the counter if he kept this up for too long. The thought made his cock throb.

After fondling and sucking Andy's balls for several more seconds and nipping at the loose skin surrounding them, he slid the tip of his tongue up the underside of Andy's cock. That broke the man. He grabbed Ken's head, spearing his hands through Ken's hair. "Suck me, right fucking now."

Ken grabbed Andy's wrists and pulled back to look at him. "I'm driving tonight. Get used to it."

"Fuck, Ken. I can't do this."

Ken grabbed his hips and shoved him back against the counter. "Yes, you can."

"I don't—"

Ken stood up and moved into Andy, wrapping a hand around the back of his neck and pulling him toward Ken until their lips were almost touching. "Tonight, you do."

"Ken." The word was a plea.

He cupped Andy's face and rubbed his thumbs over his cheekbones. "Let me do this."

Andy nodded. "Okay, but I can't promise not to fight."

"What did you say to me the first time? What would be the fun in that?"

Andy smiled then, and Ken knew he was doing the right thing. He lowered himself to his knees again and took Andy's cock into his mouth. Andy hissed and thrust into him, but Ken grabbed his hips and shoved him back into the counter. Andy didn't fight him anymore. This time, he let Ken suck him. Ken slid his lips along Andy's cock, teased with his tongue, and pulled the most amazing sounds from him.

Just when Ken was sure Andy was right on the edge, he tightened his grip on the base of Andy's shaft and pulled off.

Andy glared at him.

"You wouldn't want it to end so soon would you?"

"What I wanted was to come down your throat. You know once won't be enough."

Ken grinned. "Maybe later. Go get on the bed."

Andy scowled at him and Ken braced to fight some more, but Andy pushed away from the counter, kicked off his pants and boxers, and sauntered to the bed, clearly knowing just how gorgeous he was. Ken swallowed hard as he stared. The man's ass was true perfection, just as he'd known it would be the first time he'd seen it outlined in tight, threadbare denim.

Andy stopped to reach into the nightstand drawer and pull out a box of condoms and lube that he tossed on the bed. Then he stretched out on his back and dropped his legs open.

"Getting into your role?" Ken asked.

"You said I didn't have any choice. I wouldn't want to disappoint the boss."

Ken saw red. "If you think for one damn minute that this has anything to do with you working for me—"

Andy grinned and Ken realized he'd been played. "Get over here and fuck me."

"I'm going to make you beg. I'm going to make you tell me exactly what you want and why."

The color drained from Andy's face, and he squeezed his eyes shut. What the hell had Ken said to cause that reaction?

"Andy?"

"Just keep pretending everything's okay."

"Okay, yeah. I… I will."

Uncertain now, Ken stripped and approached the bed. He stared down at Andy, wondering if he was heading somewhere he didn't really want to go.

"Wondering if you can take me after all?" Andy asked, that mocking gleam back in his eyes.

Ken glared at him, confidence returning. "Fuck no."

"Then stop thinking so much. Thinking only gets you in trouble."

"Actually, I believe it's the other way around."

Andy shrugged. "Maybe, but I think you like trouble."

Ken smiled at him. "With you I do anyway."

"I think you like the idea of taking out all that anger on me. You looked so fucking hot when you stormed off the porch."

Ken was mesmerized by Andy's smell, his taste, the way he felt in Ken's hands. He'd forgotten why he was so angry. It wasn't just because Andy had been out fucking someone else, if that really was what he'd been doing. It was because he was lying, hiding, and maybe putting everyone at the ranch in danger. Ken was really a hell of a lot angrier at himself than at Andy because he couldn't shake off what Andy made him feel, couldn't stop needing him no matter who he was.

"I'm going to show you what you were missing while you were off chasing someone else, and then I'm going to make it clear that as long as we're fucking, it's me and only me."

"Possessive son of a bitch, aren't you?"

"Yes, on both counts."

Andy grinned. "Show me what you got."

He reached for the headboard, displaying himself once more, but the submission was fake. Ken had no doubt Andy would try to roll him once he settled on top of him.

"I changed my mind. Get up."

Andy frowned. "Don't be a fucking cock tease."

"Like you need more anyway after where you've been."

"Ken, please. There's…"

"What? Say it, goddammit. Say what you really mean."

"There's no one like you."

Ken smiled, trying not to reveal how hard that confession had hit him. "You'd do well to remember that. Now get up."

Andy sat up, but he didn't get off the bed. "Ken—"

Ken grabbed his arm and jerked him to his feet. He stumbled as Ken dragged him toward the back of the couch. "I want you here instead. I want to hold you in place while you fight to stay on your feet. I want you struggling so you don't forget what's happening to you."

"There's no way in hell I'm going to forget."

Ken's breath caught. Andy's voice was filled with the

same tangle of emotions that were swirling through Ken: anger, fear, desperation. "Have you ever—"

"Bottomed? Yes, but not in years."

Ken shuddered. "Fuck."

"Yeah, that's what you want, isn't it? What you're demanding from me?"

Ken considered changing his mind for half a second before saying, "Hell yes."

———

ANDY COULD HAVE FOUGHT. Ken's grip on his hair was firm, but Andy could have escaped him easily. If he'd wanted to. But he didn't. He was enjoying the hell out of this. The adrenaline rush from meeting the mysterious asshole face to ski mask had been further fueled by Ken's anger and the urgent need Andy felt every damn time he saw Ken, even if they'd just fucked each other's brains out.

Ken pushed Andy down until he lay over the back of the couch and then kicked at his ankles, telling him wordlessly to spread his legs. Andy did, never even considering a protest. Ken stepped up behind him and pressed his hard cock against Andy's ass as he laid a hand to the back of Andy's neck and pushed until he bent double over the back of the couch. When Ken tightened his grip on Andy's neck and thrust against him, pinning him to the cushion, Andy shuddered. He normally hated being helpless, but Ken made it feel so good.

"You better hold on," Ken said, his voice low and sultry. "This is gonna get rough."

"I'm counting on it."

Ken groaned. "I'm going to own you, Andy."

You already do. Andy didn't trust himself to speak.

"Don't move," Ken ordered.

Andy nodded, no longer able to fight. He wanted Ken, wanted to see if it felt as good to have the man inside him as he'd imagined it would.

He heard a tearing sound that had to be Ken opening a condom, then Ken pressed the heel of his hand against the base of Andy's spine. He slid his hand upward, pressing his fingers into Andy's skin, making him have to bite his lip to keep from letting Ken know how much he wanted to feel him anyway he could.

Ken drew the fingers of his other hand along the crack of Andy's ass and teased his entrance, pushing only the tip of a lubed finger into him. "I'm going to fucking ruin you for anyone else. From now on, if you want to fuck, you come find me."

Andy swallowed hard as Ken pushed deeper into him. He worked his finger in and out, then added another.

"You're gonna give me what I need no matter when or where?" Andy asked, the words coming out hoarse and choked.

Ken added a second finger before he answered, and Andy hissed at the intrusion.

"I don't even give a damn if I'm with a customer. I'll fuck you in the tack room with them right on the other side of the door."

Andy groaned. The thought of that—being pressed up against the wall with a snooty couple from Houston looking over a prized horse not ten feet away—was all it took for the last of the tension to drain from him. He sank into the couch and pushed back against Ken's fingers, trying to take them deeper.

Ken found the right angle to brush over his gland. Andy bucked against the couch, fighting Ken's hold. "No, you stay right here. You're all mine." Ken kept working him, and

Andy bit down on the couch cushion to keep from crying out until finally, Ken pulled his fingers from Andy's body.

While Andy had the chance to speak, he tried to take back some control. "You know you love submitting to me. I've heard how you beg when I go as deep as I can, fill you up, take you without mercy."

Ken positioned his cock and surged forward, cutting off Andy's ability to speak again. Apparently, he wasn't going to be gentle even knowing how long it had been for Andy. That was exactly what Andy wanted. He hoped Ken would split him in two. If there wasn't any pain to ground him, he might give up every single one of his secrets to Ken.

Ken kept a hand on the back of his neck and grabbed Andy's hip with his other hand, holding him tight. Ken kept moving forward, slowly, opening Andy up until Andy was sure there was no way in hell he could take all of him.

"Fucking God, you're too big for this."

Ken gave an evil laugh. "You're going to take it, all of it."

"Fuck!" Andy writhed, not sure if he was trying to get free or to get more.

Suddenly, Ken was all the way in, his pelvis pressed against Andy's ass. Andy panted, fighting to get enough air not to pass out. All coherent thought was gone. Ken had completely broken him.

"So tight. So good," Ken murmured.

Andy bit his lip, but a whimper escaped.

Ken chuckled. "Yeah, you like this."

Against his will, Andy nodded. Ken let go of his hip and reached around to stroke his cock. More needy sounds slipped out as Andy thrust into his hand.

KEN GROANED. Being inside Andy was even better than he'd imagined, and he wanted to stay there forever. "I'm going to take you so hard, make this perfect for you." He pumped Andy's cock a few more times before grabbing his hip again. The room seemed to spin around him, forcing him to need an anchor. His body screamed with the need to drive into Andy and use him as hard as he could, but he had to give the man time to adjust.

"Fuck me, Ken. Now!"

Ken pulled out a fraction of an inch before pushing back in. "I am fucking you. I would've thought you'd notice."

Andy growled. "Move. Now."

He slowly pulled out almost all the way, deliberately tormenting Andy and making sure he couldn't think about anything else. Andy was panting by the time Ken was ready to drive back in. His ass squeezed Ken's cock like he was trying to hold it inside him. His hand tore at the couch cushion, and Ken was sure he was going to rip it. Then he pushed back in, not as hard as he wanted to, but hard enough to make Andy cry out. This time he didn't slow down; instead, he set up a rhythm that was fast enough to keep Andy from catching his breath. Within seconds, Andy was cursing, yelling, and calling Ken's name. He was close and so was Ken, but Ken wanted more than just to make Andy come. He wanted him to give up as much as Ken had. "Who's fucking you, Andy?"

"You are. Now get on with it."

"You love it don't you?"

Andy snarled. "Fuck yes."

Ken gasped as Andy's muscles clenched around him. "Tell me how much you want this."

"Goddammit, Ken."

"Tell me!"

Andy was close. Ken was sure of it, so he wrapped his

hand around the base of Andy's cock, preventing him from coming.

"No," Andy yelled as he pushed back into Ken, trying to take him deeper.

Ken kept him pinned down and pulled out slowly, ignoring Andy's desperation. When he thrust back in, he made sure he was at the perfect angle to hit Andy's gland.

Andy sucked in his breath, biting his lip so hard a drop of blood welled up and rolled onto the couch. Ken didn't give a fuck about the fabric. All he wanted was Andy's surrender.

"Give in," he demanded.

"Can't."

"Yes, you can. Just open up for me."

"I fucking am."

"No." Ken wasn't going to let him give any less than he'd made Ken give.

Ken kept fucking Andy gently, knowing it wasn't enough to get him off, dragging in and out, making him really feel everything.

Finally, words burst from Andy. "I need you, okay? I fucking need you. All over me, in me, holding me. Fuck, Ken, is that enough for you?"

"Yes!" Ken shouted. He let go of Andy's hip and lay over him, pressing as much of their bodies together as he could.

"Yes," he said again as he fucked Andy hard and fast. "Come for me, Andy."

Andy gasped and did exactly as Ken commanded. As he shuddered, his ass tightened around Ken's cock, threatening to send Ken over, but Ken held back, wanting to feel every twitch, every pulse of Andy's body before letting go.

When Andy sagged against the couch, thoroughly spent, Ken moved again, slowly at first, then faster.

"I want to feel it," Andy whispered. "I want to feel you give it up just like I did."

"You know I already have," Ken said. "I've given you everything." He drove in one final time before pleasure so intense he couldn't tell it from pain slammed into him. He came and came and came, thinking it would never end. Even if it did, he would never fully recover from what they'd done.

KEN WASN'T sure how long he lay there, pressing Andy into the couch. When he finally summoned the strength to stand, both men groaned as his cock pulled free of Andy's body.

Andy lifted a hand, and Ken grabbed it and helped him up. The couch had moved several feet across the floor. When Ken looked down, he saw deep grooves driven into the wood.

Andy rubbed a toe over one of them and laughed. "Worth it?"

Ken grinned. "Hell yeah."

When he looked up, the humor disappeared from Andy's eyes, and the pain that replaced it hit Ken so hard he could barely stay on his feet. Andy swayed, obviously just as affected by what was between them. Why? Why was this happening now, with this man he couldn't trust? And why did Andy show every sign of feeling the same way? Was it all a con? Ken might just shoot him if he found out it was.

"Go lie down. I'll get something to clean you up."

Andy stumbled toward the bed and fell onto it.

Ken stepped into the bathroom, wet a washcloth, and wiped himself off. He tossed it in the basket at the bottom of the linen closet and got another one for Andy. He made sure the water was warm, laughing at how he was babying Andy.

He probably expected Ken to just walk away, but he wasn't going to make it that easy for him.

Andy was curled on his side, asleep. He looked so young and innocent when he relaxed like that. Ken debated curling up beside him and enjoying the moment, but he rolled Andy over on his back. Andy murmured something, but Ken couldn't make out the words. Ken cleaned him up and carried the cloth back to the bathroom. When he came out again, Andy was sitting up, looking out the window. Ken wondered if Andy was about to tell him to leave.

When he didn't say anything, Ken sat down beside him. Finally, Andy spoke. "I just wish…"

Ken's heart pounded. What did he wish? That this could be more? That he wasn't lying to Ken? "What?"

He shook his head. "Nothing. If wishes were horses, right?"

"Beggars would ride."

Andy turned around, his jaw tight, but there was vulnerability in his eyes. "But you've never been a beggar."

"Except with you."

Andy squeezed his eyes shut. When he opened them, Ken was sure they were wet with unshed tears.

"Lie down," Ken said.

Andy did and Ken spooned around him, loving how they fit together. He kissed the back of Andy's neck, and Andy sighed. The sound made Ken's chest tighten, and it was a long time before he fell asleep.

CHAPTER FIFTEEN

Andy helped hide the next shipment of drugs, but he still wasn't any closer to finding out the identity of the man who was running the show. The man wasn't at the shed when the drugs arrived. He'd left Ben, Andy, and the door guard in charge of getting the product hidden. Andy wasn't invited to meet with the buyers the next night. He'd watched from the woods, though. Everyone important was masked again, the buyer and the mysterious asshole. He'd gotten some photos, but they wouldn't be worth shit.

That had been several days ago, and he'd yet to receive any more messages. His nerves were on edge. The only thing keeping him in one piece was spending each night fucking Ken. That and Ken holding him through bad dreams and restlessness. He was falling for Ken, letting him in way too deep, but he didn't have the strength to pull away, not when Ken's arms felt so right around him. He was the only real thing in Andy's life, even if their relationship was based on lies.

The flashbacks were coming more frequently than ever. He'd nearly fallen off a horse the day before because the whole world had flipped and he was in a warehouse, not galloping over a field stretching a horse's legs. If the animal hadn't been as well trained as he was, Andy might have ended up with a broken neck. How much longer could he hold back the darkness?

You're not fit for this.

Fuck that. I'm going to finish it.

Gomez was pushing for results, and he wasn't about to tell her how close he was to falling apart. Ken had gone to Houston to take care of business and intended to stay the night, and Andy was on his own, so bad off his hands were shaking. He'd just poured himself a drink, thinking that would be the only way to get any sleep when his phone rang.

It was the asshole himself.

"Andy. I've got a problem."

Andy's instincts told him he was in trouble. "What's that?"

"The little shit who brought you in. He's decided you're a cop."

Andy forced out a laugh. "What? That's bullshit."

"So you're not a cop, then?"

"Hell no."

"Thing is, it's hard to trust a man in this business, so I had one of my men check you out. Dig around a bit."

Andy grabbed his gun. If he'd been made, there was probably someone on his way to kill him right now. "And?"

"He didn't find a fucking thing. I think the little shit's jealous. He wishes he was as good as you."

Andy snorted. "Cocky son of a bitch."

"He is, and now he's become a liability. I'd like you to make sure he won't be a problem anymore."

Andy's hand tightened around the phone. He almost hung up, called in, and said he was done, but somehow he held it together. "Taking care of him would be my pleasure."

He'd figure a way out of this.

There hadn't been an out with Charlie, and there wouldn't be one now.

He'd known Ben was trouble, but how the hell had he figured out who Andy was? Maybe he hadn't. Maybe it was nothing more than the worst slur he could think of.

"Do it tonight."

Andy's mind raced. He needed time to put the plan in place. "I'm not sure I can get away that quickly."

"I thought you'd be eager to get this done. Do I need to reconsider his accusation?"

Andy swallowed and found his voice. "No, sir. I'll take care of him."

"I'll need proof. The whole body is too risky, but a hand or something will do. Leave it where you two first met."

Fucking sick bastard. "Will do."

"You have until dawn. Text me at this number when it's done."

The man hung up before Andy had to speak again. He tossed the phone on the bed and ran to the bathroom where he puked up what little dinner he'd eaten.

Andy tried to think of a solution that didn't involve ending the investigation, but he couldn't. He was going to have to get Ben to safety and disappear. He wouldn't even be able to say goodbye to Ken. Maybe someday he'd come back and explain, but it wasn't like Ken was going to want him after he broke his trust. He fought to ignore the wet streaks on his cheeks as he packed enough stuff to get him through a few days. Gomez could figure out how to get the rest, not that he gave a damn about most of it anyway.

He'd known that, however the case ended, he'd have to walk away without Ken knowing the real him. Hell, he wasn't even sure who he was now anyway. A fucked-up mess. That much he knew, but he'd fallen into his role here so deeply he'd almost convinced himself he really was a ranch foreman.

He tried to contact Ben, but the little shit wouldn't answer his phone. He probably thought he was too important to bother talking to Andy. He would most likely put up a fight when Andy found him, even though Andy was giving up goddamn everything to save him—all the work he'd done here, Ken, a chance to prove he could still do his fucking job.

Andy threw his bag into his truck, and he was about to call Gomez and tell her about the goatfuck this case had become, when his phone rang. He checked it. The asshole again.

"Andy."

"Change of plan. Sorry to deprive you of all the fun, but the little weasel showed up at my fucking house, whining about how he'd get proof. I shut him up."

Andy's stomach knotted, but he forced out the words he needed to say. "Wow. Wish I could have been there."

"Yeah. It was too fast. I lost my temper."

"He was at *your house*."

"You feel me, right?"

"I do."

"Good. We'll talk soon."

He ended the call before Andy could say anything.

Andy fell against the side of his truck. Dead. Ben was dead. He looked down. Blood. On his hands, dripping on the ground, spreading. It was going to drown him. *Why can't you keep them alive? Why do they all die?*

He dropped to his knees and pressed himself against the side of the truck. Someone was coming. They were going to kill him too.

Get up. Run.

He couldn't move. He deserved to die. He couldn't save anyone.

Footsteps. Closer.

They were coming. They were going to kill him. They knew he was a cop, and he was going to die just like Charlie and Ben.

"Andy! Andy! What's wrong?"

Someone was calling him. Why? Why not just kill him?

"Andy?" A man reached for him, and he flinched and fell back, hitting something. Metal, not wood. Not the warehouse. He lifted his hand to touch it. It was dry, not wet with blood. Metal. The truck. His truck.

Andy blinked and looked up. Ken stood in front of him. His eyes were wide, and he was watching Andy like someone would a dog that was prone to attack.

Andy used the side of the truck to pull himself to his feet. He grabbed the door handle, pulled it open, and slipped inside. Before he thought about what he was doing, he'd started the truck and taken off. He had no idea where he was going or why, but he had to get away from Ken, from death, from everything he no longer wanted to be.

KEN WATCHED Andy's truck tear down the driveway. Had Andy been having a flashback? He'd seemed to come out of it, but…

Ken's thought process was interrupted when he registered what it meant that there were boxes in the back of the truck. He raced up the guesthouse steps. The door wasn't locked. Andy had left things there, but Ken could tell that a lot of his stuff was gone. He'd actually been planning to leave, and Ken would never have known if he hadn't come home. He'd driven back from Houston because he'd missed the fucking bastard.

Why was he going to leave and where had his mind taken him that had made him look so scared?

He's not who you think he is.

Apparently not, because the man Ken thought Andy was wouldn't run off like that without having the courage to say goodbye. Ken looked around again, still not really believing Andy was gone. Why had he left some of his stuff? Then he saw it, a folded piece of paper with his name on it. He reached for it and then pulled back his hand. He didn't want to know what pathetic excuse Andy had made up for leaving him.

He thought about Andy taking off, still shaking from whatever hell he'd visited. Should he go after him? He'd recognized Ken before he'd taken off; Ken was sure of it. But Andy had no business driving when he was that shaken up. He could be out there, hurt or unsure of where he really was. He needed help.

He was planning to leave you.

He might be hurt or in trouble?

You're not his keeper. You're just the man he's been lying to.

Ken slammed the door of the cottage and stomped toward the barn. A hard, fast ride, that was what he needed. If Andy did come back for the rest of his stuff, Ken didn't want to be there. Because chances were, whatever shit story Andy told him, Ken would believe it or pretend he did, and they'd end up in bed again. When it came to Andy, he was a fucking addict.

He saddled Jekyll, wanting the wildest possible ride. When the horse was ready, they took off down the road that circled the ranch. Ken would rather have raced across the fields, but he wouldn't risk his horse like that. Even with a full moon, the road was much safer.

After nearly an hour of riding, Ken gave up on settling himself with speed and fresh air, if the muggy nighttime of a Texas May could be considered fresh. He slowed Jekyll to a walk and returned to the barn.

When the horse was cooled down, groomed, and settled in his stall, Ken stalked to the house. Clearly, he needed something stronger to blot out thoughts of Andy, naked, willing, open to him. *Fucking son of a bitch.*

He banged open the door and walked into his house through the kitchen. He opened the liquor cabinet and chose a bottle of tequila. This night called for something serious. When he needed to make himself comatose as fast as he could, tequila was his best friend. He reached for a glass but changed his mind. This was a full-on drink-from-the-bottle-until-you-couldn't-stand-up occasion. Instead of setting the glass back, he hurled it across the room, loving the sound of it shattering. He longed to smash the rest of the glassware, almost as much as he wanted to smash Andy's face.

The man needs help just like Renata said. He needs you.

He's been lying to me for weeks.

With his words, but the fucking you've been doing is too real to be a lie. There's something you're not seeing.

He was leaving without saying goodbye.

You might be his only chance.

Shut the fuck up.

He got the lid off the bottle and took a huge swallow. He could have gotten a lime and some salt to make the liquor more palatable, but he didn't. He just needed to stop the voices in his head. Stop thinking, stop wanting.

He took another long sip, and his body started to tingle just like he wanted it too.

Andy makes you tingle.

Fuck that. He was clearly not drinking fast enough.

"MARIA?" Andy didn't have the energy to care that fear came through in his voice. He'd pulled off the road to make the call, but he wasn't sure where he was.

"What's wrong?"

"He killed him."

"Who?" She'd obviously been sleeping, but she sounded fully awake now.

"Ben. The kid who got me in."

"Oh."

Andy knew Gomez would make the connection to Charlie. He didn't have to say it. "Ben accused me of being a cop, but they didn't believe him."

"Thank God."

"The man in charge ordered me to kill him, but Ben tracked him down to try to make him listen and the man killed him. I was going to find him and get him to safety. I was going to shut everything down so I could save him, but I was too late."

"Where are you now?"

Andy ignored her, not wanting to explain that he'd freaked out and run. "He's going to ask me again."

"Ask you to kill someone?"

"I won't do it."

"Andy, you need to get out. We'll find another way to get this guy. You've given us a lot to go on."

"No, I have to go back. I have to finish it." He sounded crazy, even to himself. Gomez was never going to let him stay.

"Andy, tell me where you are. I'm going to come get you."

"No, I've got to go back. I don't want them to have died for nothing. This is our best chance."

"Are you sure this is the same man who killed Charlie?"

"Yes." The man looked so much like Ken. But he wasn't Ken. No fucking way.

"But you don't have any proof."

"His voice, his build, they're all the same. He's the same. I know he is." Fuck. He still sounded crazy. Gomez wasn't going to trust him, and she was right.

"Andy, where are you?"

He looked around. "I'm not exactly sure. I'm on some back road not too far from the ranch. I just started driving after…"

"After what?"

He couldn't tell her about his flashback. She'd pull him out and shut the whole thing down—exactly what she should do. "After I found out Ben was dead."

"It's time to pull you out, Andy."

"No. I've got this."

"You don't. You're too emotionally invested. I shouldn't have let you talk me into this."

"Maybe not, but you did, and I'm here. I'm sticking it out."

"Andy, I can hear how off-balance you are."

"I'll pull it together. Tonight was just… hard, okay? I needed someone I could say that to. I don't need you to come out here."

"Andy, what are you going to do now?"

"Go back home and get drunk."

"Home?" He heard the judgment as clearly as if she'd

said it outright. UCs walked a fine line. Immerse yourself in the role, but never forget your real purpose.

"I'm going to go back to the ranch and get drunk. How's that?"

"Will Ken be waiting there for you?"

Fuck her for asking. "Yes, he's there, but I ran out on him."

He heard her blow out a breath. He could see her in his mind, sitting there in bed her forehead wrinkled, hand rubbing her eyes, looking as exasperated with him as she always did.

"I'm okay."

"You're very far from okay. There are other ways for us to get these men."

"Let me stay."

She sighed, and he knew he had her because it was her I'm-about-to-do-something-stupid sigh. "Fine, but if anything else like this happens, you're out."

He ended the call. Now he had to slink back to the farm and deal with the consequences of his meltdown. He wondered if Ken had seen the boxes in the back of the truck or the note he'd left. Andy hoped to hell not. Answering questions about why he'd planned to take off for good would be even harder than asking forgiveness for being a fucking freak.

He whipped the truck around and took off, hoping instinct would lead him back to the ranch. Later he wouldn't remember anything about what happened between his decision to drive back and seeing Ken standing in the doorway, a bottle of tequila in his hand.

Ken took a step and fell against the doorjamb. "What are you doing back here, you fucking bastard?"

Andy's instincts told him to run, but he walked up the

steps. "Don't say a fucking word about tonight," he ordered. "I was stupid. I get that. I'm back now."

"I fucking hate you," Ken said, gesturing wildly with the bottle.

Andy grabbed the bottle out of his hand and tipped it back, swallowing slowly enough to really feel the burn. He wiped his mouth with the back of his hand and held the bottle up so he could observe the level of liquid. "Tell me this wasn't full when you started."

"Was brand dew. Few. Fuck it."

"Yeah, I guess it was," Andy said, laughing.

"I should send you…" Ken gestured toward the road.

Andy nodded. "That would be the right thing to do."

Ken laughed, and it took him a while to stop. "Can't do it."

"I wouldn't go anyway."

He needed to be with Ken. He could tell himself he'd insisted on staying because he had to see the case through, and he did, but he was also there because of Ken. He couldn't stand the thought of leaving him, and he sure as hell wasn't going to let anyone hurt him. "Ken?"

The man looked up, a goofy smile on his face.

Tell him.

"I…"

Ken probably wouldn't even remember the conversation the next day. And what good would it do? He'd waited too long, gotten too close. He'd screwed up his chances the second he'd kissed Ken without telling him who he really was.

Andy's chest tightened, and his breath caught. Panic was closing in on him again, and he knew where it would send him. He took another long pull from the bottle.

"You gonna say somthin'?" Ken asked.

Andy shook his head.

Ken turned and stumbled into the door. Andy put a hand around his waist and helped to right him. "Office?"

Ken gave him a crooked grin. "Hell yeah."

Fucking was not going to solve this, nor was drinking himself into oblivion, but he didn't care. Apparently, he'd stopped making reasonable choices a long damn time ago.

CHAPTER SIXTEEN

Andy woke in the predawn hours on the floor of Ken's office, his limbs entangled with Ken's. They were both naked.

A few seconds later, he crawled to the adjacent bathroom and was violently ill. When he gained the strength to move again, he grabbed his clothes and walked to the guesthouse still naked.

Shower. Coffee. More toilet hugging. More coffee, slower sips the second time. Then the call came. One of the mares had decided to have her baby that morning. At least it would help him avoid any awkward talk with Ken. Though he couldn't be sure his head wouldn't roll right off his shoulders into the mare's stall.

As soon as one foal was born, another mare went into labor. Forty-eight hours passed before Andy had time to think again. He was bone tired, starving, and happier than he'd been in ages. Working with the horses let him turn off all the shit that usually buzzed around in his head. Since he'd gone to the barn two days ago, he hadn't had a single flashback.

The sick feeling that was always there in the pit of his stomach had left him.

Now, the sun shone into his kitchen, birds chirped, the sky was clear, and anyone else would be happy as hell to face a beautiful day with nothing to do. He wanted to go right back to the barn and work himself to exhaustion again.

Gomez had called him at least four times during the mares' labors. He'd finally returned her call as he'd fallen into bed the night before. If he didn't give a full report soon, she'd show up and pull him out. He was sure of it, but he wasn't up for talking to her yet.

Breakfast. He'd start there. He could go grab breakfast at the bunkhouse, but he didn't want to talk to anyone, so he opened the fridge and looked in.

As he'd suspected, there wasn't much there. At least he had coffee. He took another sip and almost spilled it on himself when someone knocked on the door. He hadn't heard anyone approaching. How could he have let his guard down so thoroughly?

He set his coffee down and walked to the door. The hair on the back of his neck stood up. Trouble. He was so certain of it he considered grabbing his gun.

He pulled the door open. Ken stood on his porch. He'd been right, but this wasn't the kind of trouble a gun could solve, more's the pity.

"Morning," Andy said.

"Have you had breakfast?"

Andy shook his head. "Just coffee."

"Follow me." Ken turned around and walked down the porch steps.

Andy wanted to refuse. He'd gotten a reprieve because of the horses, but now Ken was sober, rested, and ready to confront him about the other night. So much for a good start. Andy now felt nearly as bad as he had when he'd woken up after helping Ken finish off the tequila.

"I'm not hungry."

Ken glanced over his shoulder. "Yes, you are."

Andy sighed and followed him.

"Take a seat," Ken said in what Andy thought of as his CEO voice.

Andy didn't bother to argue. He slid onto a stool at the counter as Ken served him a plate with bacon, eggs, and a biscuit. Maybe he was hungry after all. The biscuit was big and fluffy and looked homemade. "Did Renata make these?" he asked.

Ken smiled, looking much too pleased with himself. "No. I did."

Andy stared at him. "You?"

"I spent a lot of time in the kitchen as a kid. Renata taught me her secrets."

Why was that so fucking hot?

"What do you take in your coffee?" Ken asked.

"Black's good."

Ken raised a brow.

"Cream and a fuckload of sugar."

His smile widened. "That's what I thought."

"Fucker."

Ken poured a generous amount of cream into the mug and then handed it to Andy along with a sugar bowl. "You don't have to hide from me."

If only that were true.

"Some of the guys at the stat—uh, ranch I worked on before this one used to tease me."

"Aww and you couldn't handle the mean old ranch hands?" Ken laughed.

Andy scowled at him. "I handled it just fine, but I didn't feel like taking shit from you this morning."

"Coffee is the least of your worries."

Andy tensed. "Look I told you I wasn't in the mood for company."

"Eat."

"What the fuck put you in this I'm-in-charge-of-the-world mood this morning?"

"We have two beautiful foals. I survived two days of nonstop work with a hangover that didn't let up until day two, and it's a gorgeous day. Besides, I'm always in charge of the world."

Andy gave him a knowing look, and Ken chuckled.

"What I let you do to me is an anomaly."

"*Let* me do?" Andy asked.

"That's right."

Andy started to stand up. A fight would make this day much better. A fight and a good, hard fuck.

Ken shook his head. "Sit down and eat. We can argue when you have food in you."

Andy sighed and did what Ken said. He took a bite of biscuit, and suddenly that was all that mattered, flaky, buttery, tangy perfection. He could come from eating these biscuits, and Ken had made them with his strong, long-fingered hands. Goddamn that man. Andy realized he'd closed his eyes as he savored the taste. When he opened them again, Ken was watching him with a smirk on his face.

He had to fucking face it. Ken had him right where he wanted him, and the man said Andy was a seductive bastard. "You make orgasmic fucking biscuits, okay?"

Ken nodded. "Okay."

"Sit down, you're making me nervous hovering like that."

Ken laughed. "*I* make *you* nervous."

"Fuck, Ken, has it really taken you this long to figure that out?'

"I…" Ken shook his head. "Just eat."

Andy did, cleaning his plate and going back for more. Ken seemed to do more watching of him than eating, but Andy pretended he didn't notice. He also ignored the buzz of tension in the air. Ken surely expected an explanation for his erratic behavior the night he took off, for his dishonesty and his secrets. He stalled as long as he could by stuffing himself with biscuits, but eventually, he couldn't fit in another bite. Ken cleared their plates and poured each of them more coffee.

"So," Ken said when he sat back down. "Where did you say you grew up?"

Andy's heart raced. This was a trap. He was sure of it. The lines were blurring, his past self, his current self, his assignment. He'd known he was going to fuck something up. "I didn't."

Ken narrowed his eyes. "Yeah, you did."

Fuck, why was Ken asking questions now. "When?"

"The other night."

Andy's stomach flip-flopped. "The tequila night?"

Ken nodded.

What else had Andy said that night? Something that could compromise all he'd worked for? All he remembered about that night was sucking Ken off, begging to swallow his load and then wanting more. He'd never let a man come in his mouth before, but he wanted to do things with Ken that he'd never even considered. He was so fucked. "Don't push. Please."

KEN RAN a hand through his hair wishing he could do what Andy said, but ignoring his lies was getting more and more dangerous. "You're running my ranch. How am I just supposed to be okay with the fact that you refuse to answer normal everyday questions?"

Andy shrugged, but Ken could see through his attempt to act casual.

"I worked my ass off to get this ranch and make it mine."

Andy looked him in the eye, and Ken saw emotions he'd only seen during sex. "Trust me, okay?"

Ken laughed, but the sound had no mirth in it. "When your hands are on me, that seems so easy. I'd believe almost anything that comes out of your seductive mouth, but I've got to stop being such a fool."

"Don't. Not yet, please."

He couldn't wait for a confession any longer. "Andy, I know. I checked up on your background, and I know."

Andy looked away for a few seconds. When he faced Ken again, he looked hard and angry. "What exactly do you know?"

Ken shook his head, his lip curled in disgust. "Are you really going to make me spell it out?"

Andy didn't say a damn thing.

"The drugs, the possession charges, all the things you just managed to skate away from or get only the minimum punishment."

"And you're assuming I'm still involved in shit like that? You know people change. You've seen it in Rusty."

"Funny you should mention Rusty. He thinks something strange is going on out by the border with Lawson's and that you might be involved."

The color drained from Andy's face, and he grabbed onto

the edge of the counter. For a few seconds, Ken was afraid something he'd said had triggered a flashback.

"What gave him that idea?" Andy asked, his voice hoarse. The man was scared of something. Ken wished to God he'd say what it was.

"He went out there to meet someone and found some very interesting crates that sure as hell didn't belong there."

"Probably liquor. Just a bunch of kids taking advantage of an unused place to have a party."

"Rusty didn't think that's all it was."

Andy looked like he might be sick. "Did you tell him to stay away from there?"

"He decided that on his own. The last thing he needs is to get mixed up in trouble."

"Good. I'll check into it." He pushed away from the counter and turned like he was going to leave.

"Andy, don't play me."

He faced Ken again, and Ken was sure he was going to deny what he was doing, but he simply watched Ken, studying him.

"Are you in some kind of trouble yourself?" Ken asked.

"Nothing I can't handle."

"No matter what you're involved in, I can help." The offer was out there before Ken could stop himself. Renata had said Andy needed his help. He did not need to get mixed up in Andy's bullshit, especially not if it was something his family could use against him, but he couldn't help himself, and Renata was more important to him than almost anyone.

"No. Not with this."

"So you admit that you've been lying to me?"

Andy sighed and nodded. "Please don't ask any more questions."

"Goddammit, Andy!" Ken slammed his hand down so

hard he was lucky he didn't break something, the counter or his hand. "If you're fucking up my ranch, if you're using my land for something illegal, I will hunt you down."

"It's not what you think." Andy no longer looked angry or defensive. He simply looked sad.

"Then what is it?"

"I can't tell you."

"How the fuck can I trust you if you won't talk to me?"

"What do your instincts tell you about me?"

Ken blew out a long breath. "That I'm a fucking fool."

Andy raised a brow. The bastard knew there was more.

"My instincts also say you're a decent man."

"That may or may not be true, but I swear to you, I'm not going to harm this ranch. Please give me a few more days to take care of my problems."

Ken sighed. "You're asking too much."

Andy nodded and turned to walk away, but Ken grabbed his arm. "Look, just promise you won't hurt—"

Andy held up a hand. "Don't. Don't ask me that. Please."

"What do you think I'm going to ask you?" Ken fought to control his expression. He didn't want Andy to know how twisted up he was inside.

"I…" Andy squeezed his eyes shut and Ken watched a bead of sweat roll down his face. "I thought you were going to ask me not to hurt you."

Ken's snarl was so savage, Andy took a step backward. "Fuck you, Andy. Now you want me to admit to being way more invested in this"—he gestured back and forth between them—"whatever the hell it is than I have any business being. Well, you're not getting that. I don't give a damn what you do. Go fuck your life up, but do not hurt this ranch. And if you want to run away again. Run. You're a damn good fuck, but I can find another one."

Andy swallowed visibly. Ken's heart pounded, and he felt as sick as Andy had looked earlier.

A few seconds later, Andy nodded. "Me minding my own business is probably for the best."

Ken gave a single sharp nod. "It would have been even better if we'd never started this at all."

"I didn't start this. You did," Andy said, his voice ice cold.

Ken wasn't feeling icy. He was running as hot as a volcano. "Are you going to finish it?" He asked, spitting the words at Andy.

Andy shook his head.

"Really? This sounds an awful lot like goodbye." Ken knew he should walk away, but he stayed right there, staring at Andy, challenging him to make the next move.

Andy took a step toward him and then another until he'd backed Ken against the wall.

Ken almost pushed him away, ordered him to either be honest or get the fuck out, but Andy grabbed his hips and slammed their bodies together.

"A fuck as good as you isn't all that easy to find, and I'm not ready to give this up, not yet." His tone was harsh, but Ken saw through him. Andy was as desperate to cling to whatever they had as Ken was.

"Show me how much you want me," Ken demanded.

Andy crushed him against the wall and leaned in close, hovering with his mouth a fraction of an inch from Ken's. Ken expected a bruising, punishing kiss. Instead, Andy brushed his lips across Ken's cheek and then whispered in his ear, making Ken shudder. "Not now. Not here where anyone could walk in on us."

Ken growled. "You're going to push too hard one day."

"So I'm the one who's pushing?" Andy asked. Ken

shoved at him, but Andy shoved back, preventing Ken from moving. "I need privacy and more time for what I want to do with you."

Ken glared at him. "I need your bed and me in charge."

"No. You need my cock in you, and that's what you're going to get tonight."

Ken saw desire in his eyes and the same desperation Ken felt. "You think I'm going to let you fuck me after this?"

"I think you still want me to make you scream."

"Fuck." Ken didn't know what else to say.

Andy grinned. "Oh yes."

"And after you make me lose control again, you're going to leave."

Andy looked stricken.

"You hate staying the night. You always want to run as soon as you've gotten the surrender you want."

"I've never gotten the surrender I really want, and I'm not the kind of man who sticks around."

Ken nodded. "Yeah, I'd guessed that."

"I'm coming for you as soon as I finish up in the barn tonight. Be naked and ready."

"I'm *always* ready for you. That's why you're so good at playing me."

Andy reached between them and palmed Ken's cock, rubbing up and down until Ken couldn't hold back a groan. "Don't you dare come before tonight."

Ken grabbed Andy's ass and thrust against him. "What if I want to come right now?"

Andy shook his head. "No."

"Bossy son of a bitch, aren't you? Especially for a man who won't tell me who he really is."

"You fucking love it."

Ken felt his vulnerability like a stab to the heart.

Andy's expression softened, and he cupped Ken's face with one hand. "I love that you're willing to let me take charge, and I know that it's something special for you. Watching your face as I push into you is my favorite thing in the world."

Ken didn't know how to deal with that knowledge. Andy hadn't said "I love you," but his words were likely as close as he could come. For a few seconds, the two men simply watched each other, their breathing the only sound in the kitchen.

Then Ken pushed Andy away. "Get out of here."

"Yes, sir," Andy replied. He winked at Ken and walked away.

THE NEXT DAY while he was tacking up Honey, a fidgety bay who needed some exercise, Andy's phone vibrated. He pulled it from his pocket and checked the messages.

Tomorrow night. Customer arriving. You will clear the area and assist in the sale.

Andy squeezed his eyes shut and took a deep breath. This was the invite Andy had been waiting for. Why did he feel so sad? He'd known his time at the KC wasn't going to last forever. Had a part of him really believed he could just become Andy Watson, ranch foreman? Apparently, he had.

Darkness threatened to close in. He clutched the edge of the nearest stall.

Breathe.

He tried to take another deep breath, to smell the horses, the hay, the leather tack. Not blood, anything but that.

"Andy?"

Rusty was calling him. Rusty wasn't from the past. He

was from right now. He squeezed the stall door tighter, letting the rough wood scratch at his hand. "Right here."

He heard Rusty approach, and he turned to face the younger man still dizzy and half in the past. "Whatcha need?"

Rusty was frowning at him. "Are you okay?"

"I'm fine."

Rusty frowned. "Really?"

"Just tell me what you need!"

Rusty took a step back.

Why the fuck was he yelling at the kid? Rusty hadn't done a damn thing to him. He couldn't resent him for suspecting Andy after seeing him at the shed. Going to Ken with his suspicions was exactly what he should have done. "Sorry. I'm just having a bad morning."

Rusty nodded. "I... Never mind. I just wanted to see if you were going to exercise Honey or if I should."

"Would you? I need to make a phone call."

"Sure."

Andy nodded to him and headed out of the barn. He started walking, needing to breathe fresh air, even if heat surrounded him like a suffocating blanket. Feeling it pressing on him meant he was alive and in this moment. When he was far enough from the barn not to be heard, he called Gomez.

When she answered, he started in with no preliminaries. "The man in charge contacted me. There's a buyer coming tomorrow night. He should be there along with all the major players. There will be product there to show the buyer. I think this is our chance to nail them."

"Can you handle this?"

Andy scowled at the phone. "I'm not going to fuck it up now."

"What if things go down like they did last time?"

Andy shuddered, torn between anger that she would bring

it up and fear that's exactly what could happen. "No, no one's going to die unless it's that murdering bastard."

"Andy, you know you can't be sure of that. Be reasonable"

"Fuck reasonable. I'm telling you how this is going to go down."

"No, I'll be telling you how things are going to go. If you think this is going to mess with your head, then—"

"I'm going in. I have to. If I don't show, they might bail."

"If you show and freeze, things will go worse."

Maybe for him, but not for the rest of them. "Ben's already dead. It's not going to go down like before. I'm not invested in any of these men."

She sighed. "What are you invested in, Andy?"

Ken. Becoming someone else. Nothing and everything. "Ending this."

She sighed.

"We've got to move on this. Ken's been looking into my background. He's questioning me, and Rusty has noticed activity where the meet is tonight. I won't risk them by prolonging this."

"Fine. I'll put together a team and take care of it."

"Without me? Fuck that. This guy is good. He'll sense something's wrong and call it off if I don't do exactly what he says."

"Andy, I've put myself on the line for you already. You are not going to push me anymore on this."

"Maria, please. Don't shut me out now. I'll hold it together."

"And after this? What happens then? I know you're close to a meltdown out there. I can't send you undercover again."

Andy ran a hand through his hair. He didn't really give a

fuck about what happened next. "We'll figure that out when this is over."

"Andy—"

"You need me to make this bust. If for no other reason than to prove you aren't crazy for trusting me."

"I'm not sacrificing you so I can get a pat on the back."

No, I'm sacrificing myself. For you. For Ken. "I'll be fine."

"Do you think the leader knows about you?"

"No." *Maybe.* "Everything will be fine. If he's made me, I'm counting on him thinking I won't call in backup this early."

He heard her sharp intake of breath. Fuck, he should have kept that to himself.

"This is a fucking suicide mission for you, isn't it?"

"No. I don't want to die." But he was willing to if it came to that. No one else was going to die because of him.

"You do not owe your life to that boy."

"He…" No, there was no point in saying more. Andy had had this conversation a thousand times, with the department shrink, with Maria, with himself. With Charlie's fucking ghost. "I took this assignment, and I'm going to finish it."

"For the wrong reasons."

He paced back and forth along the fence line, barely seeing the beautiful horses trotting around in the pasture. "You agreed to this."

"Because I'm a fucking idiot. Andy, I can't—"

"Stop this from happening. But you can send a team and bring these guys down."

"You do not tell me what I can and cannot do. I have every right to order you out of there."

He leaned on the fence and closed his eyes. This had to work. "But you're not going to."

"Have you ever thought that maybe I actually care what happens to you? That I don't think you're expendable."

He knew that. Maria was one of the few actual friends he had. "It's because you have a heart that you're not going to stop this. If Ken and Rusty keep digging into this, they're going to be targeted. I can't allow that and neither can you."

"And you're one hundred percent sure they're not involved?"

No way could Ken have played him that deeply, and Rusty for all his bravado was too naive. So the leader was Ken's size and build. That didn't mean he was Ken. The things their bodies said to each other couldn't be lies. They just couldn't. No one had ever stripped him of everything like Ken did. If he was wrong, then he might as well let Ken kill him because he would be dead anyway.

"I'm as sure as it's possible to be."

He heard Maria exhale, and he could see her running her hands over her hair, smoothing down the strands that had escaped from her ponytail. "I'm going to let you go in, but you're going to play this exactly like I tell you to."

"Of course I will."

"Don't fucking act like you're all compliant. I've got to be able to count on you to follow procedure with this."

"Procedure goes out the window in shit situations like this. You know that."

"Other detectives manage—"

"If you wanted a kiss-ass, you'd have sent one in and he'd be dead now. I'll listen to your plan, and I'll do my best to stick to it. That's as much as I can promise."

"I'll be in touch within twenty-four hours."

Andy smiled. He could feel her seething through the phone. "I await your orders."

She ended the call without saying more.

Andy realized someone was close by, maybe close enough to have heard. He'd been too involved in convincing Gomez to keep him in the loop to pay attention to his surroundings.

He pocketed his phone like he hadn't sensed a thing, wishing he had his gun. He'd just have to charm his way out of it. He turned and saw Rusty. Fuck. He'd rather it be someone the leader had sent to spy on him. Had he been intentionally spying on Andy? Had he overheard anything?

"What's up?" Andy asked. "I thought you were exercising Honey."

"Um… I had a question first."

Rusty wasn't looking at him, and even considering the heat, his cheeks were red. He'd deliberately followed Andy, not that Andy could blame him. He'd have to figure out what, if anything, to do about it later.

CHAPTER SEVENTEEN

Sam hadn't succeeded in finding out any more about Andy. Ken's investigations hadn't turned up anything either, and he was more frustrated than ever. He wanted answers even if they tore him apart because he couldn't stand pretending anymore.

But when Andy turned up at his door after dark, he didn't interrogate him. He yanked him through the door and crushed him up against the wall. Ferocity pounded through him as he felt his barriers crumble. Andy didn't fight like Ken had expected, he sank into the wall and let Ken assault him.

Ken kissed him, holding his head in place as he probed his mouth, wanting him to fight, wanting him to admit who he was, to end this one way or another. Yet he couldn't ask that of him, not with words.

Andy pushed his hands under Ken's shirt and caressed his back, the soft, soothing movements contrasting with the angry heat running through Ken.

"Are you trying to get me out of your system?" Andy asked, perceptive as always. Before Ken could answer, Andy sank his teeth into Ken's shoulder and held on, sucking and marking him. So much for gentle. Ken growled and tried to pull away, but Andy reached between them and pressed his hand against Ken's cock. "Fuck," Ken hissed and ground against him, pinning him tighter to the wall.

Andy laughed against his neck. "Is it working?"

Ken glared at him. "What do you think?"

"That you're as gone for me as I am for you."

If Andy was really saying shit like that then Ken's instincts were right; Andy wouldn't be around much longer. Every day he seemed more and more restless. If only Ken *could* fuck him out of his system, but every time they were together he only wanted him more.

Ken slid his hand into Andy's hair and massaged his scalp. Andy dropped his head back and made a sound like a fucking purr.

"You put some kind of fucking spell on me," Ken accused.

Andy started to laugh, but Ken tightened his grip on Andy's hair, jerking his head to the side. He licked at the outer edge of Andy's ear until the man trembled. "You going to fuck me tonight?"

Andy sucked in a breath.

"I want it. You know I do. I want you to use me, to hurt me so I feel it in my ass instead of here." He let go of Andy and touched the center of his chest with a shaky hand.

Andy covered Ken's hand with his own. "I feel you there too."

"Make it stop."

Andy shook his head. "I can't."

"What the hell have we done?" Ken asked, his voice raw.

"I-I don't know."

"Fuck me Andy. Make me forget what a fool I am."

ANDY NODDED. His eyes stung, but he was not going to fucking cry. Not now and not in front of Ken. If he lived through the night and brought down the fucking bastard who'd killed Charlie, Ben, and countless others, if he walked away and was still sane enough to know what he'd done, then he could cry. But that was very unlikely, because even if the leader of the drug ring didn't kill him, he wasn't sure his mind would ever find reality again.

"That I can do."

Ken smiled, and Andy took the opportunity to catch him off guard and flip their positions.

He grabbed Ken's wrists and dragged his arms over his head. "Mine," he growled against Ken's lips.

"You wish," Ken responded before Andy kissed him.

You have no idea how much.

Ken fought him for a few seconds, refusing to open to him, but Andy thrust against him, rubbing their cocks together and tightening his grip on Ken's wrists. Finally, Ken gave in, opened up, and sagged against the wall.

Andy released his mouth and slid his lips to Ken's ear. "That's it, surrender to me. Let me have what I need, what you need."

"Yes, God, yes."

He put his hands on Ken's shoulder and shoved him to his knees.

Ken went down without protest.

Andy unfastened his pants and freed his dick as Ken looked up at him, all challenge gone from his hazel eyes. He was ready to do whatever Andy asked.

"Hands behind your back."

Ken sucked in his breath as he obeyed.

"Good." Andy couldn't hold on to anything else in his life. He couldn't even make his own mind behave like he needed it to, but he could control this, at least for a little while. He'd own Ken until whatever burned between them stole everything from him, forcing him to let go. "Keep your hands there while you suck me."

He rubbed his cock over Ken's lips before letting the man draw him deep inside. He held onto Ken's head, positioning him so he could thrust into his mouth. Ken had asked to be used, and Andy was sure as hell willing to do just that.

Ken took everything he gave, even when he started driving in hard enough to choke him. Ken never moved his hands from where he'd clasped them at the base of his spine, and his surrender was the hottest fucking thing Andy had ever seen. If he didn't pull back, he was going to come any second.

"I'm not letting you off that easy." Andy pushed himself away from the wall, and Ken let his cock drop from his mouth.

Ken raised a brow. "I wouldn't call this easy. You're quite a mouthful."

Andy growled as he grabbed Ken's hair and tugged upward. Ken gracefully placed a foot under him and stood, not even flinching from Andy's vicious treatment of him.

"Don't push me right now," Andy ordered.

"But you see, that's exactly what I want to do, push you until you take me as roughly as I want."

"Goddamn, Ken. Don't make me really hurt you."

Ken smiled. "You won't."

But he would. He would rip Ken's heart to pieces and teach him not to ever trust anyone. "You're trying to make me hurt you so it's easier to say I'm too much of a bastard and walk away."

Ken scowled at him. "Do it, Andy. Take me the way you want to."

Andy grabbed the back of Ken's neck and crushed their mouths together, tasting himself on Ken's tongue. He wouldn't give Ken that kind of out. He was going to fuck him, hard and deep like a wild animal, but they were both going to enjoy it. This was goodbye, and it was going to be so good, so sweet that neither of them would ever forget it. This night would become the thing they measured any future pleasure against.

Neither of them had wanted to feel more than lust for each other. Both of them were going to be hurt, maybe too much to recover. But Ken had his ranch and his friends to give him the hope of salvation. Andy could walk away and leave him that, but he was too damn selfish not to leave his mark. "You're going to love every second of this night, and you're never going to forget what I can do to you."

"Son of a bitch," Ken said, but there wasn't any conviction behind it. He pulled Andy back to him and kissed him. Somehow they ended up on the floor, tearing at each other's clothes, both struggling for dominance. When they were naked, Ken got onto all fours and spread his legs, displaying himself for Andy, but Andy wasn't fooled. Ken wasn't open or vulnerable. He was hiding.

"Turn over."

"No!"

Andy grabbed Ken's hips and shoved. Ken rolled, but he raised up and took a swing at Andy that Andy barely dodged. Ken used the moment of surprise to pin him. Rather than fighting, Andy relaxed under him, letting his legs fall open.

Ken growled. "You want me to fuck you instead? You want my dick in you, fucking you until you scream?"

"If that's what you need," Andy said, refusing to look

away even though his mind was screaming for him to fight, to run.

"Goddamn you, Andy."

"I'm not fucking you while you hide from me. You're going to look at me when I push into you, or you can just go without." He almost never fucked face to face, but when he'd taken Ken like that before, watching Ken's face as he entered him, it had been one of the hottest things he'd ever done.

Ken had loosened his hold, so Andy rolled them again. "Anger makes you vulnerable."

Ken growled and bucked under him. "Don't I know it."

Andy groaned. "This is exactly how I want you. On your back. Fighting me. Desperate with need."

"I fucking hate you."

"I wish I hated you. It would make my life so much easier."

KEN GAVE A BITTER LAUGH. "No, it wouldn't. I might hate you, but I still need you so bad it hurts. That hasn't stopped."

Andy ground against him, working their cocks together. Ken bit his lip, refusing to let any sounds of pleasure escape, but Andy already knew how turned on he was and how desperately he wanted to give in. Andy was desperate too; Ken was sure of it, but he was too much of a fucking coward to look Andy in the eyes while they fucked so he could see what he felt. Soon, Ken was going to have to watch the bastard walk away, because whether he admitted it or not, Andy was saying goodbye.

"Tell me you don't want this," Andy demanded. "Tell me, and I'll stop."

Ken had told a lot of lies in his life. He'd looked his father in the eye and lied for the good of everyone involved in Carver Pharm. He'd spent years lying about his sexuality to his family, to his friends, to the media. But he couldn't lie to Andy, couldn't say he didn't want something his body—and his heart—were screaming for. "I can't."

Andy slid a hand between them and wrapped it around Ken's dick. This time he couldn't stop himself from thrusting into Andy's hand and making those needy sounds Andy loved so much and Ken fucking hated, at least when he was the one making them.

Andy worked him slowly up and down, twisting his palm over Ken's cockhead. "Relax," he said, his voice low and seductive. Ken's body obeyed even as his mind screamed in protest. He dropped his head back against the carpet.

"Mmm, that's it," Andy purred.

"Thought you liked it when I fought you."

"This is good too."

Ken closed his eyes and turned his head to the side.

Andy stilled his hand. "You're going to watch me while I open you up."

"So I can remember what it's like to be ruined once you leave?" The bitterness came through in his tone, but the croak in his voice betrayed his overload of emotion.

Andy sucked in his breath. "You think I'm leaving?"

"Andy." The word was a warning.

"Let's go to your room. Actually fuck in your bed. We never have, you know."

"Promise me you'll still be here next week," Ken responded, knowing Andy never would.

"Ken."

"I've never had a man in that bed." He'd wondered when Andy was going to ask why they never went to his room.

He'd hoped the agreement about giving up control when they were in his office would keep him from bringing it up. Ken knew it was ridiculous, but he couldn't bring Andy to his bed unless he knew he was staying. He needed someplace he could go after Andy left that wasn't full of memories.

"We should break it in."

Ken shook his head. "That's my space. I don't let anyone in there."

"Maybe you should."

"I might if that person wasn't about to walk away."

Pain showed in Andy's eyes. "You don't understand."

"No, I don't."

Andy looked so sad that Ken almost changed his mind, but he couldn't let Andy in any further. It was just a room, but it was a room he'd added on to the house just for him and a bed he'd bought to start this new life. He wasn't ready to share.

Andy sighed and sat back. He took Ken's hand and pulled him up. Was he going to walk away after all? Had Ken ruined the chance to say goodbye with his refusal? No matter what he'd said, he wanted every second with Andy that he could get.

He reached out and caressed Andy's cheek. "Kiss me."

It was the sweetest, softest kiss they'd ever shared. Andy's lips barely brushed his at first. Andy tasted him slowly, sliding his tongue over Ken's bottom lip, and Ken shivered, ready for more. He opened to Andy, and Andy cupped his face with both hands, holding Ken in place while he explored. Ken fell under his spell. Maybe he could pretend for just one more night.

When Andy pulled back, the each pulled their pants back on and grabbed the rest of their clothes. Then Andy took Ken's hand and led him through the French doors, across the patio and to the guesthouse. Neither of them spoke as Ken stretched out on the bed, on his back, and studied Andy.

Andy settled between his legs. Ken held his breath when his lover ran his hands over Ken's torso slowly, like he was memorizing him. "Want you," Andy whispered, making Ken's chest tighten.

Ken nodded, incapable of speech. Then he watched, mesmerized, as Andy rolled on a condom and slicked his cock, making himself ready for Ken.

His gaze locked with Andy's as Andy pressed his cockhead against Ken's entrance. "Right here, right now, you're mine. I don't want you to think about anything else or feel anything else. Just me inside you. You got that?"

"Yes," Ken whispered. Andy seemed to see right through him to the insecurities and secrets he held inside. No one had ever read him so well.

Ken sucked in his breath when Andy breached him, and Andy drove forward until he was all the way in. Ken panted, trying to adjust to being stretched wide as Andy forced him to feel more than he wanted to. It was terrifying, and it was the best thing he'd ever experienced. Hard, angry sex with Andy was fantastic. The dirty, get-each-other-off-like-wild-beasts sex was incredible too, but this—sex tinged with sadness, with need too deep to express any other way—was more powerful than anything else they'd ever done. Part of him wanted to shove Andy off and run. But Andy touched something inside him that bound them together, no matter how much Ken wanted to fight it.

Andy pulled back, slowly, carefully, almost coming all the way out. Ken whimpered and wrapped his legs around his lover, pulling him closer.

"Don't leave." Andy had to know he wasn't just talking about sex.

Andy thrust in hard, jolting Ken. He didn't slow down this time. The harsh rhythm had both of them dripping with sweat in no time.

"Is that enough? Is that what you wanted?" Andy demanded.

"Never enough. Nothing is with you."

"Goddamn right it's not."

A storm swirled around them, one made of emotions neither man was willing to acknowledge. Ken felt it building and pressing against his skin. Andy must have too because he started moving faster and thrusting harder. "Need you. Damn it, Ken."

"Yes!" Ken shouted. "I feel you. In me. Around me. You're killing me."

"Me too. Too much. Too fucking much."

They bucked against each other, riding out the storm until it crashed over them, and they both came, calling each other's names, clinging to what they both assumed was their last time together.

When they could breathe again, Andy left the bed long enough to clean up and bring Ken a washcloth. Neither of them spoke as he settled beside Ken and pulled the covers over them. Ken turned over and allowed Andy to spoon him. Cuddling was worse than fucking because Ken knew it would be a very long time before he'd let another man hold him like this. He might never be able to do it again.

CHAPTER EIGHTEEN

Ken didn't know how much time had passed since Andy had gone to sleep. He'd dozed, but his mind was racing with questions about Andy—who he really was and why Ken hadn't pushed for a confession. How was he going to survive Andy walking away?

You don't know how to deal with it because you always get what you want.

That's not true.

You didn't get your family, but otherwise, if you set your sights on something, you take it and make it yours.

I can't buy Andy.

How do you know?

I want him here because he wants to be here, not because I forced him.

That's sweet.

He's going to destroy me. I knew better, but I couldn't stop myself.

You could have, but you refused to, and now it's too late.

Ken couldn't lie there listening to the sarcastic voice in his head anymore. He slipped out of bed, pulled on his clothes, and stepped outside. The night air was stifling, but he didn't care. He wanted to be outside. He considered riding, but the horses deserved their rest. He headed out across the field on foot, toward the place where the road curved and the forest encroached on his pastureland. It was his favorite spot on the ranch. Maybe he could find a few moments of peace there.

KEN WAS GONE when Andy's alarm woke him at one a.m. He missed the man's warmth, but it was easier not to have to explain why he was getting up. In one hour, all hell would break loose, and then one way or another, Andy would be leaving. He rubbed his thumb over his lips, still swollen from Ken's kisses, and wished he could kiss him one last time.

Fuck. He had to stop thinking like that. He turned the shower on as cold as he could stand it, hoping to wake himself up, but the water beating on him reminded him of shivering in the rain the night Charlie died. He turned the heat up as memories threatened to take over, cursing himself for being such a fucked-up mess. If he managed to live through this night, what was his next move? Keep taking undercover jobs until he got killed? Probably. That sounded like what a fucked-up cop whose lies were about to wreck his chance at happiness would do.

Andy dried off, dressed, and checked his weapons. His phone buzzed as he was cleaning his gun. Once and then again. Two messages.

The first was from Gomez. *Everyone's in place.*

The second was from the man he hoped to see in cuffs or, better yet, dead by the end of the night. *Get over here now. We've got trouble.*

Had he spotted the team?

Andy texted Gomez back. *Possible problem. I've been called in early because of "trouble."*

We're ready for anything.

Were they really? Was Andy? Hell no, but he was going anyway.

KEN WAS STANDING by one of the pasture fences looking out at the horses who were spending the night outdoors and watching the grass sway as a slight breeze ruffled the ground. He tried to block out everything except the sounds and sights around him, but he couldn't loosen the knot in his stomach. Something was wrong, something to do with Andy keeping secrets. He knew it. Even with a breeze, the very air felt tense. Something was about to blow up, but he didn't know where the bomb was or how to defuse it.

Ken's phone rang. He pulled it out of his pocket and saw Rusty's name on the screen. Heart pounding, he answered. "What's wrong?"

"I went back out toward that old shed I was telling you about."

"Rusty, I told you not to—"

"Andy got this phone call today, and I got curious."

"You need to—"

"Listen to me. There are men out here, and they're heavily armed. I don't think they're having a party."

Ken felt hot and cold at the same time. He had to get Rusty out of there. "Go back to the bunkhouse now."

"I can't."

Ken's hand tightened around the phone, fear and anger revving him up. "Rusty, get out of there. I'll handle this."

"I'm hiding. If I move, they might see—"

"Rusty?"

Ken heard a gunshot.

"Rusty!"

"I got him," a man called. Rusty grunted, and Ken heard a sound like someone being punched.

Rusty didn't make another sound. Why the hell hadn't Ken done something when Rusty had first talked to him?

Because you refused to believe Andy was involved.

But he wasn't, was he? He was back at the guesthouse, in bed.

Ken ended the call with Rusty and dialed 911 as he started running for the house.

ANDY WAS NEARLY THERE. He focused on the road, telling himself he could do this for Ken, for Rusty, for the vengeance he sought for the dead. He was there, in the moment. There wasn't any blood on his hands. Not yet.

His phone rang, and he glanced at the screen. Ken.

"This isn't a good time," he said when he answered.

"Where the hell are you?"

"Out."

"Fuck you, Andy. Rusty's in trouble."

Nausea curled in Andy's stomach. "What happened?"

"He went poking around that shed. The one I told you about."

"What? Start over. Tell me exactly what happened." Andy's heart thumped hard against his ribs, and a cold sweat dampened his body.

"Andy, where are—"

"Not now. Just tell me exactly what happened."

"Rusty called me a few minutes ago. He said he'd gone out to the shed and there were armed men there. I told him to get out of there, but he was hiding and didn't want to move. He was talking to me and then someone must have found him. I heard fighting and a gunshot. I called 911, and now I'm headed that way—"

"No. Stay where you are. I'll take care of it."

"You? What do you mean? Who are you Andy?"

"Just stay where you are and trust me."

He ended the call and hit the brakes, no longer able to see the road.

Rusty. Shot, bleeding, maybe dead. This was worse than Charlie. Rusty was innocent, Rusty was under his protection. How could he let this happen?

Blood so much blood. Everywhere.

Fight it. Stay here. Got to save him.

Andy knew if he opened his eyes the truck would be covered in blood, so he stayed curled in on himself, eyes closed, begging his mind to listen to him.

He fumbled with his phone and forced himself to open his eyes long enough to text Gomez.

They have Rusty. He may have been shot.

He's alive. We're proceeding as planned.

Alive. That was good.

Do not let anything happen to him.

Just get your ass out here.

Andy started driving again. A minute or two later, he pulled his truck into the grassy area in front of the shed and hopped out.

The same asshole who'd guarded the door before pointed a gun at him.

"It's me, asswipe. Seriously, you need to calm down."

"Boss just caught someone spying on us. Did you send the little shit? 'Cause I think he's a friend of yours."

Andy rolled his eyes. "I didn't fucking send anybody. Is it that kid who was fucking Ben? Carver's cousin or nephew or whatever? He comes out here sometimes."

"Yeah, it's him. But of course you already knew that."

"Course I did. He's the only one from the ranch who comes out here."

The man glared at Andy, but he stepped aside and let Andy enter the shed.

When Andy saw Rusty, his knees threatened to give. He had to pretend to trip over something on the floor. "Fucking nails coming out of the floor. That's dangerous, man."

The leader looked up at him, ski mask still in place. At least now, he knew it wasn't Ken. He did, right? Ken didn't call him to get him here after catching Rusty himself. Did he? "Are you drunk?"

"Hell no," Andy answered, surprised his voice sounded steady.

"You'd better not be. We've got us a problem here." He inclined his head toward Rusty.

"I can see that." Thank God Rusty didn't appear to be injured beyond a few scrapes and bruises.

Rusty's eyes widened when he saw Andy. "You son of a bitch."

"Mouthy, isn't he?" the asshole asked.

Andy laughed, but when the leader turned away, he mouthed, "Trust me" to Rusty.

Rusty scowled at him and looked away.

"It's cute how he trusted you and Ben, isn't it?" the asshole asked.

Andy nodded, not trusting his voice.

They heard a commotion outside. "Fuck!" The leader slammed his fist against the wall. "What now?"

Before Andy could register what the man was doing, he pulled out his gun and pointed it at Rusty's head. "Who's with you? Who the fuck else did you bring out here?'

"N-no one," Rusty said.

Andy stared at the gun in horror. This wasn't going to happen. He'd stayed in to protect Ken and Rusty. Whatever he had to do, he was not going to let Rusty die.

He was about to make a grab for the gun, when the door guard shoved Ken into the room. "Found another one."

Andy should have been horrified that they now had both Ken and Rusty, but he was simply relieved to see both of them alive and to know for certain that Ken was innocent. He was the man Andy thought he was. Now, Andy had to keep him alive.

Ken jerked his arm free of the guard's hold and brushed at a mud stain on his thigh. He glanced at Andy and gave no indication he even recognized him. "Do you have any idea how much these jeans cost?"

He was doing a damn fine job of looking like a man with serious entitlement issues who was certain he'd get out of this like he did everything else, but Andy knew the real man under that armor. He was sure Ken was as scared as he was.

"Give me one reason why I shouldn't shoot you?" the leader demanded.

Ken gave him a disdainful look. "I could give you several billion reasons." His voice was as cool as if he were standing in a boardroom.

The leader turned to the door guard next. "What the fuck are you doing bringing him in here? He's fucking Kenneth Carver. You understand that, right? People will notice that he's missing."

The guy shrugged. "He was snooping around."

For a second, Andy thought the leader was going to shoot the guard, but he lowered his gun and said, "Get back out there, and don't bring me any more trouble."

The guard scurried away.

Andy grabbed Ken's arm and jerked him toward where Rusty sat. He hooked his leg around another old chair he pulled away from the table Rusty had used for his art. "Let me take care of these two. You get ready to meet our customer."

The man raised his gun. "I'll take care of them now."

Andy held up a hand, praying it didn't shake. "Rusty used to be in the business."

The leader glanced toward Rusty and then back to Andy. "Interesting."

"And Carver's brother's a doctor."

The man looked at Ken while Andy tied him to the chair, making sure the ropes were loose enough that he could easily get out of them.

"You gonna help us out?" the leader asked Ken.

Ken didn't respond.

"I got ways to persuade him," Andy insisted.

The leader narrowed his eyes. "We'll hold onto them tonight. See what you can do. If they won't cooperate, you can kill them later."

"Good plan," Andy replied.

When the leader turned to crack open one of his crates, Andy pulled out his phone and texted Gomez. *Need a distraction.*

KEN KNEW he couldn't let his shock or his anger show, and

he sure as hell couldn't let this bastard—or Andy—realize how close he was to falling apart. Andy had sworn that whatever he was lying about wasn't what Ken thought, but that's exactly what it was. Renata had been wrong after all. And yet, he'd tied Ken so he could easily slip out of his bonds. Why?

Ken glanced at Rusty. The kid looked terrified, and Ken hoped to hell he could hold it together until he could figure out how to safely escape. The police should be there soon, but he wasn't sure what their chances of survival were if cops raided the place. He needed to get them out of there as fast as he could, preferably after shooting Andy's lying ass.

The guard stuck his head in the door again, and the leader jumped and then pulled his gun. From what Ken could tell, the man in charge was crazy as fuck. He was also on edge, which meant he could lose it any minute and just start shooting.

"I told you to stay out there and quit bringing me trouble."

"Someone else is out there," the man said.

The leader whirled on Ken. "Who is it? Did you call someone?"

Ken stared him down. "I have assistants to make calls for me."

The man growled and pointed his weapon at Ken's head.

Andy fought for calm. "Go deal with it," he said. "I'll take care of these assholes. Just handle it, or the whole night will go to shit."

The man glared at Andy, and for a few seconds, Ken thought he might shoot him. Ken should have been cheering him on. Instead, he tugged on his bonds, ready to tackle the man. He wanted revenge for what Andy had done, but apparently he didn't have the stomach to watch anyone else hurt the bastard.

Andy faced the man without flinching. "Come on. Let's try to salvage this."

After a few seconds, the man dropped his gun and pushed through the door with the guard following him.

Andy pulled a knife and crouched beside Rusty.

Ken didn't think Andy would hurt the kid, not when he'd left Ken's ropes loose on purpose, but he had to be sure. "You hurt him, and I'll make you pay."

When Andy looked up at him, the pain in his eyes hit Ken like a tangible force. What the fuck? Andy was the one who'd betrayed Ken, who'd lied to him. The fucking asshole had seduced him, not just his body but his heart. He was in love with a lying piece of shit who was working for a fucking psychopath.

Andy looked away and used his knife to cut partway through the ropes binding Rusty's hands and ankles. "When the police get here, run as fast and far as you can," Andy said.

"Why?" Ken asked.

Andy looked at him like he was crazy. "Because he'll kill you. No matter what he says, he's not going to ransom you or get you to help us. He's going to kill you both before the night is over. You've got to get the fuck out of here."

"I meant why are you helping us?"

Andy didn't answer.

Ken glanced at Rusty. He was pale, but he didn't look like he'd been badly hurt. The shot he'd heard must have missed or been intended as a warning.

"Can you run?" he asked.

Rusty nodded.

The door creaked and the man in charge returned. Andy drew his gun and jammed it against Rusty's head.

Ken fought not to react. This was an act. It had to be. Why help them then shoot Rusty?

Andy had PTSD, but he wasn't crazy, and Ken had never seen him hurt anyone. So what the hell was going on? Had Andy gotten in over his head? Was he in debt and desperate for money? What would make him do this?

Rusty was shaking, obviously not so sure Andy wouldn't hurt him. Andy jerked on Rusty's wrists, loosening the bonds so he could slip out of them easily.

"There, that tight enough now?" Andy asked. "Quit your squirming, or I'll make sure you never move again, you got that?"

"Y-yeah."

"Remember it."

Ken watched Andy and the leader, hoping Andy had a plan for giving them a chance to get away. "Who was out there?" Andy asked.

"No one, probably a fucking coyote or something."

"I guess he's jumpy after these two got the drop on him."

"Yeah, fucking idiot. I should've put you out there."

"And left him to deal with these two and the merchandise?"

The leader rolled his eyes. "Right. He'd fuck that the hell up."

Ken heard a vehicle approaching, a good-sized truck if he guessed right.

"They're here. We're going to give them a good show," the leader said.

The wild look in his eyes scared the shit out of Ken. Andy tensed when the man turned away. Most people wouldn't have noticed, but Ken knew his body and its signals well after the last few weeks—had it really been such a short time?

The leader opened the door, and Andy glanced at Ken and Rusty before stepping out.

Ken wondered if they had time to get away before Andy and the man came back in, but seconds later, just as Ken almost had his wrists free, the door swung wide and Andy, the leader, and a man he didn't recognize stepped in, followed closely by the man who'd been at the door and four other men Ken had seen guarding the area.

Andy was fiddling with something in his pocket. What was he up to? The leader looked at Ken, and Ken dropped his gaze, not wanting the leader to wonder why he was watching Andy. Why the hell was he protecting the man who'd betrayed him?

He's helping you.

Yeah, helping us get loose from the killers he's working for. I guess that makes him less than completely horrible.

Ken looked over at Rusty. The kid was struggling to hide how terrified he was. How the hell had he survived in the criminal world? Maybe he was so scared now because he knew how ruthless men like this one could be.

A man with sharp features and dark hair in a crew cut entered, but the men behind him were held back by Andy and the guard who was apparently named Ed. "My men go where I go," the dark-haired man insisted.

"There's no need for them here," the leader said. "We're simply doing business. All the others can wait outside."

He gestured for his men to leave, but Andy remained behind.

"What about him?" the man asked, indicating Andy.

"He's going to be assisting. We have something special planned."

"Ah," the new arrival said. He surveyed the room, and his gaze landed on Ken and Rusty. "A present for me?"

The leader laughed. "We shall see."

Andy glanced at Ken, and his look seemed to tell Ken to wait. How much longer could he just sit there?

"Let's see what you've got," the dark-haired man said.

The leader opened the crate, and the man—presumably a customer—gazed at the pills inside.

Suddenly, someone outside screamed. "Cops! Get out of here."

The leader pulled his gun and pointed it at Andy's head. "Ben was right, wasn't he? You are a fucking cop."

Andy had his hand on his gun, but the man had been too fast for him. "Drop it," the leader ordered.

Andy tossed it, right at Ken's feet.

"Go!" he yelled.

Ken broke free, grabbed the weapon, and put a bullet through the leader's head. The man hit the floor with a thud that scattered dust. Andy looked at Ken, wide-eyed, and then one of the cops grabbed him.

Ken took Rusty's hand and pulled him toward the back door of the shed. He glanced back once and saw Andy in cuffs. So much for the theory that he was a cop.

"Run for the house," Ken shouted, not willing to take a chance on one of the men escaping.

CHAPTER NINETEEN

When two FBI agents came knocking on the farmhouse door, Ken answered it with a rifle in his hand and Andy's gun tucked into his waistband.

"Put the weapon down, sir."

"Show me some ID, and I might." He was not in the mood for any bullshit.

The two men held up their badges, and reluctantly, Ken let them in. The last thing he wanted to do was talk to them about how thoroughly Andy had played him. Rusty was sitting on the couch, also armed to the teeth, like he thought a strike team was going to storm the farmhouse.

"Why did you leave the scene?" one of the agents asked.

"Because they were going to fucking kill us."

The shorter of the two men scowled at him. "We can do without the hostility."

"I could have done without being taken hostage," Ken responded, but they were right. They didn't deserve his attitude. He just wasn't sure he could turn it off, not for a while.

A woman pushed her way in. "I'm Special Agent

Gomez." She looked at the two agents who'd gotten there before her. "I've got this."

"Did you come to play good cop?" Ken asked.

"No, I came to get your statements so we can put these assholes away and hopefully find more of their associates."

"I don't know shit about their associates. Apparently, I don't know shit about anything."

Rusty put a hand on Ken's shoulder. "Let's just get this over with, okay?"

Rusty shouldn't have to be the grown-up, but Ken was seething with rage and full of adrenaline. He wanted to rip someone apart, almost as much as he wanted never to feel anything again.

"Let's focus on what happened tonight," Gomez said.

"Yeah, tonight." *The night my world blew up.*

"I went out to that shed. I'd been using it as…" Rusty glanced at Ken.

He's a kid, and you've taken responsibility for him. Help him.

Ken drew in a breath. Time to man up and handle this. There'd be plenty of time to fall apart later. Days. Months. Years.

He nodded, hoping he was communicating that Rusty needed to be completely honest. No more fucking secrets. He'd kept them and look what he'd gotten.

Rusty finished his sentence, "…an art studio and a place to meet someone."

"Meet someone? For what?"

"I was meeting a guy, okay? Hooking up."

She smiled. "Okay."

"He suggested we meet there. I think he was involved. He disappeared a few weeks ago, and no one on his ranch has heard from him."

"Ben Rawlson?" she asked.

Rusty nodded. "That's him."

"I'm sorry to be the one to tell you, but Ben is dead."

Rusty didn't look surprised. Ken assumed he'd already expected that. "Thank you for telling me," he said, and then he continued his story, explaining that he'd gone out to collect some art supplies he'd left in the shed and seen men there.

"Why didn't you report that?"

Ken interrupted. "He mentioned it to me, but I dismissed it, thinking they were kids from around here using it for a party. Obviously, that was a mistake."

She nodded. "And tonight?"

"I went back out there," Rusty said. "And the men were there again, but they were armed and unloading a truck. I hid in the bushes, afraid they'd notice me if I tried to head back. I called Ken."

"And I called 911," Ken said.

"But you went out there too?"

He nodded. "I wasn't going to let them hurt Rusty."

"I suppose lecturing you about how stupid that was wouldn't do any good?"

"You suppose right."

She sighed. "Tell us what you saw while you were in the shed."

They did, but Ken wasn't sure if Gomez fully believed them or not. She wasn't easy to read.

"You shot a man during your escape."

"Yes. Who the hell was he and what was he doing on my land?"

"We're looking into that. You do realize there could be serious consequences for—"

"Bullshit. It was self-defense. He was going to kill Andy,

and he would have turned on us next."

Gomez nodded, not at all ruffled by Ken's anger. "Based on other reports I've received, your story holds up. I'm going to have more questions for you later, so I need you to stay in town."

She started to say something else, but one of the detectives rushed in.

"Detective Wofford's been shot."

The color drained from her face. "What?"

"One of the men we were taking in had a weapon no one found. He shot Wofford as they started into the precinct."

"Is he—"

"On his way to the hospital, but he took a bullet to the chest."

"I'll be in touch," she said, tossing a card at Ken before heading out the door yelling, "Get me to him now."

Rusty looked green. "You don't think Andy was involved in that, do you?"

Ken shook his head. "I... How am I supposed to know what the fuck he'd do?" Would Andy shoot a cop so he could get away? Ken didn't think so. When they'd captured him, he'd looked worried, defeated, and scared. And Ken still didn't know why he'd helped them.

Because he cared.

Just not enough to be honest and let me help him.

"Ken?"

He looked up. Rusty was staring at him, worry in his eyes. This wasn't the time to fall apart. Not yet.

"Sorry. I'm fine."

Rusty laughed. "Yeah, right. Your lover turns out to be running a drug operation from your ranch, and we both get taken hostage and nearly killed, but you're fine."

Ken wished Renata was there. He'd sent her to visit her

family, not wanting her to be around if something dangerous was going on at the ranch. Obviously, he'd made the right decision, but he really needed someone to take care of him. "You want a drink?" he asked Rusty.

"Hell no. I want a bottle or two."

"How about something to help you sleep instead, something that won't make you feel as bad in the morning?"

"No, I'm not taking anything like that." He looked terrified.

"Okay. Sorry." Rusty was proud of having gotten clean, and he was obviously scared that even a sleeping pill might cause a setback.

Ken poured Rusty a drink and started to pour himself one, but he realized he didn't really want it. Part of him craved oblivion, but he was still jacked up from their escape, and what he really wanted was a way to work off all that excess energy. "I'm not even sure this is going to help."

Rusty frowned. "You want to talk about it?"

"No. I just want…"

"To pound someone into the ground and or fuck them until they can't stand up?"

Perceptive little shit. Ken turned away and looked out the window.

"Go on if you need to," Rusty insisted.

Ken shook his head. "No, this is better. I might kill someone in the mood I'm in." If he went out, he was likely to get himself arrested. Hell, if he beat someone up at a bar the press might dedicate the whole front section of the local paper to his meltdown.

Rusty raised his drink for a toast. They clinked glasses and both downed their drinks in one go.

"All this is going to be in the papers, so get ready," Ken said.

Rusty nodded. "I am."

"Everyone is going to know what a damn fool I was. I hired a man to be my foreman who was dealing drugs on my ranch. They'll think I don't even bother to background check my employees out here."

Rusty raised a brow. "But you did check him out."

"I did, but there were things I didn't follow up on. I wanted to pretend everything was okay."

Rusty smiled as he poured them each another drink. "You're allowed to be human, you know?"

"I just thought maybe I could…"

"Relate to people like a person instead of the son of a billionaire who made his mark by using people's weaknesses to screw them over?"

Ken laughed. "How'd you get so smart?"

"I watch things, and nobody notices me."

"I notice you." Ken thought of all the people at Carver Corp and Carver Pharm who worked in the background. All the people he'd ignored. All the men he'd fucked and treated like they were nothing but a convenience. Maybe tonight was exactly what he deserved.

"Whatever you're thinking, you're wrong," Rusty said.

"How do you know?"

"Because I can tell your thoughts are dark and full of shit."

Ken glared at him. "Like yours are all sunshine and rainbows?"

"I was as much of an idiot as you were. I should never have gotten involved with Ben."

Ken frowned and picked up the bottle to pour them round three. "Neither one of us is drunk enough to handle this shit."

THE NEXT MORNING Ken woke up on the floor of his office. He considered lying there for the rest of the day, maybe forever. He should never have let Andy have so much power over him that he could make him feel like this, make him want to crawl into a hole and die. Without consideration for Rusty, who was curled in a chair nearby, Ken grabbed a vase from a nearby table and threw it at the French doors Andy had been so fond of slipping through.

Rusty grabbed his head and groaned. "What the hell?"

"Sorry. I…"

Ken couldn't finish his sentence. He barely made it to the bathroom before his stomach gave up its contents. When the spasms had finally passed, he forced himself to shower. If he lay back down, he might never get up again. When he was clean and dressed, he checked on Rusty. The kid was sleeping again, this time on the couch. Ken left him there.

His standard hangover cure was eggs, bacon, grits, and biscuits, but he felt too dead inside to bother eating. Disgusted with himself, he walked out the kitchen door and headed to the barn. He needed normalcy—feeding the horses, checking on the foals.

Luke and Rodrigo were there. He'd briefed them before he and Rusty had gotten seriously trashed. He was sure they had questions about what had happened the night before, but he wasn't in the mood to answer them.

"Didn't expect to see you today," Luke said.

"There's no reason for me not to be here. Somebody's got to get all this fucking work done."

Luke and Rodrigo exchanged a look but didn't say anything else. They clearly felt sorry for him, which was the last fucking thing he wanted. They didn't even know he and Andy had been lovers. At least he didn't think they did. Hell, maybe they knew that and lots more. Maybe they'd been in on all of it. Maybe they were aliens who'd come to take over the ranch and use it as a base to invade Earth. Maybe he was still drunk.

Ken worked until he was about to fall over. At some point, Luke brought him water and forced him to drink. "You're dehydrated, boss. You need to take a break."

That was the last thing he needed. Every time thoughts of Andy started to break through his numbness, he shoved them back and kept going, pushing himself harder. He stood out in the midday sun driving a fencepost into the ground, slamming the hammer down, wishing it was Andy's face he was smashing. *No, don't think about revenge. Pretend the man doesn't exist.*

At some point in the late afternoon, he must have finally passed out because he woke to Luke and Rodrigo bent over him, calling his name. "'M fine. Just leave me alone."

They forced more water on him. "You need to go inside and cool off, boss. You're going to kill yourself," Rodrigo insisted.

Was he trying to? Not really, but he didn't care about much anymore. He pushed himself up to a sitting position, and the world spun around him. He'd really fucked himself up, but if he went inside, he'd start thinking, and that would kill him faster than sunstroke.

"Ken! Ken!"

Rusty was running toward him from the house. He should have checked on him before now.

"I'm fine." He tried to yell it, but he was too weak to make his voice carry.

Rusty fell to his knees beside him. "Ken?"

"I'm fine. I'm just hot." Ken was already tired of people fawning over him. He tried to get up, but Rusty held onto his shoulders.

"No, listen. The man who was shot last night—"

"The cop?"

"Yeah. It was Andy."

"What? What do you mean?" Was he hearing things?

Rusty shoved his iPad in front of Ken and used his hand to block the glare of the sun.

A news article was on the screen.

Undercover cop shot after prescription drug bust.

"Why do you think it's Andy?"

"Look at the picture."

Ken enlarged it. It was fuzzy, and people stood in front of the man who was lying on the ground with blood all over him, but Ken could see his shirt clearly. It was the one Andy had worn the night before, the blue one that brought out his eyes. He must have grabbed it from the floor when he'd gotten dressed before going out to the shed.

The full meaning of the picture hit him, and darkness closed in on the edges of his vision. Andy was a cop.

It's not what you think.

Damn right it wasn't. Andy had helped them because he was a fucking cop. He'd been there undercover. And now he was… *Oh God*. Ken tried to stand again and nearly fell over. "Where is he? What hospital?"

"Calm down," Rusty insisted.

"Don't tell me to fucking calm down."

"I don't know where he is, but she will." He handed Ken his phone and a card. Ken looked down. Special Agent Maria-Jose Gomez. He remembered her giving it to him the night before. With a shaky hand, Ken dialed the number.

"Gomez."

"This is Kenneth Carver. Where the hell is he?"

"Where is who, Mr. Carver?"

"Andy or whatever his real name is. I know he was shot,

and I'm going to find him. It would be easier if you helped me."

"Andy was arrested, Mr. Carver."

Ken squeezed the phone until his hand ached. "Don't bullshit me. He's one of yours, and he was shot."

"Even if he was, I can't endanger him by revealing his whereabouts."

"I'm going to find him."

She sighed. "I could get in a lot of trouble for telling you this, but I think he'd want you to know. Hell, I know he would. But you're going to have to do this my way. If you go charging in there, the media circus is only going to get worse."

"I know how to be discreet."

She huffed in exasperation. "Fine. Meet me at Anton's. It's—"

"Across the street from Houston Methodist."

"Right."

KEN SAW GOMEZ as soon as he stepped into the coffee shop. When he sat down opposite her, she said, "You won't be able to talk to him. He hasn't woken up yet."

Ken nodded, trying to ignore the panic building inside him. Andy had to pull through this. He simply had to. "What's his prognosis?"

"Not as good as I'd like. He lost a lot of blood. He came through the operation, but it was touch and go for a while. There was significant damage, but the surgeon put him back together as well as he could. The main concern now is that he should have regained consciousness, but he hasn't."

"You've got to get me in that room." Ken's voice sounded

detached and far away. He thought he'd been braced for the worst, but he'd been wrong.

She frowned. "We have to keep the media away."

Ken was still angry with Andy. Maybe one day he would fully forgive him, but for now he could push that away, because angry or not, he wasn't going to let Andy die. "The way Andy was feeling the last few days, he's not going to care if he dies. I need to talk to him, to tell him to fight, to tell him there's a reason to. Even before I knew who he really was, I wanted to help him. He kept getting lost in the past."

"He worked a case with some of the same suspects. Things didn't end well, and he never got over it."

There was one question that kept circling in Ken's mind. He needed an answer to help him understand how much of his time with Andy had been a lie. "Did he think I was in on this?"

Gomez shook her head.

Ken raised a brow, not sure he believed her.

"He never did. I pushed him to investigate you, but he always swore you were innocent. I'm sure he'd kill me for saying this, but I offered to pull him out, and he insisted on finishing the mission because of you."

Ken sucked in his breath. Andy really had struggled with what was between them just like he had. "The bastard that I shot, can you tell me who he was and why the fuck he was on my ranch?"

"I can't discuss an ongoing investigation."

Ken studied her. "I understand there are rules you're supposed to follow, but I will use every resource I can to find the information I need. You might as well save us both the trouble."

"I'm putting my career on the line for you already."

"I will make sure—"

Gomez shook her head. "I don't want to owe you anything."

"Please. I deserve to know what went down out there."

She sighed. "Apparently, the man was the nephew of the previous owner of your ranch. When his uncle got too old and sick to notice, he started using the land for his 'business.' He brought Warren in to help him."

"So Warren didn't die of a heart attack?"

"Not one from natural causes."

Ken ran a hand over his hair. "How the hell did I not realize…"

Gomez gave him a sympathetic look. "You had no reason to suspect it."

"Was the man I killed part of the case Andy worked on before, the one he never got over?"

She nodded.

Maybe the man's death would help Andy move on. "I need to see Andy so I can give him something to fight for."

"You really think you can do that?"

Ken nodded.

"There's one more thing you need to know that you're not going to like."

"What about this have I liked so far?" Not the part where Andy had lied to him and certainly not the part where he was dying. Ken pushed that thought away. He would make Andy fight, no matter what he had to do. He didn't know if they'd ever be able to move past what had happened, but whether he and Andy had a future or not, Andy was going to live.

Gomez frowned. "I'm the only one at work who knows he's gay."

Ken nodded. He shouldn't have been surprised. "I can restrain myself. I'll remember not to suck his cock or anything while I'm in there."

She glared at him.

"Sorry. That was… I'm being an ass."

"I'm used to it."

Ken laughed. "If you work with Andy, I guess you are."

When Ken stepped through the door of the hospital, the bright lights and the buzz of the place made him dizzy. He hadn't eaten anything but a muffin Rusty had shoved into his hands as he'd left the ranch.

"Are you okay?" Gomez asked.

"Yeah, I got a little too much sun earlier, and I haven't eaten much today."

She smiled. "Maybe you're also a little hungover."

He nodded. "That too."

"Let's get you some food," she insisted.

"No. I need to get this over with."

Special Agent Gomez grabbed his arm and steered him toward the cafeteria. "You can't help Andy if you're about to pass out."

Ken let her pull him to the counter. "You care a lot about him, don't you?"

"We were partners before I started at the Bureau." She gestured toward the cooler case. "At least get some water."

When it was his turn to order, he got a bottle of water and a bagel sandwich.

He opened the bottle and drained half of it. "Let's go," he said.

Gomez had to run to catch up with him. Once the elevator started the climb to Andy's floor, she said. "You've got to do exactly what I say when we get up there. We cannot attract attention."

Ken nodded. "I understand."

The elevator doors opened, and they stepped out. Ken knew instantly what room Andy was in because there were uniformed policemen posted at the door. "They're not attracting attention?" he asked, gesturing toward the cops in the hall.

"Not as much as you will if someone realizes who you are."

Gomez nodded to the guards, and one of them opened the door for them. "I'm assuming you want me to wait out here?"

Ken couldn't do anything but nod because he saw Andy lying in the bed: pale, small, too fragile to be the man Ken had gotten to know.

His heart hammered, and part of him wanted to run. He swallowed hard and took another step toward the man he'd loved and hated and trusted and been betrayed by.

He told you as much as he could.

Did he? Couldn't he have at least told me when I called him to say Rusty was in trouble?

Another step. Machines beeped. Far too many cords and other equipment surrounded Andy.

Please don't let him die.

Ken pulled a chair close to the bed and sat. Had anyone other than Gomez been to see him? Did he really not have any family, or had that been part of his cover story? Did he even want to know?

"I want him to live, that's enough for now." When he realized he'd said the words out loud, he figured he might as well go on talking.

"Andy, it's Ken. I…" His voice caught and his eyes burned with tears he'd refused to shed every time he'd thought about Andy tossing Ken his gun, accepting that he'd die but giving Ken and Rusty a chance to escape. He'd kept Andy alive the night before, and he wasn't going to let him die now.

He took hold of Andy's hand. Fuck whoever might be

watching. He didn't want to hurt Andy by outing him, but he'd damn well do it if it meant he was alive. Andy could hate him for it later.

"I'm here because I want you to fight. I can imagine what's going through your head. Whatever happened in your past is still hurting you, and this case made it worse. But you saved me and Rusty. The men who tried to hurt us are in jail, and their leader is dead. You did exactly what you needed to do. I understand why you lied to me now, and I…"

He couldn't say more even though part of him wanted to. He wasn't ready to make any promises about the future. "Don't let go. You did what you were supposed to do. I sidetracked you, but you saw the case through anyway. Don't let those bastards win."

"Sir?"

Ken turned to see a nurse.

"I'm sorry, but the doctor is on his way to examine Detective Wofford, and you're going to have to leave now."

Ken nodded, but he turned back to Andy. "I meant what I said. Don't stop fighting."

Andy squeezed his hand.

"Wait," he called to the nurse. "He moved his hand."

She frowned. "Are you sure?"

"Yes… Maybe." The movement was so slight maybe Ken had imagined it.

When he left the room, Gomez was waiting in the hall. "He's going to make it," Ken told her. He wouldn't let himself think anything else because he couldn't handle the idea that Andy might never wake up, that he might never hear Andy's voice again. He would keep Andy alive by sheer force of will if he had to. He'd accomplished plenty of other impossible things that way. Kenneth Carver did not take no for an answer.

CHAPTER TWENTY

The next day, Ken's phone rang. He was in the barn, forcing himself to keep busy again—this time with a little more food and water in him. He slid it from his pocket. It was Gomez. He hesitated a few seconds before answering. What if...?

"Carver."

"Andrew's awake. It's still touch and go, but his chances are a hell of a lot better now."

Ken closed his eyes and took a deep breath.

Maybe he really had squeezed Ken's hand. "Great. I'll—"

"You can't see him today. I had to question him, and just those few minutes wore him out. He doesn't want any visitors right now."

Ken nodded, then realized she couldn't see him. He'd have to find a way to get some words out. "Okay."

Ken heard people talking. Gomez said something to them, but he couldn't distinguish her words. "Thank you," she said a moment later. "I don't know what you did, but—"

"I didn't do anything."

"I think you did. His vitals were stronger after you left."

"What I said couldn't have mattered too much if he doesn't want to see me now." Ken sounded like a petulant child, but he didn't give a fuck. He'd already exposed himself to Gomez. What was a little more humiliation?

"He doesn't want to see anyone."

"You don't have to baby me. No matter how pathetic I sound, I'm a big boy."

"Fine. I'll call you if there's a change."

"Thank you." He ended the call, shoved his phone into his pocket, and threw a feed bucket against the wall so hard it cracked.

When he walked into the kitchen that night, Renata was there.

"You're still supposed to be on vacation," he said.

"I heard what happened, and I came back. Do you think I could leave you here alone like this?"

Ken didn't ask how she'd found out. She probably wouldn't have told him anyway. "Don't you dare start in on me."

"Kenneth Worthington Carver, you could at least give me a hug hello before mouthing off."

He let her pull him into her arms and once she had, he held her tight, not wanting to let go. "I'm glad you're here."

"Me too. Now tell me why you're not at the hospital with your beautiful man."

"He doesn't want me there."

She pulled back from the hug and glared at him.

"Gomez, the FBI agent directing this operation, just called to tell me he was awake, but he didn't want to see me."

Renata drew in a shaky breath. "He's going to be all right?"

"It sounds like it."

Renata made the sign of the cross. "Thank God for that. Your man wants to see you. He's just afraid."

Ken shook his head. "Don't do this. Don't make me think…"

She laid her hands on his shoulders and stretched up to kiss his cheek. "I love you, Kenneth. I would never want to hurt you. Being away from Andy will hurt you more. Trust me."

He wished he could.

A WEEK LATER, Ken was ready to come out of his skin. The days were bad enough, but at least he could focus on work. At night there was no escape from thoughts of Andy. No matter how hard he worked to exhaust himself, he always lay awake for hours.

Rusty tried keeping him company in the evenings at first, but finally, Ken barked at him so much he gave up. Ken had tried going out. He'd told himself he was going to pick up a man, drag him back to the ranch, and wreck him the way Andy had wrecked Ken, but he couldn't stomach it. He'd left the bar he'd chosen before he'd even finished his first drink.

He'd tried washing Andy from his mind with whiskey, but then he either couldn't sleep at all or dark dreams had him waking in a cold sweat.

He'd had all he could take. To hell with what Andy or Gomez wanted, he was going to see Andy again. It wasn't like Ken had gotten what he'd wanted in any of this. He at least deserved to talk to Andy again. Maybe he was being selfish, but after all they'd gone through, he had a right to be. This time, he dressed in one of his best suits. To hell with discretion. If he had to throw his name around, he damn well would.

When the elevator doors opened on the floor where Andy's room had been, the lack of guards by the door told Ken that Andy was no longer in the same room. What if... No Gomez would have called him if Andy had died. He was sure of that.

Ken approached the nurse's desk. "I need Detective Wofford's new room number."

The nurse shook her head. "We can't give out that information."

"I've been to visit him before, but he's no longer in the same room."

"Are you family?"

Ken fought the urge to throttle her. "No, but I need to see him."

"I'm sorry, sir. We cannot give out any patient information."

"You're either going to give it to me, or I'm going to go through every room in this place until I find him."

She picked up a phone. "Security. I have a hostile visitor at—"

He grabbed the phone from her hand and hung it up. "Forget hospital security. Call the FBI. Ask for Special Agent Gomez. She'll tell you exactly who I am."

A few seconds later, Gomez stormed through the door.

"What the hell are you doing?" she demanded.

Ken ran a hand through his hair and frowned at her. What was he doing?

Exactly what Gomez had begged you not to do, making a commotion.

"Fucking up?"

IF WISHES WERE HORSES

Her mouth twitched like she was about to smile. "Yeah, you are, but I could use you right now."

He hadn't expected that. "Really?"

"Yes. Internal Affairs is here. They're grilling Andy, and you might be able to get rid of them."

"What? Why?"

"The man you shot asked Andrew to kill Ben. Ben is dead, but Andrew says he didn't do it."

Ken shook his head. "He didn't."

"I know, but Andrew's not exactly popular at his precinct. He doesn't like to follow rules."

Ken smiled. "No shit." All the anger he'd felt—at himself for not fighting harder to see Andy before now and at Andy for ignoring him—focused in on these men who'd accused Andy of something he would never do.

"Tell me what you need."

Gomez frowned. Ken wondered if she was pondering how far she would go to help Andy.

"I can—"

She held up her hand. "Don't say something that's going to get us both in trouble."

He exhaled. "Fine."

"I'm hoping the detective has an alibi for the times in question."

No matter what the time in question was, he'd say Andy had been with him. "I'm sure he does."

She sighed. "If they push this, Andrew might meltdown completely. He's never stopped blaming himself for what happened on the last undercover mission."

Ken nodded. "I've seen what the flashbacks do to him."

She rubbed her forehead. "I should never have sent him on this assignment."

She damn well shouldn't have. But then Ken never would have met Andy. "What timeframe does he need an alibi for?"

She narrowed her eyes and whispered, "Do not lie for him. If they push this, they will try to prove you wrong."

"I'd like to see them try me."

Gomez held his gaze for a few seconds. Whatever she saw must have convinced her not to bother saying more. "The night in question is May fifteenth," she said, motioning for him to follow her. They stepped into the elevator, and she pushed the button that would take them up two floors.

That was the night Ken had returned from the city to find Andy having a flashback. Andy had run, and when he'd come back, he'd said he didn't want to talk about what had happened. "That's the night Ben was killed?"

She nodded.

He didn't do it. Ken knew that, but someone could sure as hell make it look like he had if Ken didn't do something about it.

The elevator doors opened, and Ken saw two police officers standing in front of a door halfway down the hall.

"I'm going to end this right now."

"Ken, don't. Wait until they come out. I'll set up a time for—"

He pulled away from her and charged down the hall.

―――

ANDY WAS WORN out from the effort of answering questions from these Internal Affairs bastards. He wanted to tell them to get the hell out of his room, but Gomez had begged him to play nice. There was only so much she could do since it was an HPD investigation.

"So you claim to have—"

The man's snide remark was cut off when the door burst open. At first, Andy thought he must be seeing things because there was no other explanation for Ken standing there, looking ready to tear someone apart.

The two men from IA stood and faced him, but Ken ignored them. Instead, he sought out Andy, and what Andy saw in Ken's eyes made his breath catch in his throat. Despite all the hell Andy had put him through, Ken still had feelings for him.

"What are you doing here?" Andy asked him.

Before Ken could answer, Ramsay, the more aggressive of the two IA detectives said, "I don't know how you got in here, but you need to leave immediately."

Hidalgo, the other man, was at the door, summoning the guards to deal with him.

"Calm down," Ken said, shaking himself loose from Ramsay's grip. "I'm here to help you."

"Ken." Andy used a warning tone.

Ken ignored him. "You're mistaken about what happened."

Gomez entered the room right behind the officers who'd been standing at his door. The men looked from her to Ramsay, obviously confused about whose orders to follow.

"Detective Wofford didn't have anything to do with Ben's death," Ken said.

"How can you be so sure of that?" Ramsay asked.

"Because he was in my bed that night. All night."

Hidalgo, Ramsay, and the uniforms turned toward Andy. Andy had known he'd eventually be outed. Somehow he'd slip up or run into someone at the wrong time. He'd expected to feel anger, fear, something terrible. Instead, he just felt relief.

"Is this true?" Ramsay asked.

Andy's tongue snaked out to wet his lips, and Ken gave him a once-over. The bastard. "Yes, it's true."

"Why didn't you mention it before?"

Andy glared at him. "Who I sleep with is none of your concern, and I assumed Mr. Carver didn't want me discussing his private business."

Hidalgo's eyes widened. "You're Kenneth Carver?"

Ken gave the man a predatory smile. Andy was sure that look had made many hardened businessmen shake in their boots. "I am."

"So you and Detective Wofford had a relationship during the time he was investigating drug trafficking on your ranch?"

Ramsay managed to make it sound like Andy had broken at least sixteen regulations by doing so, when he'd done nothing wrong.

Ken spoke before Andy could. "Detective Wofford was undercover. Are you going to tell me your undercover agents never sleep with people in the course of their investigations?"

"What I'm suggesting," Ramsay said, "is that there's something going on here that the two of you aren't talking about, and it stinks of a cover-up."

Ken pulled his phone from his pocket and tapped at the screen. He grinned at Ramsay as he put it to his ear. "My lawyer," he said, pointing to the phone. "She's the best in the city. I'm sure she'll enjoy owning your asses."

Hidalgo spoke up. "There's no need—"

"There's every need unless you intend to drop all charges against the detective."

"Are you threatening us?" Ramsay asked, taking a step toward him.

"Threatening you? With my right to an attorney?"

Andy knew he should intervene, but Ken in protector

mode was one of the sexiest things he'd ever seen. For once, he was enjoying having someone take care of him. If only Ken could truly be his.

"You haven't been accused of anything," Hidalgo said, obviously trying to keep things from escalating.

"Has Detective Wofford?"

"He is under investigation," Ramsay asserted. "And we don't have to discuss the investigation with you."

Gomez stepped in between Ramsay and Ken, which was good, because if Ramsay said one more snarky thing, Ken was going to punch him. "Why don't we let the detective rest and finish this later?" she asked.

Ramsay glared at her. "I'm not going to let the Feds or this asshole push me around. We don't answer to either of you."

"Gentlemen, I'm sure Detective Wofford's doctor would agree he's had enough for today," she said, not rising to Ramsay's bait.

As Gomez herded the men out, she glanced over her shoulder at Ken with a combination of exasperation and pride.

Ken turned his attention back to Andy then, and Andy's stomach knotted. "What the hell was that?" he asked, his voice scratchy.

Ken grinned. "Me saving your ass."

"By outing me?"

"You're going to get pissed at me for that when I…" Ken exhaled and shook his head.

Was he going to walk out? Andy's chest ached, and he could barely keep his eyes open, but he didn't want Ken to leave.

"Thank you," he said, the words almost too quiet to hear.

Ken smiled. "You're welcome."

"I'm sorry for everything," Andy blurted out.

"I can't decide whether to be pissed at you or just damn glad you're alive."

"I figured you'd hate me."

Ken shook his head. "I always knew you were hiding something. I'm glad it wasn't that you were running a drug ring."

Andy laughed, but it sounded hollow. "I told you it wasn't what you thought."

"You did, but you could have given me a little more to go on."

Andy shook his head, the movement making him hurt even more. "I really couldn't."

Ken ran a hand through his hair. "I don't want to argue."

"Neither do I."

"If those assholes hassle you again, I'll take care of it."

Andy frowned. Ken had lied for him, and he would never have asked him to do that. "Ken, you know I wasn't—"

Ken held up his hand. "Don't. You didn't kill that boy."

"How do you know? I lied to you about—"

"You lied because you had to. I don't like it, and I don't know where it leaves us, but I know you would never kill a kid no matter how much of an idiot he was."

"The man who brought you into the shed, the one you killed." Andy winced as he said those words, but Ken just held his gaze. "He ordered me to."

"But you didn't do it."

"No, that man killed him before I had a chance."

"You're trying to scare me, and it's not working. You wouldn't have harmed Ben no matter what."

Andy hated how Ken could always read him. "I was going to take him and run. That's why I'd planned to leave that night. When you saw me, I'd just found out he was dead."

Andy wanted to beg Ken to climb onto the bed and hold him. He knew Ken couldn't take all the pain away, but touching him would help like nothing else.

"That explains a lot." Ken shifted positions and toyed with one of his shirt cuffs. Andy had never seen him look so antsy. "You going to be here much longer?"

"I should be out in a few days." Andy wanted to ask Ken if they could see each other then, but he couldn't work up the nerve. If Ken said no, he wasn't prepared to handle it.

"I'm glad you're healing." Ken looked uncomfortable. Andy should just let him go.

"Me too."

Ken looked out the window like eye contact was too much for him. "I'm sorry for outing you."

"It was going to happen, probably soon if Ramsay pushed the investigation. I'm not sure I'll go back anyway."

Ken looked at him then. "To being a cop?"

Andy nodded.

"I'm sorry."

"I don't know if I am or not." Andy wasn't sure what he would do if he quit, but if Ramsay had his way, going back to work wouldn't be a choice anyway.

"I haven't hired a foreman," Ken said.

Was he suggesting Andy should come back to the ranch? "You haven't?" His words sounded much too eager.

Ken shook his head.

"I'm sorry you haven't found anyone yet."

Ken gave a sad smile. "No one is quite like you."

Andy sucked in his breath. "You're right. Most people are actually who they say they are."

Ken shook his head. "Not really. Most people have secrets."

Andy didn't know how to respond, so he changed the subject. "How's Rusty?"

Ken frowned. "Okay but quiet. Still processing what happened."

"The cops aren't giving him any trouble, are they?"

"No, I'm making sure of that."

"I guess you're good at that."

Ken smiled. "I'm fortunate to have lots of resources, but I understand you made it clear in your report that he was never involved."

Andy nodded. "I did."

"Thank you."

"I was just telling the truth."

"You could easily have suspected him, though."

Andy shook his head. "No, I couldn't have."

They stayed silent for several more seconds.

"I suppose you need to rest."

"I hate how tired I am all the time." He didn't want to say goodbye, but if Ken stayed much longer, Andy was going to beg him for a kiss.

Ken looked down and then back up again. "You almost died."

Andy could feel the weight of Ken's emotion. "I—"

"You gave me your gun. If you'd had it—"

"It wouldn't have helped. When that asshole shot me, I was completely unprepared for it."

"No one would have been. He was supposed to have been handcuffed and searched for weapons. The officers in charge of the prisoners should be investigated by Internal Affairs, not you."

"Trust me, they are, but I think the guy was just that good."

"Or that angry."

Andy nodded. "Anger can make you good."

"But it's no way to live."

That was for damn sure. Andy took a deep breath and coughed. Ken reached for the water by his bed.

Their hands brushed as Andy took the cup, and a jolt of electricity ran through Andy and made him shudder.

"If you need anything…" Ken looked unsure how to finish his sentence.

"You saved my life," Andy said, needing to get that out there before Ken left.

"That bastard wasn't going to stop with shooting you. I was protecting all of us."

"But I'd given you every reason to—"

"I never wished you dead, not even when I first saw you in that shed."

"Thank you."

Ken took a step back from the bed. "I better let you get some sleep. Call me. If… For anything."

"You'd answer?"

Ken chewed on his lower lip and looked away. Andy's heart pounded as he waited for the answer. Finally, Ken looked back at him. "I would."

"I wish…" Andy was too much of a coward to finish his sentence. Ken deserved better than him anyway.

Ken nodded. "Yeah, me too." He turned and walked out the door.

Andy didn't want this to be their final goodbye, but he didn't have the energy to sort things out yet. Ken was open to talking to him again. That would have to be enough for now.

CHAPTER TWENTY-ONE

Gomez looked up from her desk when Andy walked into the FBI field office. "What are you doing here? Aren't you supposed to be resting?"

"I needed to talk to you."

She studied him for a few seconds, then stood and gestured for him to follow her into a conference room.

Once they had some privacy, he said, "I'm going to resign."

After several moments of silence, he got impatient. "Don't you have anything to say?"

"Oh, I have plenty to say, but I'm trying to decide what weapons I'll need to pull out to make you reconsider."

"You really think I should stay on? Wasn't this bullshit enough? Didn't you see that I have no business being in the field?"

"What I saw was a man with impeccable instincts, one I should have put more faith in."

He shook his head. "You were right to question me."

"Probably, but ultimately you were right. You're a damn good cop, and I wish you'd come to work for the Bureau."

Andy glanced out her office window and frowned. "You're the only one around here who feels that way."

"Plenty of people were very happy to see those bastards brought in."

Andy nodded. "I'm still done with police work."

"Would you consider an extended leave of absence?"

Andy closed his eyes and took a long breath. "I need out."

"You'd be out, no responsibility to check in, nothing. I hope you'll keep in touch, though, because I still consider you a friend."

Andy smiled. "If we weren't in your office, I'd hug the shit out of you. You're the best friend I've ever had."

"Then listen to me when I tell you that if you take a break, figure things out with Ken—"

"I don't—"

Gomez held up her hand to silence him. "Let me finish. Ken could help you. You need someone who understands you. If you had someone to ground you, I think you could find your way back, and I think you could be even better. Although I have to admit you did a fine job on this case even if you were crazy and strung-out."

"How long?"

"Six months, and then if you still want out, fine. If not, I hope you'll think about applying to this office."

"You can work out that much leave for me?"

"After you closed this case? Yes. You'd have at least two more months of medical leave anyway."

Andy nodded. "Fine. I'm too tired to fight you."

She pointed to the chair in front of her desk. "Sit down. You look like shit."

"Thanks. Like I said, you're a real friend." He did as she said anyway.

"I try."

He snorted. "Look, about Ken. I haven't even talked to him since the day he bitch-slapped the guys from IA."

Gomez grinned. "That was beautiful. Whose fault is it that you haven't talked?"

Andy shrugged. "Both of us, I guess."

"What do you think would happen if you called him?"

"Fuck if I know. He might have forgotten me by now."

Gomez gave him a look that said she thought he was an idiot. "Do you want to call him?"

Andy nodded. He did, more than anything. Not an hour had gone by that he hadn't thought about Ken, but even though he'd seemed interested in seeing Andy again, Andy had been too afraid of being rejected to actually call. "I was happy out there on the ranch. I kept fantasizing about staying and just becoming Andy Watson."

"Then go be him for a few months, see if that's what you want or if you miss all this." She gestured toward the rows of desks where agents were hard at work on caseloads that would keep them there until late at night.

"I don't want to come back."

"Right now you don't, and I can't blame you, but give it some time."

"Okay."

"Don't disappear on me."

He reached out and squeezed her hand. "I won't. I promise."

"You didn't drive yourself here, did you?"

Andy grinned. "Hell yeah I did."

"Fucking idiot. You aren't supposed to drive for two more weeks."

A MONTH after Ken had walked out of Andy's hospital room, cursing himself for not having the courage to tell the man how he felt about him, someone knocked on his office door. Ken didn't want to see anyone; he rarely did these days. He ran his ranch and interacted with Rusty and the other hands as much as he needed to. Renata fed him and tried to cheer him up, but he'd taken to hiding from her, not wanting to fight off her suggestions that he call Andy and end this waiting game. Sam periodically called, trying to cheer him up and reporting on Andy's progress. No matter how many times he told her to stop, she continued to keep tabs on Andy. She seemed convinced if she kept talking about it, she'd convince Ken to "go get his man," as she put it.

He no longer felt the drink-himself-into-a-stupor anger he'd experienced when he'd thought Andy was part of the drug ring, or even the ache that had settled in his chest when he realized the betrayal was part of an assignment, something Ken could—though it took work—forgive. After several weeks, Ken had finally built a wall around his heart thick enough to leave him numb.

He'd become even more withdrawn than he'd been after his parents' rejection spurred him to start Carver Pharm. The only time he felt anything anymore was when he woke from dreams of Andy wrapped around him or on his knees in front of him or behind him fucking him hard and fast or, worst of all, lying on the ground with a bullet in his chest. Those nights he felt so much he thought he might come apart, but day-to-day there was nothing but plodding on with the ranch.

The person at the door cleared his throat, and Ken reluctantly looked up. His breath caught. Andy was standing there in jeans, boots, and a t-shirt with his Stetson in his hands as if he'd never left, as if the last month had never happened, as if he were truly Ken's foreman.

"I heard there was a job opening here," Andy said.

Ken's mouth dropped open. If Andy hadn't spoken, Ken would have decided he was a hallucination. But hallucinations couldn't speak, could they? He needed to say something back, but neither his brain nor his voice would work.

Andy chewed his lower lip, and Ken stared at his lush mouth and teeth. He could still feel them sinking into his neck. He'd loved when Andy marked him.

"So are you hiring or should I… go?"

"No."

Andy started to turn away, and Ken realized he'd said the wrong thing. He tripped over his chair as he tried to get around his desk and stop the man from leaving. "Don't leave. I meant that you shouldn't go, not that I'm not… I want you here."

ANDY WHIRLED BACK AROUND, heart pounding. He still didn't have the stamina he used to.

Ken's eyes were wide, and he was breathing nearly as hard as Andy. "You're really here? You really want to work here?"

Andy nodded, reaching for the doorframe to steady himself. "I've taken a six-month leave of absence. I tried to quit, but Gomez… You've seen what she's like."

Ken grinned. "I have."

"She convinced me to take some time and then see how I felt. The only thing I'm really sure of is that I want to be here with you. During the case, I dreamed of running off, finding a job on another ranch, and becoming someone else, someone who'd never been a cop, someone who didn't have to lie all the time. But…"

Ken took a step toward him. "But?"

"You wouldn't have been there."

Ken moved closer. "No. I'm right here."

Andy nodded. "Yeah, and I want to be here too, if you'll have me."

Ken gave him a slow once-over. "I expect a lot from people who work on this ranch."

Andy swallowed hard. "So I've heard."

"I think you'd have to work extra hard to please me."

Andy grinned. "I got your extra hard right here." He stroked himself through the worn denim with the hand he wasn't using to hold himself up.

Ken sucked in his breath. "I never hired a foreman." The words came out hoarse, which made Andy smile.

"You do know I'm not actually qualified."

"Neither am I."

Andy shrugged. "I guess not."

"But together, if we don't get too distracted…"

"In other words, you're going to be hanging around the barn, second-guessing everything I do."

Ken grinned. "All the damn time."

"Then we're going to have the same rules as before. When we're here—in your office—you're mine."

"I happen to recall you enjoying being mine a few times."

Andy nodded, but he couldn't look at Ken. "I did. I want to be yours, but I've never had anything like a relationship, and if I'm here all the time, I'm probably going to fuck up and—"

"Stop," Ken ordered.

He cupped Andy's chin and tilted his head up. "We'll take each day as it comes. We'll work the ranch and—"

"I'll work you over."

Ken grinned. "Exactly, and we'll figure out where to go from there.

"This is more than sex, though."

Ken nodded. "Yes, it is, but we don't have to label it. Not now."

"So I've got the job?"

Ken's smile was the most beautiful thing Andy had ever seen. "You've always had it."

Andy was certain Ken didn't just mean the foreman position, but there were so many things they weren't ready to say, and if they let them spill, one of them might run. So he pulled Ken to him and kissed him gently. When things started to heat up, Andy stepped back. "You expecting anyone?"

Ken shook his head.

Andy grinned. "I'm going to go slower than usual today, but once I'm all the way healed, I'm going to make sure you remember exactly who's in charge when we're in this room."

"Oh, I remember. I remember so very well."

Ken was his. The whole world suddenly seemed brighter. Things weren't going to be easy between them, but his instincts said they were going to be okay.

CHAPTER TWENTY-TWO

Epilogue

Three months later

Andy had gone out to the barn to check on the foals after dinner. He'd intended to head straight back to the house, but the night was more pleasant than any they'd had during the summer. He was finally able to get through an entire day without feeling too exhausted to stay on his feet, so he allowed himself to lean against the pasture fence and watch the horses grazing lazily and resting after a day of training.

Several moments later, Andy heard footsteps behind him. Even if he never went back to police work, he didn't think he'd ever feel comfortable being approached from behind, but this time, he didn't turn around. The cadence of the steps and the way Andy's body became hyper aware told him it was Ken.

Andy's lover placed a hand on his back, and Andy leaned into him without even thinking about it. A few months ago, Andy wouldn't have thought he was capable of that kind of unconscious surrender.

"I was starting to think you weren't coming back," Ken said.

Andy tensed and turned to face him. "After all this time, you thought—"

Ken shook his head. "I didn't mean I thought you'd run. We're passed that, aren't we?"

"Fuck yes. The only way I'm leaving is if you send me away, and even then I'm going to put up a fight."

"I just meant I thought you'd fallen asleep in the barn or something."

"I told you I'm doing a lot better. I don't need naps anymore."

Ken gave him a seductive smile. "It's not like I minded, especially when I got to slip into bed and wake you up."

"And then exhaust me so much I needed another nap."

"It's not my fault that's your favorite way to wake up." Ken ran his fingers up and down Andy's spine, letting him feel their warmth through the fabric of his t-shirt. All it took was that simple touch for Andy's cock to start demanding they go inside. But Ken seemed content to stay there by the fence, and he was keeping Andy well satisfied, so Andy's cock could wait.

"Have you thought anymore about going back?" Ken asked.

"Back to detective work?"

Ken nodded, but he kept his gaze on the horses. He hadn't said as much, but Andy knew Ken wanted him to stay right there, running the ranch with him where he was, out of harm's way. He also knew Ken wasn't going to deny Andy the opportunity to go back. Ken knew firsthand what it was like to have family force you into a life that wasn't what you wanted. And Ken was family to him now. They hadn't talked much about what was between them, preferring to let their actions speak instead. But as far as Andy was concerned, Ken was it for him. This was his forever.

When Andy didn't say anything else, Ken turned to look at him. There was so much emotion in his eyes—desire mixed with concern. Was he worried that if Andy went back to the force, that would be it for them? That was the last thing Andy wanted. Maybe it was time to share some of those scary words. "I'm still not sure if I'll ever want to go back, but I am sure of one thing."

Ken gave him a rare uncertain look. "What's that?"

"I love you, Kenneth Carver."

Ken's eyes widened, and his breath caught. He lifted a hand and cupped Andy's cheek. "I love you too. I have for a long time."

"I wanted to believe that back when I was hiding everything from you, but I told myself not to hope for it. Then you saved my life, and I thought maybe… But I never thought I could really have this. I wasn't sure I deserved it."

Ken brought his other hand to Andy's waist, gripping him tightly. "You deserve this, and so much more."

"If I ever do go back, I promise I won't be leaving you, even if I'm not working as the foreman. This is where I belong, if you'll have me."

"I will always have you. You're mine, and I have no intention of letting you get away."

"That goes both ways."

Ken raised a brow. "Which way is it going to go tonight?"

The heat in Ken's eyes had Andy needing to reach down and adjust himself as he pondered the question. Things had been gentler between them as he'd recovered, and he'd mostly bottomed, but tonight... tonight he was ready for something rougher. He needed to remind Ken just how thoroughly he belonged to Andy. "Tonight I'm going to lay you out, open you up, and fill you so full you'll be sure no one else could ever satisfy you like I do."

"I've been sure of that since the moment you walked onto our ranch."

"This really was inevitable, wasn't it?"

Ken smiled. "The fucking was at least. The rest? I don't know, but I'm damn glad it happened."

"I've always believed in making my own fate, but the moment I met you, I knew I'd never really be in control when it came to you. I thought I was going to hate that."

"And now?"

"Now I enjoy surrendering to you almost as much as I love that moment when you truly give in and let me have it all."

Ken took Andy's hand and tugged him toward the house. "Maybe now that you've got more of your stamina back, you can have both of your favorite things tonight."

Heat raced through Andy, but something stirred at the back of his mind. He replayed their conversation. "Wait a minute? You said "our" ranch."

Ken shrugged. "You said you were never going to leave, so if you plan to spend the rest of your life here, I figure it's just as much yours as it is mine."

"Ken, I'm not —"

"Or... We could make it official."

"You mean you'd give me part of the ranch?"

Ken rolled his eyes. "You're really not getting it, are you?"

Andy's heart pounded. "You're not... you're not asking me to..."

"Marry me? I just said it's an option."

Andy froze and Ken stumbled, not having realized he'd stopped. "Look at me, Ken."

Ken did as Andy asked, but his expression was all false bravado, a look he'd surely used to intimidate his employees at Carver Pharm.

"No, *really* look at me."

Ken's gaze dropped to the ground, and there was just enough light left for Andy to see the color in his cheeks. "I know it's too soon, and I shouldn't have—"

"I've never known you to say anything you didn't mean."

Ken looked up at him then, and Andy could see how frightened he was. Did he think Andy would say no?

"You're right," Andy said. "It is early, but nothing about our relationship has been done by rules anyone else would play by. So if you want to make this *our* ranch, then my answer is yes."

Ken's mouth dropped open, and for a moment, Andy worried he'd forgotten how to breathe. Then he grabbed Andy and crushed their lips together. Heat flared between them, and Andy stopped worrying about what the future held. The only thing he cared about in that moment was whether they could get away with fucking right there on the dusty ground, because the time it would take to get to the house suddenly seemed too long. He needed his future husband right that second.

Dear Reader,

Thank you for reading *If Wishes Were Horses*. Blake from the neighboring ranch is getting his own story, *Ranch Daddy*.

Want more romance starring sexy policemen? Read *Fitting In (Fitting In Book 1)* or grab the series bundle.

I offer a free book to anyone who joins my mailing list. To learn more, go to silviaviolet.com/newsletter. You can chat with me on Facebook in Silvia's Salon, and you can email me at silviaviolet@gmail.com. To read excerpts from all of my titles, visit my website: silviaviolet.com/books.

Please consider leaving a review where you purchased this ebook or on Goodreads. Reviews and word-of-mouth recommendations are vital to independent authors.

Silvia Violet

ABOUT THE AUTHOR

Silvia Violet writes fun, sexy stories that will leave you smiling and satisfied. She has a thing for characters who are in need of comfort and enjoys helping them surrender to love even when they doubt it exists. Silvia's stories include sizzling contemporaries, paranormals, and historicals. When she needs a break from listening to the voices in her head, she spends time baking, taking long walks, curling up with her favorite books, and hanging out with her family.

Website: silviaviolet.com
Facebook: facebook.com/silvia.violet
Facebook Group: Silvia's Salon
Twitter: @Silvia_Violet
Instagram: @silvia.violet
Pinterest: pinterest.com/silviaviolet/

ALSO BY SILVIA VIOLET

Lace-Covered Compromise

A Chance at Love

Coming Clean

Revolutionary Temptation

Of Hope and Anguish

Three Under the Christmas Tree

Needing A Little Christmas

Ames Bridge

Down on the Farm

The Past Comes Home

Tied to Home

Fitting In

Fitting In

Sorting Out

Burning Up

Going Deep

Getting Hitched

Anticipation

Anticipating Disaster

Anticipating Rejection

Anticipating Temptation

Love and Care

Father of the Groom

After the Weekend

Demanding Discipline

Painfully Attractive

Hungry (short story)

Thorne and Dash

Professional Distance

Personal Entanglement

Perfect Alignment

Well-Tailored (A Thorne and Dash Companion Story)

Lonely Dragon's Club

The Christmas Dragon's Mate

The Snow Dragon's Mate

The City Dragon's Mate

The Island Dragon's Mate

Howler Brothers

Claiming Bite

Bodyguard's Bite

Trillium Creek

Love at Lupine Bakery

Love at Long Last

Love Times Three

Love Someone Like Me

Law and Supernatural Order

Sex on the Hoof

Paws on Me

Dinner at Foxy's

Hoofing' It To The Altar

Wild R Farm

Finding Release

Arresting Love

Embracing Need

Taming Tristan

Willing Hands

Shifting Hearts

Wild R Christmas

Printed in Great Britain
by Amazon